Praise for *Sh*

"As addictive as it is disturbing. . . .
I couldn't look away."
ALICIA ELLIOTT, AUTHOR OF *A MIND SPREAD
OUT ON THE GROUND*

"Leah Mol's debut novel explores the
burgeoning sexuality of teenaged Katie,
and delves into what it feels like to live in the
female body. . . . Mol is a brand new talent
with a sly, devastating, and remarkable eye
for details of the female experience."
HEATHER O'NEILL, AUTHOR OF *WHEN WE LOST
OUR HEADS*

"*Sharp Edges* is a visceral portrait of a
millennial teen girl exploring her sexuality,
mending broken friendships, and keeping
unspeakable secrets in the early aughts of the
digital age. Leah Mol's debut novel is a fiery,
gut-wrenching must-read."
ANDREA WERHUN, AUTHOR OF *MODERN
WHORE*

SHARP EDGES

SHARP
EDGES

a novel

LEAH
MOL

DOUBLEDAY CANADA

Doubleday Canada and colophon are registered trademarks of
Penguin Random House Canada Limited

Library and Archives Canada Cataloguing in Publication

Title: Sharp edges / Leah Mol.
Names: Mol, Leah, author.
Identifiers: Canadiana (print) 20220175217 | Canadiana (ebook) 20220175330 |
ISBN 9780385697224 (softcover) | ISBN 9780385697231 (EPUB)
Classification: LCC PS8626.O448635 S53 2022 | DDC C813/.6—dc23

This book is a work of fiction. Names, characters, places and incidents are products
of the author's imagination or are used fictitiously. Any resemblance to actual events
or locales or persons, living or dead, is entirely coincidental.

The excerpt from *Bye Bye Blondie* by Virginie Despentes, and translated by
Siân Reynolds, has been reprinted with the permission of The Permissions
Company, LLC, on behalf of The Feminist Press at the City University of New York,
www.feministpress.org. All rights reserved. Copyright © 2004 by Editions Grasset &
Fasquelle. Translation copyright © 2016 by Siân Reynolds.

Cover design by Jennifer Griffiths
Cover images: (girls) Jena Ardell, (stripes) golubovy, both Getty Images

Printed in Canada

Published in Canada by Doubleday Canada,
a division of Penguin Random House Canada Limited

www.penguinrandomhouse.ca

10 9 8 7 6 5 4 3 2 1

Penguin
Random House
DOUBLEDAY CANADA

for sixteen-year-old me

"She murmurs words she likes to hear . . ."

—VIRGINIE DESPENTES, *Bye Bye Blondie*

one

∧∧∧

I didn't get my first period until grade nine. I thought it was supposed to be red like blood, so when there were brown stains in my underpants I was pretty sure I was dying. After a couple days of stuffing my underwear with toilet paper and waiting for the end, I did a search online and found out it was my period. I wasn't excited like I thought I would be; it felt like something else. Disappointment, maybe, that something so scary had suddenly become normal, something other people dealt with all the time. Everyone knew more than I did. I just felt stupid. I went home after school on the third day and told Mom about it, but I pretended it'd just happened, that I'd known all along what it was supposed to be like. She told me periods change everything, that I had to be more careful, that I could get pregnant now.

At the end of the week, there was a bag sitting on my bed. Inside it was a ring in a small box and a card that said *Congratulations, Love Mom*. I wonder if her own mom gave her jewellery after her first time, or if she looked it up on the internet—*first period gifts*. The ring has a real gold band and my birthstone. The box it came in is plain blue, and it's soft like animal fur. That's where I keep my razor blades now.

⌃⌃⌃

LILLIAN PUTS ON Avril Lavigne because that's what we always listen to in her car. There's only a tape player and the Avril tape got stuck in it last year when Lillian put it on to bug her dad—he was the only one who drove this car back then. Lillian screams the words to "Complicated" and I laugh at her for a minute and then scream the words, too. There are lots of things I'd be embarrassed to do if Lillian wasn't around.

Lil doesn't have her full licence yet, but her parents let her take the car as long as we don't leave town. I'll be sixteen this year, but I don't know if I'll get my licence anytime soon. Lil says I'll be a horrible driver.

We go past Wal-Mart and Home Depot, past the car plant that was supposed to open two years ago. We pass the hospital where I was born. Sometimes I look at it and wonder which room it was, the first place I was on my own, not connected to someone else. My mother had to have a C-section even though she always says her hips were made for birthing.

Most of us who were born in this town are still here. We've been going to school together since kindergarten. Every year in elementary school, the teachers took a picture of the kids who'd been there from the beginning. The pictures are in a box under my bed. I used to look at them all the time. In my favourite one, Lillian and I are both sitting—it was taken before I got taller than her, before teachers started putting me in the back row. There are a couple kids between us, but Lillian's leaning all the way forward, looking right at me. New kids moved here every year, transferring from other schools, from big cities and small towns, but the original group of us—the kids from the beginning—didn't leave. We weren't all friends, but we knew one another. It felt like having a family. Now that I'm older, though, sometimes I hate it. When I'm with people I grew up with, I'm stuck with a personality. It seems like that should make things easy, but it's exhausting. I can feel myself being poured into a mould and hardening until I'm a mannequin that looks just like me. Every time I try something new, people ask me what's wrong.

Lillian rolls down her window even though it's freezing outside. Her car doesn't have heat anyway, so it's almost as cold inside. My hands are bare but I keep them warm between my legs. Snow hits us in the face and Lil opens her mouth to catch some. *This'll be the last snow of winter*, I think. But lately, every single storm feels like the last.

〰〰

WE END UP at the McDonald's downtown, because the new one by the highway is under construction again and the one inside Wal-Mart is shit, and we each get a double cheeseburger off the dollar menu. Lillian bets me she can eat hers in one bite, and watching her shove it into her mouth makes me laugh so hard it hurts.

I leave the last bite of my burger and Lillian eats it without asking. I never eat the last bite of anything; it feels horrible to empty a plate. It used to drive my mom nuts. She tried everything—pleading, bribing, forcing—but that just made it worse. I'd sit at the kitchen table for hours because she wouldn't let me leave until I finished. I guess now she doesn't care if I eat.

On our walk back to the car, Lillian stops outside a restaurant and points to a sign in the front window. "They're hiring," she says. "More than one job, too. We could work together. Want to go in?"

"Okay."

"Finish your Coke first."

I suck until I hit air, then throw the cup into a garbage can on the sidewalk.

Lillian's been looking for a job for a couple weeks. She says it's better to get one now while less people are applying, and then by the summer you can just pick up more hours instead of starting from nowhere.

The door jingles when we go in, and the only two people eating turn and watch us walk through the restaurant. I've never actually been in here before—it feels like an old-person place. I move to ding the little bell on the counter, but Lillian grabs my hand before I can touch it.

A woman comes out from the kitchen a couple seconds later.

"Hi, could we speak with a manager, please?" I'm impressed Lillian knew to ask that.

The woman smiles like she's tired, like things aren't perfect but she's trying. "That's me."

"Oh, hi. We're looking for applications for the waitress positions?"

"Lovely. Did you bring résumés?" She has a slight British accent, so slight that I bet most people just think she pronounces some words weirdly, and I wonder how she ended up here. The only British people I've ever met are the exchange students who came over last year and spent two weeks with the grade twelves. One of the girls got so drunk on their last night here that she fell and hit her face on the sidewalk and lost two teeth. Apparently there was blood all over the pavement but she couldn't stop laughing.

"No," Lillian says. "Sorry. We saw the sign so we just came in."

I wonder if it's a bad thing that Lillian's doing all the talking. Lillian always does the talking, though, so at least it doesn't feel like I'm faking anything.

"That's fine. But you'll need that to apply. Why don't you take these application forms home, and you can bring them back with résumés. But come back quickly, okay? By tomorrow. The owner wants to do interviews soon as possible."

Back in the car, Lillian says, "We should fake interview each other."

"Do you actually want to work there?"

Lillian shrugs. "I mean, the manager was nice."

"You only think that because she's British."

"What?"

"Never mind," I say.

"So? Interview me."

"What celebrity do you look the most like?"

"Seriously, Katie."

"What? It's a good question. It'll tell me if you're full of your-self, or if you have bad self-esteem, which I think is important when you're a waitress. The good ones are confident but not *too* confident, right?"

Lillian glares at me. "I'll ask you first, then." She turns a corner and drives over the edge of the sidewalk. "Oops. All right, why do you want this job?"

I think about it. I don't really want the job. It seems like a waste of weekends. "It'd be fun to work together?"

"No. Answer like I'm the owner."

"People tell me I'm really good at pouring coffee. I feel like I'm finally ready to accept my destiny."

Lillian rolls her eyes. "Come on."

I poke her elbow with one finger. "Okay. I'm sorry. Are you going to drive back tomorrow? Or should we walk?"

Lillian's focused on something in the rearview mirror. "I guess it depends on the weather. We probably shouldn't go back together, though, right? I mean, the owner might think we always want to work together or something. Next question—what are three words other people would use to describe you? Please be serious—I really want to do this with you."

It hits me that only Lillian might get the job, and if she did, she'd take it. That'd be worse than neither of us getting it. *Loser, needy, stupid*, I think. *Be serious.*

"Hardworking, responsible, punctual."

Lillian smiles. "Perfect."

〰

LILLIAN PARKS AT her house and we walk the block over to mine. My house just has a main floor and a basement, so it's not huge, but it's better than a lot of people's houses. Mom's probably lying on the couch. Lately, she spends most of her time watching reruns and soap operas and talk shows. Sometimes, if it's a good day, she goes to the grocery store or puts something frozen in the oven. Sometimes she goes on diets. A couple weeks ago she was only eating green foods. She feels better for a few days and then something happens and she ends up on the couch again. Today she says my name like a question as soon as I open the door. Lillian sits down in the kitchen to wait, on the only chair with a cushion. I thought she'd come say hi, but maybe she can hear something in Mom's voice, too.

In the living room, the TV is muted.

"Hey, Mom?"

"Hi, hon." She keeps her eyes closed.

"There's this job I want to apply for. But I need a résumé."

"That's good," she says.

"Do you think you can help me with it?"

"Yeah, maybe this week, okay? I have a migraine right now."

I bite the inside of my cheek. "I need to drop it off tomorrow, though, so I wanted to do it today maybe?"

"Katie, I can hardly open my eyes right now without blinding effing pain. And you want me to read something? Or write something?"

She says *effing* all the time now. She must have heard it on a TV show. It's kind of cute when I'm not mad at her. I've even said it accidentally. I can't help her rubbing off on me.

"Can't you wait a couple days?" she asks. "There'll be other jobs."

"Okay." It was silly of me to ask, anyway. I can do it myself, look it up online. It was mostly for her; I figured it'd make her happy. She used to help me with homework and make me feel like every single one of my ideas had potential, that I could make any project exciting. In grade nine, I had an English assignment where I had to keep a diary from the point of view of Juliet. Mom stayed in character as Lady Capulet the whole week I was doing it. I got an A-plus.

"Can you get me an Advil?"

When I pass through the kitchen, Lillian isn't there anymore, and the door to the basement is wide open—she wants me to know she went down.

I go into the bathroom for the Advil and shut the door behind me without thinking about it. I sit on the toilet for a minute because it feels like I should, but I don't even need to pee. Afterward, I look in the mirror and push my boobs together, pull up my jeans so there's no fat spilling over the edges. I feel like a mess of flesh. The Advil bottle is already open on the counter, so I shake out two pills.

The living room is dark because the curtains are closed, and Mom's face changes colours with the television. I drop the pills into her palm.

Lillian spins her chair to face me when I get down to the basement. "You okay?"

I bite my cheeks when I'm upset and I always thought nobody could tell. Then I did it in the mirror once and realized my whole jaw puffs out. But it's already a habit. I can feel my chin getting bigger, my jaw pulsing. I must look like Popeye. "Yeah, I'm fine. Why?"

"All right." She shrugs and turns back around.

Lillian and I spend a lot of time in my basement. The couch smells like mould but we don't really care if it's gross—it's private and we can do whatever we want. The computer used to be up in my mom's room, but she started worrying about the radiation.

Lillian's on the rolly chair, so I take the metal one I brought down from the kitchen table a few months ago. Mom and I hardly ever use the chairs in the kitchen anymore. The metal one gives you little shocks every time you sit down, so Lillian hates it and always calls the rolly. I don't mind, though. It's familiar. Sometimes I use it even when I'm by myself.

Lillian signs in to the chat room we've been going on the past couple weeks. Our password's just a bunch of numbers—I wanted to make it our names or something easy, but Lillian always says she remembers numbers better than anything. She says if everyone's name were a number, she'd never forget a name. She's terrible at math, but she does have all our passwords memorized.

There are chat rooms for everything. One of our favourites is for anorexic girls. There's another one we've been going on for forever that seems like it's just for regular people but it's actually full of weirdos. So many weirdos. The first time we went on it, Lillian clicked on this guy's name and typed *Hello*, and he sent her a picture of his dick. No warning. We both screamed and tried to close the chat window and Lillian fell off her chair. When Mom yelled at us to see if everything was okay, we couldn't stop laughing. We've seen a lot more dick pics since then. We had internet boyfriends for a while last year—we called them our IBs. We acted like it was a joke, but sometimes I had dreams about mine. Lillian's IB told her he loved her and then disappeared from the chats; mine just disappeared. There are a few people we talk to all the time. None of them know who we really are.

Lillian waits until I'm paying attention before she clicks on a name and writes, *ASL?* Age, sex, location. The response is just a link to another site. Lil clicks on it and there are pictures of a girl wearing a bra and underwear and nothing else.

"Stop it," I say, batting at her hand. "You shouldn't click on random things."

"I just wanted to see."

She clicks on a thumbnail and there's a photo of the girl's ass, her underwear pulled to the side. Another one shows her from the chest down. And then there are pictures of her underwear, stained with something dark.

Lillian has to lean forward to read the posting because she never wears her glasses. "She's selling her underwear," she says.

"This is insane." I laugh when she laughs, but not because it's funny. I think most of the time when I'm laughing, it's only because I'm supposed to. That's not true for Lillian; she'd never laugh just to fit in.

She clicks through to the main website and there are hundreds of posts. Most of the girls seem pretty young, but there's one lady who must be at least sixty. She looks like a swim instructor, or a gymnastics coach. Another girl looks even younger than me and Lillian; her pubic hair is dyed blond. *My boobs are worth millions*, it says on her profile. One girl says she's looking for a daddy. She says she'll be everything he's ever dreamed about. Lillian and I laugh at all the things she's willing to do just to get an old man to buy her things.

Lil gets bored after a while. She pushes off the desk with her hands to spin her chair in circles. I keep looking at the website. I'm not bored at all. This isn't like the dick pics or the random porn that sometimes pops up—those things feel awkward, kind of funny since we didn't mean to see them. They've always been an accident. This feels like a choice. It feels like a million tiny hearts beating in my stomach. I can't tell if I'm dizzy because of what's on the site or because Lillian is spinning right beside me.

When she gets too close and hits me in the shoulder, the chair stops fast. "Oh my god, I could throw up," she says.

I close the browser window because it seems wrong to keep clicking through the profiles, looking at women and their dirty laundry. If I'm looking with Lillian, I have permission—it's not weird. But I don't think I was supposed to keep looking when she stopped.

Lillian stands up like she was never spinning, like she's never been nauseous in her whole life. Maybe she's just a good actress.

"I have to go in a minute. I have that essay due Monday and I haven't even started."

For Lillian, "haven't even started" means she's been thinking about it for weeks and already has an outline.

"You know, I had to do a résumé for theatre last year," she says. "I mean, I need to change it for a *job* job, and add some stuff, but I could send it to you. I can come over later, or in the morning, and we can work on them. And then we can still drop them off tomorrow. I'll drive us."

I glance at her but she's looking through my cardboard box of DVDs. I used to get them for every birthday and every Christmas because Lil and I spent so much time watching movies. Mom thought it was my favourite thing, but really it was just something to do.

"Shouldn't we not go together? Because it looks bad or whatever?"

Lillian looks right at me. "Fuck it."

"Yeah, okay." I nod. "Fuck it."

∿∿∿

MY ROOM IS at the front of the house. I used to have stuff up on my walls but I took it all down to start over and I haven't put anything back up. I have a window that I keep open except on the very coldest days. I still have a collection of animal figurines set up on my dresser from when I was a little kid.

I try to read the newest *NYLON*, but I can't stop thinking about the girls on the website, the way they didn't even seem to care if people knew who they were. I throw the magazine onto the floor and lie down, but my heart is pounding in my ears.

Some of the girls online were hot, but some of them were fat or had shitty skin. Lots of them weren't even pretty. I think about their boyfriends or husbands, the people who touch them in real life. I move my hand under my jeans but it just feels stupid. Sometimes I can't tell what kind of mood I'm in.

I can hear the TV in the living room. Mom likes to have it on all the time—she says it stops her thinking so much. It's the only time her head is quiet. She used to use music; she'd listen to it so loud I could feel it in my body. I loved that. Mom said we were the same, that we both needed to stop thinking so hard and just listen. She'd put on the music and we'd sit there together. Sometimes we'd shake our bodies like we were being electrocuted or lie down on the carpet side by side. But at some point Dad always came home. He'd turn the knob all the way down, tell her she'd make us both deaf. But we didn't go deaf. She doesn't need to listen to the TV extra loud because it's got a lot already—it has sound to listen to and video to watch and subtitles to read. It's not about the volume; it's about *more*. We both found other ways to quiet our heads.

I take my ring box out of my purse and pull my sweater off. My skin is red in a few places from the wool. The inside of my left arm is already covered in straight lines. Some are bright and new, some pink and scabbed; others are ghosts, almost invisible. I've been retracing a star above my hip bone for months—I want it to last forever so I'll always know who I was right now, this year of my life.

I pull the blade along the soft skin halfway up my forearm, crossing over scars so old I can only see them in the sun. I make three cuts and then I lie down in bed and watch myself bleed. It's so quiet that I can hear my heartbeat slowing down. The tightness in my throat and stomach loosens and I can feel it seeping out of me, like a monster leaving my body.

∧∧∧

IN GRADE SEVEN, I made up Lipstick Day. I didn't actually make it up. I read about it in some book. On Lipstick Day, everyone took lipstick from their mom or bought it from the dollar store—bright colours were best—and by noon all of us were covered in kisses. It was mostly the grade sevens and eights, but lots of the younger kids had big red and pink and purple smooches on their foreheads and cheeks, too. It didn't matter if people had boyfriends or girlfriends—we all kissed everyone. It only happened once, but it was the kind of day everyone would talk about for years, the kind of fun kids live for.

After lunch, the principal called all the older classes to the gym for an emergency assembly. "Whose idea was this?" she asked. "This is serious. If nobody tells the truth, you'll all be punished."

Everyone knew it was my idea. They all knew I was the one who started it; I'd even brought a plastic bag full of weird-coloured lipsticks for people who'd forgotten or hadn't heard about the plan. Black and green and orange and blue.

The principal stood at the front of the gym, her frown falling and falling like the sides of her mouth were melting. But it was quiet.

Nobody said anything, and everybody got a week of detention. We all had to stay in at lunch and the teachers found us extra homework every day. Sometimes I worry I might be a follower, that I'm not special and no one will ever have a reason to remember me. But I've never felt so powerful in my life as I did in the silence of that gym, boys in lipstick and girls in lipstick and all of us in it together.

〰

WHEN I WAKE UP, I'm holding my arm against my chest like it's a baby, and there's blood all over my tank top and on my pillow. I wrap a towel I keep in my bedside table around my arm and hold it tight. There's dried blood on one side of the towel, but I make sure only a clean section is touching the new cuts. They're dry anyway. The blood looks like a desert that hasn't had rain in months, cracked and curling. It flakes off onto my sheets when I touch it. I still feel almost like I'm floating, like I've dropped twenty pounds. Everything feels far away, like white noise, like putting my hands over my ears when the vacuum is on.

I take off my top in front of the mirror. I suck in and my stomach looks flat and smooth. I run my hands over it, lean forward, and kiss myself.

Lillian texts to ask if I'm ready to work on résumés. She wants to go to Dairy Queen first even though it's freezing outside. I guess she finished her essay, or maybe she just needs a break. I pick my coat up off the floor and empty the pockets. There's a couple dollars in change and a five-dollar bill folded up into a tiny origami heart. I throw my coat into my closet and put on two sweaters instead. I'm tired of winter.

two

∧∧∧

In the cafeteria at lunch, Lillian won't stop talking about Steve Hamilton. He said hi to her in the hallway this morning and she lost it. Apparently he's been telling everyone how pretty he thinks Lillian is, how amazing she was when the school did *Jesus Christ Superstar* last year. He's two years older than us, but he's not popular. Lil's a real virgin; she hasn't done anything with anyone. She hasn't even kissed anyone yet. She came close once at an after-party for one of the plays she was in. There was a drunk guy there from another school who kept hitting on her. He sat beside her on the couch and gave her sips of his beer and tried to get her to smoke pot, but she never smokes pot without me. She thought she got a little high just from sitting beside him, just from smelling him. I didn't tell her that's not possible because I wasn't really sure. He leaned in to kiss her a few times, but she rolled off the couch and called her mom to come pick her up.

The first person I French kissed was this guy named James in grade seven, and I hated it. At first, I kept my mouth shut tight in a line and he licked right underneath my nose. It smelled like rubber. When I finally opened my mouth, his tongue felt smooth and everything was warm in the wrong places. I wondered why everyone wanted to do it so bad when it felt like exactly what it was, licking something wet, getting someone else's spit all over your mouth.

A few weeks after that, though, I couldn't stop thinking about the kiss. I still remembered how I felt when it happened, but now there were new things, new parts of it that made me want to do it again. I thought about the moment when I was so close to him I couldn't see his face anymore. The smell of his breath, like old gum. His tongue beating like a baby animal's heart against my lips. The way he pushed into me like he wanted to fill me up, touch my insides.

"Steve is so cute," Lillian says.

"So go out with him. Nobody cares."

I brought carrots for lunch today. You can eat as many carrots as you want and not gain any weight. They're negative calories. They were wet and slimy when I got them out of the fridge, but I washed them and peeled them and put them into an old yogurt container. I left the peels, spotted with dirt, in the sink. Mom was watching a morning show and I could hear it through the window after closing the front door behind me.

"You don't have to be a bitch, Katelin." Lillian always uses my full name when she's mad at me. She was named after a famous writer and her own grandmother. I wasn't named after anyone. She picks up one of my carrots and throws it at me. It hits me in the shoulder and bounces onto the floor.

"I just mean you should do whatever you want," I say.

Lillian always does what she wants. She doesn't really go to parties, and she hardly drinks at all. Sometimes I wish I was more like her, that I cared less about what people think.

"Maybe he won't ask me out. I don't even know if I like him." That's what she says when she really likes somebody, when she wants to talk about them but she doesn't want me to know she wants to talk about them.

I don't say anything. I look down at the rest of my carrots—I think they might taste weird but I'm not sure if I remember what carrots are supposed to taste like. I wonder if I can get someone to lend me three dollars for curly fries.

Lillian pushes her middle finger into one half of her egg salad sandwich. It leaves a dent in the white bread.

〰

I GUESS I was wrong when I said Lillian has never kissed anyone. When we were in grade three, these two grade-six guys were obsessed with us. One of them called Lillian's house every night and she'd always run to answer the phone and then tell her parents it was me who was calling. The guy who liked me used to sit with me at lunch recess and poke my shirt where my nipples were. He didn't always poke the right places. It only lasted for a couple weeks, but we got a lot of attention. All the other girls were jealous. One day, the boys chased us to the edge of the schoolyard and pinned us up against the fence. We pretended to struggle, like we wanted to get away, and they kissed us on the lips. Lillian cried on the walk home from school, but we didn't talk about it. I don't even remember their names.

〰

MARCY SHOWS UP at our table halfway through lunch. She's wearing a *Magic School Bus* tank top that's supposed to be pajamas.

I only know that because I used to have the same pair. It actually looks pretty cool as a regular shirt—I wish I thought of doing stuff like that.

She throws her bag in the middle of the table. "Guess what."

We both just look at her. Marcy always knows more about what's going on than we do.

"I went to a party at Niall's this weekend and that picture of Emma is still up on his fridge."

"Such a dick," Lillian says with a mouth full of crust—she always tears it off and eats it first so her last bites all have sandwich filling.

At a party a few months ago, Emma got tag-teamed by two older guys who used to go to our school. Apparently she let other guys watch. When she went home, she left her bra in their bathroom and her coat on one of their beds. I wasn't there that night, but we went to a party at Niall's the next weekend, and there was a drawing taped up on the fridge. In pencil crayon, it was Emma as a cow, with spots and an udder, getting fucked from behind and giving another guy a blow job.

"I might have done something I shouldn't tell you about." Marcy looks between me and Lil and smiles with one side of her mouth. "With Niall."

"Marce." Lillian's mouth actually drops open.

"What? Katie thinks he's hot. Right?"

Lil shakes her head. "She does not. She thought he was cute for like a day in grade nine, and that's before he started shaving his head."

I laugh. "He is kinda gross now."

"Meh, we made out. And I was drunk. It's like a 3 on a slut scale of 1 to 10. Or, like"—she points a thumb at Lillian—"from Little Miss Innocent over here to Emma."

"Yeah, she won't be down at number 1 for long," I say, glancing at Lillian.

"What! Steve Hamilton?"

"Oh my god, guys, I hardly know him."

"So if you fuck him, you'll go straight up to at least a 6, maybe a 7," I say.

Lillian rolls her eyes. "It's not like that. How'd you know about Steve, though?"

Marcy shrugs and takes one of my carrots. "Saw you talking to him in the hallway this morning. It's obvious."

Marcy's always been good at figuring out when people like each other. In grade eight, she predicted Alex and Jonah would end up dating even though they have completely opposite friends, and now they've been together for longer than anyone else at school.

Marcy takes another carrot and I push the whole container toward her. "Thanks—I didn't bring lunch today. You should do it, Lil. He dated Jess last year and I heard he's a good kisser."

She sounds so happy for Lillian, like this is a good thing, and I wonder what's in it for her. Or maybe that's just how she feels; maybe that's how I should feel.

Lillian changes the subject to the math test she and Marcy have next period. Marce is amazing at math. Like, genius level. Sometimes people joke that she must be fucking the teacher, but she's always been like that. In elementary school, the teachers gave her a high school textbook and let her work alone.

I don't have Math this semester, and lunch is almost over anyway, so I say bye and leave Marcy the rest of my carrots.

"See you after school?" Lillian asks. There's a hockey game tonight—we've been going to the arena for all the Junior B home games for like two years now.

"Yeah, I'm covering Jonah's library duty, though, so I'll just meet you at your house and we can go from there." I'm in the Library Club. It sounds stupid, but I like it. We get to suggest books we think the library should stock, and we help one day a week organizing and putting books back on the shelves. It always smells nice in there, and the librarian whispers when she gives me instructions, even when no one else is around.

〰

EMMA USED TO be friends with all of us. Lil and I only really spent time with her at school. Emma and Marcy were closer—their moms both worked at Wal-Mart and they took the same bus to school. But then in grade seven Emma had sex with Russell Daniels, and when they broke up, she told everyone that he raped her. She even went to the principal. But we were all pretty sure he didn't rape her; he didn't even get suspended. We all knew how much Emma liked him. They kissed at recess all the time. After that, people stopped inviting her places, and she mostly hung out alone during recess. She stopped taking the bus and got a ride to school every day. I never say anything when I see her in the hall-way. She forgot the rules.

In grade two, the most popular boy at school had a pool party and invited everyone but me because he said he didn't want to see me in a bathing suit. Another year I was the only girl invited to a boy's party and all the girls whispered about me so I could hear it; they all said I was loose. Mom made me go to the party but I refused to talk to any of the boys the whole time. We went to Burger King. There was a ball pit and all the boys went in while I sat at a table with someone's mom and ate fries dipped in sweet and sour sauce.

|Now that I'm fifteen, things are even harder. Boys want you to do things, but they hate you when you do them. The rules are: never say no and never say yes.|Marcy said no to a guy who wanted a hand job and he told everyone that she gave him a blow job and he was embarrassed because she's so ugly. If you say yes, you're a slut. Always do something, but never do as much as they want.

⋀⋀

THE BACK WALL of the school library is filled with old graduation pictures. Lillian's parents are both in the one from 1981. Her mom looks like she's trying not to laugh, and her dad looks like a nerd. They weren't together then, not for another couple years. My parents aren't in any of the pictures because neither of them are from here. They met in Toronto, but once they decided to have me, my dad thought they should live somewhere quieter. My mom was always the one who liked the city—now he's back there and she's stuck here.

The librarian had to go to a staff meeting, so she left me alone with two carts full of books to reshelve. She said I could just leave and close the door behind me when I'm done.|At first, the quiet feels like a kind of violence. But if I'm in the library for long enough, the buzzing in my head breaks like heavy rain.|

I pull my sleeve up to scratch my arm. I love the way my cuts look the day after, so straight and clean. I keep them covered now, ever since Lil saw them a couple months ago and freaked out. She made me promise not to do it anymore. Every time I cut, I wonder if maybe this is the time they'll be permanent, the time they'll stay bright and sharp, but after a couple days, they always start to fade. I heal fast, maybe because I'm young. Maybe because I just do. Sometimes I put on Polysporin and bandages because it feels nice to take care of myself.

Once I'm done with what's on the carts, I walk through the aisles and reshelve anything that's not in place, then I tidy the librarian's desk. Those aren't things we have to do, but I asked once if I should and the librarian was so happy it almost felt sad. Whenever I come here with classes, she smiles at me like we know each other. The other kids are just regular students.

I leave school through the back doors, and Alex is smoking outside. As soon as I see her, I can't get enough air—I pretend I have to retie my shoe and crouch on the ground so she won't see me freaking out, pursing my lips to slow down my breath. We used to be really good friends, best friends, really—her and me and Lillian. We dressed up like the Spice Girls and won a lip-synching contest. We had sleepovers and made up our own Sailor Moon characters. Once we pulled our scabs off and rubbed our bloody knees together.

When we were in grade two, she taught me how to do it. Sex. I thought it was the only way, that everyone just rubbed up against each other—boys, girls, everyone. I didn't know anything could go inside anything else. We never kissed because we didn't put that together as part of it. Kissing was for love; this was for something different. We knew that without ever talking about it. Once Alex told me people do it with each other's faces, too. She rubbed against my nose and I laughed so hard that we had to stop. It smelled like hay. Every time after we did it, my body would crash with guilt. I'd swear I'd never do it again. But I could never stick to my promise.

One day, after we'd been doing it for more than a year, I told Alex I wanted to dress up, that I'd be a cool tomboy, way cooler than the popular girls, and she could be the popular guy who liked me. She looked right at me and said she'd never do it again. She was so much better than I was. I was disgusting; I was going to hell. For weeks, I thought she hated me. We hardly talked at all. The shame was a rock in my stomach. And then it started seeming like we were okay again. I would've given anything to go back, to never have done it. But that was impossible, so instead I tried to convince myself that Alex had already forgotten, that it was so unimportant to her there wasn't even a place for it in her memory. When someone says no to me, I think about it forever.

But in grade five, we stopped spending time together. There wasn't a clear ending the way there was with Emma. It's less like we stopped being friends and more like we started being people who used to be friends. I thought we'd always be close, that I could trust her with anything. But Alex was hanging out with girls who were already in high school, and she was allowed to date, and it just seemed like she was older than we were even though she had the latest birthday of anyone in our grade. She used to have blond hair but it's dyed black now, and she has cheek piercings that must've hurt like a bitch.

When I feel like I can breathe again, I stand back up, and she waves at me from where she's sitting on the fence, so I walk over and lean against it.

"You want one?"

I nod, and she passes me a smoke from her pack of Player's, then pulls out her lighter. I lean toward her to use the flame.

"What are you still doing here?" I ask.

"Waiting for Jonah."

"Is he here? I thought he had a family thing—we switched days in the library."

"Shit. That's why he hasn't texted me back. I forgot."

She's wearing a short dress, so most of her ass must be right up against the wood of the fence. It's a warm day; there are piles of snow melting on the side of the road. It smells like spring, like melting dog shit.

"You're gonna get splinters," I say.

"Nope." She pulls her dress up to show me she's wearing boxers, probably Jonah's. "I'd wear nothing but boys' clothes if I could."

In grade six, all of the girls were standing around one recess and Alex used the word *rendezvous* and Marcy asked what it meant. Alex said it was when people meet in secret, sometimes for sex. She looked right at me and smiled and said, "Katie and I used to rendezvous. Right, K?" My whole body froze.

Marcy broke the silence. "You guys used to have sex?"

Alex looked at her like she was disgusting and said, "Don't be an idiot, Marce. It doesn't have to be for sex."

I tried to laugh with the other girls, but my face felt bright red. Now just seeing Alex makes me sick to my stomach. She'll always have something on me, this secret. I try to tell myself I have something on her, too. But I can't help thinking I care more than she does, that she'd throw us both over the edge if she had to.

She takes a drag of her cigarette, deep like she wants the smoke all the way down into her arms and legs, and we both watch a blue truck—the back filled with grade-eleven boys—pull out of the parking lot, squealing into the empty street.

∧∧∧

THE SIDE DOOR isn't locked at Lillian's, so I let myself in. They're in the middle of dinner. It's just Lil, her dad, and her little brother, Dougie—her older brother's in college and her mom's probably at work. Dougie's the reason we started going to Junior B games in the first place. He used to think he was obsessed with sports, so Lillian's mom asked us to take him to a hockey game. We spent the whole time drinking hot chocolate and eating french fries and making fun of how serious it seemed. Dougie got cold and bored halfway through and wouldn't stop whining—hockey wasn't his sport—so the next time the team was playing, me and Lil just went alone.

"Hey, Katie. Hot dog?" Lillian's dad asks. "There are still a couple left."

She looks at me and rolls her eyes. "Katie can't eat hot dogs, Dad. Not since she ate three that time at Canada's Wonderland."

Sometimes Lil talks for me, but I love it. It's not like she's trying to tell me what to do or think—it's more like she remembers everything about me. Like I'm so interesting that she wants to prove she knows every detail.

I sit on the empty chair beside her.

"Oh, yes, the infamous hot dog-puke incident. How could I forget?"

Lil slides me her plate. "Finish my fries? I have to get a sweater."

Once she's gone, her dad asks, "So how was today, Miss Katie?"

I think about how to respond—I want to tell him something true. Lillian's dad is better than regular dads. He helped us make a piñata out of papier mâché for Alex's seventh birthday. He took us to laser tag an hour away once, on a normal day, just because we wanted to go. He makes dinner almost every night. When we were little, he used to take us to gymnastics, and he braided our hair better than any of the moms could.

Before I can answer, Lillian's already yelling at me from the next room. "Ready! Let's go!" I hear the side door slam behind her; she didn't even say bye. Sometimes it makes me mad, the way Lil acts like her family will always be there. It's like she doesn't know how cool it is to have people who ask you how your day was for no reason other than they care.

∧∧

THE GAME'S ALREADY started when we make it to the arena. Lillian buys large fries even though she just ate some for dinner. She always ruins them with vinegar.

We like to sit in the seats right at the top, closest to the entrance. There's a bar in front of the seats that you can put your feet up on. We have favourite players, Number 27 and Number 4, and when they score we shout things toward the ice, things that have nothing to do with hockey: *Your thighs are rock hard. I want to have your babies. Suck my face.* Hardly anyone ever sits on this side, and the acoustics make it impossible to hear anything from across the rink.

We only really pay attention when there's a fight, which happens a couple times every game. Today one of our players gets mad and breaks his stick against the boards. It's only interesting for a minute, though, and then he picks up the pieces and everyone goes back to skating around.

The guy who does the music plays the same five songs over and over again. When "T.N.T." by AC/DC starts playing for what feels like the millionth time, Lil sighs. "Why do we do this to ourselves?"

I put my head on her shoulder. "This Tim Hortons makes the best hot chocolate in town."

"True," she says. Then she presses her head onto mine like a hug.

three

^^^

L illian didn't want to hang out with Steve by herself—she said that'd be rushing things—so she made me come to the movies with them. He invited his cousin, too.

Before we left her house, she tried on four different outfits. I kept catching her rubbing her palm across her lips, which is something she only does when she's anxious. It looks weird, but I do weird shit, too. Now that we're at the movies, though, she doesn't seem nervous at all. She even asked Steve for some of his Junior Mints. Me and the cousin haven't talked. It's obvious why we're here.

There's almost no one else in the theatre. The movie hasn't started yet, and Lil tries to include me in the conversation, but she has to keep turning back and forth between me and Steve and it's awkward. I wish she'd just leave me out of it.

She's explaining her theory that everyone has two favourite movies—the one they tell other people is their favourite, and the real one. Hers are *It's a Wonderful Life* and *Grease*. "What are yours?" she asks Steve.

"Umm, so I tell people it's *Ghost World*."

"Katie loves that movie. Hey, Katie? That's one of your favourites."

She's trying so hard and it just makes me want to hit her. I nod. She turns back to Steve. "And the real one?"

"Umm. Honestly? *Jurassic Park*."

"That's hardly even embarrassing, though." She swats at his arm. "I mean, Katie's is *Crossroads*. *That's* embarrassing." She says it like it's admirable and my heart doubles in size.

"What's that?" Steve asks.

"The Britney Spears movie."

Steve leans forward to smile at me, but I know he's only doing it for Lillian. I guess we have that in common, too. I try to imagine what it'd be like to have sex with him, but I can't. Even kissing him seems impossible. It's not that he's ugly; I can just tell there's nothing special about him.

I started rating people when I used to go to church. Mom never went, just me and Dad. Back in elementary school, I did all the steps: communion, confession, confirmation. Every Sunday, I used to stay in bed for as long as I could until Dad came to wake me up. I always hoped he'd forget about me and go by himself so I could sleep in. It never worked, not even once. He was always right on time.

Dad and I always sat on the far left, next to the aisle, close to the front. After people got communion, they passed by me on their way back to their seats. I'd hold the host on my tongue as long as possible and play a game called yes/no, where I'd look at every person and decide whether or not I'd do it with them. I knew there were some people I wanted something from. People I wanted to like me.

Steve is definitely a no.

⌃⌃⌃

THE MOVIE'S JUST OKAY. And we don't stick around long afterward. I can tell Lillian and Steve are both drawing out their goodbyes, but it's cold, so I tell Lil we should start walking—Steve and his cousin are going the opposite way.

When we're out of earshot, Lillian says, "He kissed me."

"During the movie?"

"While you were in the bathroom."

"He just did it?"

"He asked first."

"And you said yes?"

"Yeah." She goes up on her tiptoes and runs on the spot, thrusting her arms above her head in celebration. It's like she didn't even hear the sarcasm in my voice. "And he asked me to come over. I said I couldn't now but I would next time."

We get to her house before mine. She shuffles foot to foot, and her hands are pulled up into the sleeves of her winter jacket. I don't feel cold anymore.

"Is it bad that I really wanted to go?"

I shrug. *Next time*, she said. *Next time* she won't need me there at all.

⌃⌃⌃

WHEN I GET HOME, I grab a granola bar to eat in front of the computer. Mom bought the good ones with chocolate chips and peanut butter; I'm not sure if she knows they're my favourite. Maybe they're her favourite, too.

It's colder in the basement than it was outside. I turn on the heater in the corner, put a blanket around my shoulders, and sit down in the metal chair. I get a shock and I can feel the static in my hair.

I log in to MSN, but nobody good is on. A guy from my English class says hi, but he always says hi, so I set my status to Busy. Everyone else must be out doing something. I go into a chat room instead, the one that's full of weirdos. It just makes me think about what happened the last time I was here. Once I start thinking about it, my whole body feels like it's humming, like there's a machine where my brain used to be. I still remember the URL. My finger hovers over the keyboard for a few seconds, one last chance to stop, before I hit Return.

I find underwear ads from all kinds of women. One says you should hold her panties over a kettle of boiling water for a few seconds before you use them. They'll be moist, like fresh, she says. I can't swallow past the lump in my throat; it's like I brought up part of my body and it needs to work its way back down, like when you eat too much bread too fast and can't get a full breath. I read the comments from customers who buy underpants, who love to smell them or put them in their mouths or wear them under their clothes and walk around in public. It's mostly men who are looking and buying, and their words make me feel light-headed and hot like I've been sitting in the sauna at the public pool for too long.

I don't know what to look at next, so I just type *porn* into the search bar. And there's the word on the screen over and over and over. *Porn* is everywhere. First I find videos of girls touching themselves. Some girls look right at me but others don't show anything above their bellies. One girl has a black square over her face, but I can hear her moaning behind it, asking herself for more. I have the sound on as quiet as it'll go without being off. I can hear Mom upstairs in the kitchen.

I find another video where a girl is in a cage. A woman opens a little door in the side and the girl puts her ass right up to it. The woman hits her with something that looks like a tennis racquet. There's a close-up on the girl's butt, bright red while the rest of her is pale like she's never been out of that cage.

As soon as I come, I feel guilty, like somebody knows what I did. I feel like someone's watching me. I even get up and check behind the door, but there's nobody there.

I put my hand on the desk as I sit back down, and my nail catches a crack in the wood. I've been growing them out and painting them different colours every day. My fingernail bends backward like it's going to come right off. Nothing happens—it doesn't even hurt afterward—but thinking about the way it bent, the panic, is horrible. There's a crack in my nail polish where it folded. I hold my finger in my other hand, pressing down like I'm holding all the parts together. I cry even though it makes me feel like an idiot, and later I scrub off the polish and bite all my nails until you can't see the white anymore. Only a couple of them bleed.

∧∧∧

IN GRADE TWO, Lillian and I were walking to the corner store, and a man yelled at us from his front door. His house had apartments in it where other people lived. People he wasn't even related to. The only people who lived in our houses were our own families, so having a neighbour on the other side of your bedroom wall seemed exciting. The whole side of the house was covered in ivy and we used to dare each other to run up and pull some down, sure that at some point the whole wall of vines would fall right on our heads.

When the man called out to us, we stopped to see what he wanted. Most of the neighbours were old and just wanted to say hi. Mom said it made them feel young and happy. One of them had a dog Lillian and I visited every few days—we weren't allowed to have pets. I'd never seen the man leave his house. We could only see his top half through the screen door, and when he opened it, he was naked from the waist down. His penis hung out, soft but huge like an elephant trunk, old-man saggy. It's the first penis I remember seeing. Lillian and I ran all the way to the corner store like someone was chasing us. We bought candy, and Lil held a piece of licorice down by her crotch and flopped it around, and I laughed so hard ginger ale came out my nose. My mouth stung from Sour Patch Kids. When we walked home, he wasn't in the doorway anymore.

We didn't tell our moms because I was worried we'd get in trouble. From then on, we usually walked around the other side of the block when we went to the corner store. We still took the old way once in a while, though. We'd dare each other to do it, or sometimes we just turned to go that way without warning, like a decision we made without knowing it. Our conversations were louder, our voices higher pitched, and we bounced on the front of our feet as we got close to the house. My breath would catch in my throat, and I'd feel hot and scared, and then relieved when there was no one in the doorway, nobody calling us over. But I felt other things, too. The rest of the walk was always filled with a kind of disappointment, something I couldn't say out loud. I used to think Lillian felt it, too, but now I'm not sure. Now I wonder if there was always something wrong with me.

〈〈〈

LIL AND I have nicknames for all the girls at Tim Hortons. There's one we call Stupidbitchuglyslutwhore because she always rolls her eyes when we order and never asks us if we want mugs instead of to-go cups. She obviously hates us. Another girl is called Glasses. We saw her wearing glasses once, and none of the other girls wear them. My favourite is Brown-Shirt Girl. We couldn't come up with a better name for her, because there's nothing exactly special about her. They all wear brown shirts.

Lillian gets a coffee and I get hot chocolate. We always sit in the same spot. If someone's already there, we sit as close as we can and Lillian stares at them until they go. They always leave eventually, but I don't know how much that has to do with Lil. We don't have to do any staring today.

Lillian takes a sip of her coffee and her whole face is a grimace. She hates the taste of coffee but she loves the idea of it.

"I sucked Steve's dick," she says.

It's not what I was expecting her to say. I'm impressed, and I guess something like jealous. Not because of Steve, obviously.

"Did you like it?"

"It was all right. His mom was there."

"What?"

"Oh, not like *right* there. But she was in the living room. We were in his bedroom. And their house is really small. It was weird."

"When?"

"Thursday after school. It just kinda happened, I guess?"

It shouldn't be a surprise—he asked her to be his girlfriend the morning after the movies. At first she asked him if she could think about it, but she called him back the next day and said yes. When she told me, I tried to be excited for her. It was always going to happen eventually—someone was going to realize Lil is the best. I tried to tell myself if she likes Steve, there must be something okay about him. We don't have to like the same people to be best friends. But she's never kept a secret from me before. If someone asked me how quick Lillian would tell me something like this, I would've said she'd call me on her drive home. But it's been a whole two days.

I didn't think Lillian was the kind of girl who gave blow jobs. Maybe every girl is that kind of girl.

"I didn't hate it or anything. It was just weird." Lillian takes another sip of her coffee but this time her face stays like normal, like she grew up completely in the last two minutes.

"Cool," I say.

I want to ask her more about what it was like, how it made her feel, because I want to know exactly what girls are supposed to feel. I've told her about stuff I've done, but not everything.

At the beginning of the school year, Lil and I went to this party at the Mariner Motel, right across from the population sign on the highway. Mostly people live there, but it's a real motel, too. We'd never been to a party there before, and it was pretty weird. Some of the rooms had no doors at all, and this old lady was telling people's fortunes with tarot cards. At one point, Mark Dresler snuck up behind me and put an open bottle of beer in my jeans upside down. Everyone saw it but they all still joked that I'd pissed myself, except this guy Nate, Dresler's best friend. Nate's the kind of guy that makes other people cool just by hanging out with them. He was so nice. He found an empty room and waited on the bed while I went into the bathroom and soaked up some of the beer from my jeans using toilet paper.

When I came out, he smiled at me like we knew each other already. "Sorry," he said. "Dresler can be a dick."

I just shrugged because it didn't feel like that big of a deal anymore. My pants were just damp now. Plus, it gave me an excuse to be in a room with Nate Murray.

He reached over from the bed and grabbed my wrist, pulled me over so I was standing between his wide-open legs. He was wearing a Hawaiian shirt that was way too big for him, like he was playing dress-up. I wanted to see it open, his bare chest a strip of shining skin. But I knew I wouldn't be able to undo the buttons because my hands were numb. I felt like I'd been out in a snowstorm with no clothes on.

He started kissing me on the arm. It seemed weird at first—I just stood there not moving—but eventually he made it all the way up and was kissing my neck and then my lips. He pulled me down onto the bed, then stood up and took his pants completely off, and when he tried to undo my jeans, I said no. I don't even know how I managed to say it; I could hardly talk around him. We kissed for a while and then he tried again, and I said I wasn't sure.

"Look how much I want you," he said.

It was true. He did want me. He wanted me so bad and I could see it. It felt like my whole body was made of cicadas and they were all about to shed their skins and fly away. *This is what it's like to be a woman who's loved,* I thought, *a woman somebody wants.*

When I put my hand on his dick, he acted like he liked it, and I was relieved because it didn't even seem that difficult—it felt like something I couldn't mess up. But pretty soon he said, "Is that all? I could do that myself," and I felt so stupid, like I'd misunderstood.

I said, "I just wanted to do this for a minute first," but he probably saw right through me, saw I didn't know what I was doing. I moved down to give him a blow job like I'd been planning it all along.

When he came, I couldn't keep everything—his semen and my spit and maybe a little puke—in my mouth. I couldn't breathe; it was just reflex. I got it on his shirt and my own shirt and the bed. He just walked into the bathroom and closed the door behind him, and I knew right away that I'd broken some kind of rule.

There was knocking on the motel room door and I ignored it until I heard Lillian yelling for me. It took me a minute to open the door because it was double locked, and when I finally got it, Lillian tried to look into the room behind me. She asked who I was with and if I was okay—she sounded so disappointed and I felt like such a failure that I just said, "Nobody. I'm fine." I wanted to tell her she wouldn't understand because everything's perfect for her, but that would have been stupid.

I wonder if Lillian will have sex before I do, and if she'll tell me about it right away. She always says she's going to wait until she's older, but maybe she's older now.

Glasses and Stupidbitchuglyslutwhore laugh behind the counter. I'm always sure they're talking shit about us. Lillian thinks so, too. Part of the reason this spot is our favourite is because we can see everything behind the counter. We always talked about getting jobs here, but we swore we'd only ever do it together.

〰〰〰

MOM IS OBSESSED with infections right now. The house has smelled like bleach for a week. She ordered a new keyboard and mouse for the computer because she read about all the viruses that can live in them. My nose was running the other day and she made me stay in the bathroom until it stopped so she knew it was just from being outside. I'm not like Mom. I know a cut doesn't kill you.

None of the doors in our house lock, so I told her I'll clean my room and she shouldn't go in there. But when I get home from Tim Hortons, she's in my room anyway. I think sometimes she uses cleaning as an excuse to look through my stuff. She secretly wants to find something just so she can hold it over my head. Once she was in there and she found an old pack of cigarettes. She got so mad at me even though I know she smokes sometimes. I told her that—it didn't help. The smokes were hidden right beside my ring box, but she didn't say anything at all about that. Maybe she didn't look inside, but I doubt it. She's the best at only seeing the things she wants to see.

Today she's vacuuming under my bed, bent all the way over with her back to me. I yell at her and wave my arms but she can't hear me.

When she stands up and turns around, she bumps right into me and then screams louder than the vacuum. She bends over again and when I pull the plug, I realize she's laughing.

"Sorry," I say.

She can hardly breathe she's laughing so hard. She's not wearing any socks and her toenails are painted green. They match the carpet. There's a smear of green on the side of her left big toe, too, so I know she must have done them herself sometime today. Dad used to paint them for her. She'd whine that she couldn't reach her toes, but in a way that always made him laugh. He'd sit with her legs over his lap and paint while we all watched TV together.

"You scared the shit out of me," she says, holding her hand over her heart.

She looks young right now, maybe too young to be a mom. And happy, like all she needed was a really good scare.

"Can we get pizza for dinner?" I ask. When he left, we ate pizza for a whole month, but I never got sick of it.

She nods really slowly. "Okay. You call, I'll pay." She puts her hand on my cheek and I tilt my head like a little dog, push my face into her for just a second before I pull away. Her fingers smell like nail polish and dish soap.

∧∧∧

I LOOK ONLINE for other sites where people are selling their dirty clothes. They're everywhere. One girl is selling a pair of shoes. They used to be white. She got them in high school and she's been wearing them for a decade. She wears them without socks for long shifts as a waitress, she says. There are comments asking for pictures of her feet, descriptions of the smell, what her toes look like, if she paints her nails. Someone asks if she has any worn-out slippers.

Most of the people want underwear and socks. Bras are popular, too. There's a man who wants women to sell him designer shirts that they've puked on after drinking a bunch of milk. I wonder if I could do that.

I end up on other sites, where you can put up ads asking for anything. There are lots of ads from men. The usual things. But there are ads from women, too. Women who want everything.

Women who want someone to spank them or fuck them in the ass. Women who don't want boyfriends at all.

I love the way people just ask for things, the way they say exactly what they like. These women are allowed to talk about their bodies—they're allowed to do whatever they want, and all the men want is more. It's like it doesn't matter that they're completely fucked up, because there's always someone else who's just as fucked up as they are.

〰

THE FIRST TIME I stuck my fingers inside my own vagina, it was because I read about it in *Cosmo*. I'd tried lots of other things before but this felt like I was suddenly a different person, like my skin was changing colours and my head was getting bigger and bigger like a balloon.

I was worried I wouldn't be able to stay quiet, that I'd yell out without even realizing it was happening, that I'd wake up the whole neighbourhood. I was worried I'd lose control. But instead my mouth opened wide and I squeaked a little. And then I stopped. I didn't move for I don't know how long. I left my fingers inside me until everything was quiet and calm and my head was a normal size again. When I couldn't feel my pulse in my eyes anymore, I started moving my fingers in and out all over again.

I've heard stories about girls who had to go to the hospital because they got a carrot or a hot dog stuck inside them. If you get caught, everyone will know who you really are. If anyone asks, you have to deny it. *Honestly, I don't. Never. I can find someone to fuck me. So gross.* Those are just some of the things you're supposed to say.

Last week at school I had to go to the bathroom to touch myself because I was reading *American Psycho* in class and there was a scene where the narrator has sex with two women at once. Before he hurts them, they do all kinds of things. They fuck and fuck and fuck. I read it over and over again and then put my hand up to ask to use the washroom. I tried to make it seem casual but my arm felt so straight, like I couldn't bend it if I tried. It felt like everyone could see me.

four

〽

There's a girl who used to go to our school whose boyfriend stabbed her six times. I didn't know her. She's older. They were both high and he thought she cheated on him. Maybe she did. Everyone always asks that question, but nobody knows the answer. He left her lying there, soaking in her own blood. Then he took a shower, put on clean clothes, and went to the police station and said he killed her. It took them a long time to do anything because he was so high they thought he was lying. Everyone knew he was an idiot. When they found her, she was hardly breathing, unconscious in a puddle.

Sometimes I think about what her body must have looked like with all those holes. What it looked like all sewed up. I wonder about her scars and if she can look at her own body without thinking about him, if she feels like it's not really hers anymore. I wonder if she thinks about how easily it can fall apart, how easy it is to break someone.

Or maybe she thinks about how many things can happen to a human body before it dies, how she regrew all the bits he took away. How bodies are just machines that break sometimes. How fixable things are.

She works at the grocery store now.

〜〜

MY MOM'S BODY is broken, too. But she did it to herself. It wasn't always like this. Right now she's sure she has leukemia. She says it explains everything. She's weak and tired. One day she asks me to feel her throat, and then every hour she knocks on my bedroom door to ask me to feel it again, tell her if she's swollen. She got a bloody nose this morning and she saved the Kleenex the whole day to prove it to me.

I used to believe her but I don't anymore. Sometimes when she tells me her ankles are swollen, they really look swollen. And sometimes it really seems like her head or her tongue or her hands hurt. But the doctors don't believe her, and doctors are the kind of people you're supposed to trust.

Maybe things are more complicated, though. Once I pretended I was sick on a long drive just because I wanted my dad to carry me inside from the car, and by the time we got home I was hallucinating with the flu.

〜〜

IT'S LIKE LILLIAN'S a different person. We already weren't hanging out at school much now that her new play has started, but she spends all her free time with Steve. He picks her up every morning even though she lives like four blocks from school. She called me last night and told me they make out everywhere.

She said his mom loves her and hopes they'll get married. That's all she talked about for half an hour. At one point I used the toilet as loud as I could—I even flushed it—and it was like she couldn't hear me.

When she started talking about how he got them tickets to see *Hairspray* in the city on Monday night—not some kiddie matinee—I interrupted. "Isn't there a Juniors game Monday?"

Lil cleared her throat like she hadn't swallowed in hours. "I mean, do you even like doing that anymore?"

"It's the playoffs."

"Katie. We never even watch the games."

It's not that I ever actually cared about hockey. But I kept going because we always went. I thought that was enough.

"We'll do something Wednesday, okay? And I'll call you after the play and tell you how it was?"

"That's okay. I've seen the movie."

There was another heavy pause, then she said, "This is my thing, Katie."

All of a sudden I felt so angry—that she knows what she wants, that she already has the thing she likes. That part's almost as bad as her ditching me for Steve. Lillian has known forever that she loves acting—plays, musicals, anything on a stage. I don't have a thing like that. I worry all the time that I'll never really be good at anything. I started realizing when I was just a kid that it was already too late. When I was twelve, I told a teacher I wanted to do ballet, and she said I should have started earlier. You couldn't learn to be a ballerina once you were already a person. I was stubborn; I took out all the ballet books I could find from the library—I'd learn on my own and surprise everyone. I'd be a winner. But it didn't work; I didn't know what I was doing, I got bored, I gave up. I was so jealous of the girls whose parents made them start figure skating or playing piano or swimming or doing gymnastics when they were little so that by the time they were older, they had this thing, this skill, that was part of who they were. Their bodies carried memories.

I wonder if it would feel so bad if Lil wasn't going to the show with Steve; maybe then I could be excited for her.

"Are you mad at me?" she asked.

I could have told her the truth—how it felt like the blood was rushing out of my head, how I didn't know what to do instead of going to the arena, how not spending the night with her meant another night alone with Mom—but I was worried I'd tell her and she'd still go to the play. "No. I'm okay. I'm just really tired. Are you mad at me?"

She laughed. "Of course not. I love you."

Her words hung there. We say *I love you* all the time. Maybe we say it so much it stopped meaning anything. The silence started feeling awkward, like there was suddenly space neither of us knew how to fill. So I told her to have a good time and we made plans to watch a movie during the week, and then we said goodbye.

⋀⋀⋀

I GO ON the site every day now. I haven't signed up for a full account, so I can only look at some of the ads and I can't comment, but that's okay. I don't know what I'd say anyway.

I've started to think about my own clothes, the things I wear under them—socks, bras, panties—differently. I used to try to see it all the way a boy might. What would they want to see, touch? Every time I got dressed, I was thinking about the right choice.

But now each pair of socks and underwear, each bra, feels like the right choice for someone. No matter what I feel like wearing, someone would like it. Some days, I walk to Wal-Mart and look through the underwear hanging in plastic. There are thongs and briefs and bikini cuts in beige and bright colours, in satin and polyester, with lace and without. There are white cotton packs of three. I imagine the man who'd like each style, colour, brand, and I can see their faces, hear their voices, feel their fingers tracing lines on my body when I'm in bed at night. They all like something different. They all want separate parts of me.

〜〜〜

LIL USUALLY GOES out for lunch with Steve now. She invited me a couple times, but spending a whole hour pretending to like Steve sounds exhausting. When I think about sitting in the back seat of his car while they laugh at some joke I don't get, my brain feels like it's going to throb right out of my skull. I spent lunch in the caf for a couple days, but it was all the same people—there's always someone to sit with, but never anyone I really want to sit with. Sometimes Marcy's there, and she always comes to say hi, but she never sticks around for all of lunch. A few days ago, she asked me where Lil was and I realized I haven't talked to Marcy alone since elementary school. All of Lil's and my friends are like that—they're ours, not mine. And I don't know if *ours* exists anymore. When I was in grade six, I made a list of all my friends on Post-it notes and plastered them on my bedroom wall. It felt so good to see them written down, like the friendships were official, like I could keep them. Lillian was right at the top of the list. Maybe it was stupid to keep one person there for so long.

So I have a plan. If Lillian's going to ditch me for Steve, I'll get better friends. The past few days I've been standing out at the back doors during lunch. That's where the cool people hang out. We have some jocks at our school and whatever, but they're mostly losers. Being cool means you make the rules. Cool people just know what to do without having to think about it. It seems like freedom.

Smoking is the only way standing around alone out here doesn't look weird. A few months ago, I started stealing Mom's cigarettes and keeping them in a plastic bag in the back of my closet. I took one from her pack in the freezer every few days, not enough that she'd notice. I've been going out to smoke one at the beginning of lunch and one at the end. Nobody talks to me. The first day, I tried to say hi to Alex. She smiled and nodded at me, but then she started talking to someone else, and they acted like I wasn't even there. I stood there, half listening to them, half looking around even though there was nothing else to look at, feeling like an idiot. By the time I finished my smoke, Alex's back was to me and I went inside without saying bye.

A few days later, it feels less and more embarrassing at the same time. I'm not as nervous as the first couple days, when my hands were shaking. But people must have noticed me by now— my friendlessness stands out like something to fear. I'm not brave enough to keep coming out here forever.

When I get out back today, Cassie Cunningham is leaning up against the brick wall. She only started going to my school last year, but everyone already knew her. She used to go to TCI, the big high school. Her hair's tied in a bun right on top of her head, and she has a blanket around her shoulders instead of a jacket. She's popular because she doesn't try to be. There are three guys standing around and it's obvious they're all trying to impress her, trying to say something cool enough that she'll notice. She gives off this thing like if you touch her she might burn your skin. I feel like if I tried to talk to her, my throat would close up. But I also want to be close to wherever she is, catch a word she says, see how she holds her body so I can copy it later. There are some people it's impossible not to want to be around, even if you hardly know them.

The first person who comes out alone is this guy named Ivan. It's obvious he's not alone the same way I am. He's confident like this is where he belongs. He's two years older than me, and he's friends with everyone but it also seems like he doesn't want to be friends with anyone at all. It's like he doesn't care about anything. Once he slapped a teacher in the face and got suspended. The vice-principal called the police and an ambulance even though it wasn't a big deal. Ivan has great hair. He's been in jail—he pulled a knife on a cop when he was really high. Once he got super drunk at a party and threw up in someone's purse.

I decide to take my chance before Ivan joins a group. I walk up to him and ask if I can buy a smoke for a quarter. He acts like it's nothing, just gives me a cigarette and drops my quarter into his shirt pocket.

"I've never seen you out here." Ivan says it like it's true, and I want it to be. He's standing right under the sun and I have to squint to look him in the face. His shirt collar is so white it's shiny. It looks like it would snap in half if you tried to bend it. This moment feels better than anything else this week.

"I don't smoke much," I say.

"You should. Anyone who says smoking isn't cool is a liar."

From the side of my eye, I see Cassie push off the wall. She moves toward the doors but she nods at Ivan as she passes. Her pupils are big like they're trying to take over all the white. It feels like Ivan's being approved of.

Then someone calls him over, and I'm alone again. I try to look at him without getting caught. He laughs at everything. He's poking the girl beside him and she's acting annoyed, but I wonder if she likes the attention—I wish someone would poke me. This smoke tastes better than Mom's, but it's gone too fast. I look down at the ground for a minute, toe a crumbling piece of wall with my Converse, and tell myself when I look up, Ivan'll be back, standing in front of me again. Instead, he's gone.

∧∧∧

IT POURS ALL morning on Friday, the first thunderstorm of the year, so I skip my first cigarette and go straight to the caf. I find a dollar fifty in change in the bottom of my purse and ask Marce if she wants to split nachos. She says she ate during her spare. There's a couple other girls at the table with us, April and Hanna, but they're already eating stuff from home. I listen to them talk about someone's older brother while they chew cold-cut sandwiches and veggie sticks with their mouths open, and my stomach growls. I press into it with the heel of my hand, but it rolls over and over like the storm outside. I didn't eat breakfast. I can't afford anything with a dollar fifty.

"Can someone please lend me money? Just a dollar? I'm dying."

April sighs. "You always do this." I don't know April that well. She does theatre with Lillian, and she hates me. "Just ask Suze for a tab."

Suze, the lunch lady, won't give me a tab anymore because it took me months to pay one off last year. I look down at the dirty coins in my hand. Maybe I should get a chocolate bar from the vending machine.

"Oh my god," Marcy says, "you look like a dying puppy." She reaches into the front of her bag, pulls out some change, and throws it on the table toward me.

I pick it all up, even the nickels and dimes and pennies. "I'll pay you back."

"Right," she says.

They all go back to talking like I've already left. My face burns. The rain is stopping, so I leave school to get a slice of pizza across the street. I like the plain cheese and the Hawaiian, but all they have is pepperoni. I don't even care. I'm so hungry my stomach hurts, and I finish most of the slice on the walk back.

I'm almost at the school's parking lot when someone yells, "Hey!" I snap my head up and see Ivan jogging over.

"I've been looking everywhere for you," he says.

I haven't been out to smoke since meeting him. I wonder if he looked anywhere other than here.

"Can I have your crust?"

I almost forgot about my pizza. I probably have sauce all over my mouth. My lips feel slick with cheese grease.

"Umm, yeah. For sure." I pass it over. I never eat the crust anyway.

He tears off a piece with his teeth, then takes the backpack off his shoulder and opens a side pocket, pulls out a full pack of Du Mauriers. The plastic isn't even broken yet. "For you," he says, holding it out to me.

"Like, to keep?"

He smiles. "Yeah, I got them for you. I was buying smokes last night and kept thinking about you and how you don't really smoke and what a shame that is."

I feel a blush starting at the sides of my nose, and I try to breathe. "Why is it a shame?"

"I only spend time with smokers."

I take the pack and throw it into my purse like it doesn't even matter, on top of my plastic bag of Mom's cigarettes.

"What's your name?" he asks.

"Katie."

"I'm Ivan."

"I know."

The grin on his face should be worth the worst kind of embarrassment, but it's a good day. Maybe I'd tell him anything.

"Cool," he says.

∧∧∧

I GET MY period on my walk home. It's that sudden feeling, like not realizing something is happening until it's over. My underpants are dry and the next second they're not.

Once I got it and I didn't have a tampon or anything, but I figured everything would be fine. I didn't worry about it at all. And then when I got home after school, there was a big stain all through the back of my jeans, like I'd been sitting in blood, like it had pooled in one place. I hadn't even felt it after the first bit. I thought about how many people had seen me, had seen my blood, and I knew I should be embarrassed. I thought about the way people had looked at me through the day, and I wondered whether they'd talked about it, about me and my disgusting hygiene, how dirty I was. I wondered if there were smears of blood left on my chairs, if other people touched it, if it got on anyone's bare skin. I took my leather boots out of the hiding place in my closet, put them on over my jeans, and zipped them up. I lay on the floor with my legs up against the bed, high in the air so I could look at myself, at how long I was. I thought about someone touching my dirty jeans, their finger bright red like a new fingerprint.

It always feels great in the middle, like there's a fire burning my insides until I'm empty. But then I'm back, heavy on the earth, in a second. And I never want to come again, until the next time.

Today, I can feel the blood, but I don't rush home.

〰

I DON'T EVEN go to the bathroom right away. Instead, I go down to the computer and sign on to the site. I read through the instructions for how to become a panty seller, the list of rules and tips. I read everything again. And then again.

I feel great—confident and sexy. I feel like an adult. I feel ready to do something.

There's a site all the women use that lets people send you money from almost anywhere in the world. It only takes a few minutes to set up my account.

five

ᐧᐧᐧ

Mom's supposed to have a job interview on Saturday, but she's been on the couch for days. She says she can't feel her legs.

I only know about the interview because there was a message about it on the answering machine yesterday. The person called her Mrs. Henry, which I guess is her name, but it doesn't sound right anymore. When your husband leaves, you should at least get your name back. I could change mine to match hers, even.

"You have to do anything today?" I ask.

"Nothing except hang out with my amazing daughter." It sounds like she's talking around something, like her mouth is full, but I haven't seen her eat since Thursday morning, cottage cheese.

I want to tell her I know about the interview, that this is all her fault, that she's ruining everything, but I don't know how. Instead, I walk to the video store and rent *Moonstruck* and *Mermaids*. This store has everything, even the old ones. Mom's always loved Cher, but we don't own any of her movies. I get a whole bag of nickel-and-dime candy for myself and a box of Smarties for Mom. I make juice from a frozen can and bring her a glass, and all we do for the rest of the day is watch movies.

∧∧∧

THE NEXT MORNING, the house phone rings. It's probably Lillian. She's one of the only people who ever calls the house phone, and we haven't talked yet this weekend. Maybe she misses me. Maybe nothing has really changed and everything can just go back to normal. It's not her on the phone, though—it's Ivan.

"Oh, hey," I say. I sit down on a chair and then stand up again, pace the kitchen tiles.

"Hi," he says. "Guess how I got your number."

"Magic?"

"Is that your actual guess? I thought you were smart."

I haven't talked to a boy on the phone since grade eight, when we'd have sleepovers and call people we had crushes on. This doesn't feel like that, and I'm glad he called me because I wouldn't have called him first. Hearing the rings on the other side is the worst because you have no idea what's going to happen—waiting for an answer and half wishing to hear a voice, half wishing the answering machine would just pick up.

"Did you ask someone for it?" My arm is itchy where it's healing in a couple places. I press my finger hard onto one of the lines, and the scab breaks; a dot of blood pops through.

"I told the secretary you left your asthma inhaler in the cafeteria. She wanted me to just give it to her, but I told her you could die if you didn't get it right away."

I don't have asthma. In elementary school, we took turns using Emma's inhaler because we thought it would get us high. I remember her passing it to me under a desk before I went to the bathroom. Then I sat in a stall and tried to talk myself into it. I was too scared to do it, but I told everyone I did. I pretended to be high; I don't know if everyone else was pretending, too, or if they really felt it.

"Okay. So why didn't the secretary call me, then?"

"She likes me," he says. "A lot. She calls me her work son."

"Okay." I twist the phone cord around my pinkie, try to cover my skin with it. My fingertip gets red and swollen with blood when I pull the rubber tight, and bright white flesh sticks out between the curls of cord.

"So what do you think?"

"About what?" There's a long pause and at first I think I lost him. I put my mouth right up to the phone so my lips are touching it, like a kiss. "Hello?"

"You coming over today?"

I make sure I'm not smiling in case he can hear it in my voice. "Okay."

"Jesus. Is that the only word you know? My house is on Clover. Three forty-one."

He hangs up without telling me anything else, like when he wants me to come or what we're going to do. I wonder if I'll be the only person there, if he'll tell other people that we're hanging out. I wonder if it's a date.

My phone vibrates in my pocket, so I check it, then hit Ignore. Lillian. She probably just wants to rub in how great it feels to be in love.

〰️

I DECIDE TO kill some time before I leave for Ivan's, because I don't want to seem too excited. It's always embarrassing to want something. Being cool means not wanting anything at all.

I need some pictures for the site, so I go to my room and take out all my bras and underwear. I was in grade seven when I bought my first thong. Most of the girls in my class had one already. I couldn't ask Mom because I knew she'd say no. She bought all my underwear from Zellers—white with little pink and blue flowers on them. The Zellers in town went out of business a couple years ago, and she hasn't bought me underwear since. I buy all my own now. I keep the sexy ones in a bag in a drawer so Mom doesn't see them. I wash them once in a while in the bathroom sink. Once I didn't clean them for a few weeks—I just left them in the bag— and when I opened it, there were little worms all over them. When I think about that, I get a shaky feeling in my legs and my throat hurts like I've already thrown up. But now I wonder if that's something a man would like, if there's someone who wants me to make that happen again. I wonder what would be too dirty.

I put on my favourite bra—black with lace all along the top— and matching underwear. My phone takes pictures; the quality is shit, but it's all I have. I put on my black boots with the high high high heels. I've never worn them out of my bedroom. I look better with them on. They make my legs go all the way up. The same year I bought my first thong, some of my friends and I decided to make the perfect body using parts from girls in our class. Marcy's hair was the hair. Lillian's mouth was the mouth. This girl in our class, Izzy, didn't have any friends, but we all still agreed her boobs had to be the boobs—she was the only one in class with a C cup. My legs were the legs. That was back when I was a size zero and didn't have any boobs at all. My legs wouldn't be the legs anymore, but I still love the way they look in heels.

The pictures are okay—they only show my body, no face. I look slutty, but in a good way. I'm really going to do this. I put my hand down my underpants while I take a picture of everything from my waist down. I'm a whore. I'll do anything.

∧∧∧

I KNOCK AND knock at Ivan's. I think about going home; I wonder if maybe this was all some kind of joke and he's watching me from somewhere, laughing. *He'll tell everyone*, I think. The house is red-brick, in an old part of town. Most of the kids at our school live around here. We walk or borrow bikes, go from one house to another—it never takes more than half an hour to get anywhere. None of the adults who live here walk anywhere.

I'm ready to leave, but I knock one more time. A woman comes to the door, but she's not speaking English and she seems confused about who I am.

"Ivan?" I almost yell it even though she can obviously hear me.

She says something and it seems like a question, so I nod. She smiles at me and kisses me on both cheeks, then pulls me inside and points to a glass sliding door at the back of the house. I can see Ivan outside sitting on a reclining patio chair. It's stuffy inside, like someone doesn't know the seasons are changing, like someone put the heat on and forgot about it. It feels like sitting in a car that's been in the sun with its windows up all day. Ivan's mom motions at my shoes with her head, so I take them off and carry them through the house with me.

It's pretty warm today, basically spring—the last few icicles on people's gutters are all shiny and slick, in a hurry to melt—but Ivan's wearing his winter jacket. When I step out onto the porch, he doesn't even open his eyes.

"Why didn't you answer the door?" I ask. I don't know if I should sit down or not, if he actually wants me here. Maybe I made a mistake, misunderstood the way things are.

"My mom was inside. You got in." He pats the cushion on the seat beside him. "Russian," he says.

When I don't respond, he finally opens his eyes. "That's what she speaks. She doesn't want to learn English because she already knows a language."

"I get that," I say. And I do. Sometimes it's easier to avoid change, to keep doing things the way you do them, even if it's not really working anymore.

Through the glass, I see Ivan's mom go into a room and shut the door behind her.

"She won't come out for the rest of the night," Ivan says. "And my dad's never here." I don't know if he means at home or in town or what, but I don't ask.

Ivan's backyard is green because of all the pine trees. It looks like most of the backyards in town. People here like trees. Every year or so, there's an article in the paper about someone wanting to cut down a tree and the rest of the town being against it. Not respecting history is the truest crime there is here. Everyone feels it—the druggies and the moms and the rich people who live on Mott Avenue. Some people are more than one thing, but they always fit one category most. And they all hate change.

Ivan lights a smoke and then lights one for me off his. The filter is a little soggy, soft when I put it in my mouth. I don't hate it. We're sharing. We don't talk while we smoke, but it's not weird. It feels like we're both doing it on purpose, like we already know what the other person is thinking so we don't have to say it. I look at his wrists and notice how thin they are. His legs are probably smaller than mine but I don't have to be jealous because he's a boy.

"What's the worst thing you've ever done?" he asks.

In grade two, Alex and Lillian and I were playing out by the baseball diamond at recess. We were skipping with Lillian's long rope from home. Izzy from our class came over and asked me if she could play. Everyone always made fun of her because she was poor. She pissed on the floor once, and we had to have class in the library while the janitor cleaned it up. I told her we only needed three people to skip. But Alex said she could stay. She said we weren't skipping anymore; we were playing prisoner.

She said, "Let's pretend we're queens and, Izzy, you're our prisoner, so we have to tie you up." I remember the look on Izzy's face. I still don't know if she was excited or scared or surprised or confused or a combination of everything. But she said okay. Alex chose a tree and made Izzy stand up against it. Then she took the skipping rope from Lillian and told us to help. She said queens have to do everything together. So we wrapped the skipping rope around Izzy, around the tree. We all started laughing, even Izzy. I thought she'd probably go inside after recess and tell everyone how much fun it was hanging out with us.

When she was all tied up and couldn't move, we just stood there for a couple minutes. I was waiting for the next part of the game—I didn't know what we were supposed to do. Alex went over to the baseball diamond and got a handful of rocks and sand and brought it back and put it right down Izzy's shirt. Then she walked over and grabbed more and Lillian did the same thing and

I held my breath until I thought I was going to turn blue. "What are you doing, Katie?" Alex said. "Are you a baby?" Alex always knew how to get me to do what she wanted.

I picked up a handful of sand and walked over to Izzy. She didn't make any noise. Her pants were elastic around her waist so they were easy to pull open. I let the sand fall through my fingers until it was gone. I could hear it running against the fabric on the way down. Some of it fell out of her pants at her ankles. We put rocks and sand and dirt down her top and her pants and underwear and in her boots and all over. Izzy started to cry and her face got red and the tears made her face clean where it used to be dirty.

And then the bell rang to go inside and Alex and Lillian started running back to school. Izzy's pants turned darker blue at the crotch, wet. She wasn't crying anymore and her stare was a bullet. I looked at her for a few more seconds, and then I turned and ran toward the portables, to my classroom, where I knew I'd lie when the teacher asked why I was late. I thought for sure there'd be punishment, but Izzy never told on us.

I still go to school with Izzy. Her house is great for parties because her mom doesn't give a shit about anything.

I tell Ivan some of that stuff.

"You're friends with Alex?" he asks.

"Kind of," I say. "Not really. What about you? What's your worst thing?"

He takes a long drag and puts his smoke out on the arm of his chair. It leaves a black burn mark. "There's a new worst thing every day."

I want to know all his worst things. I want him to trust me enough that he'll tell me all his secrets. I want to know all of Ivan's faces. I've met his mom; I know things about him. That means something. It feels nice to be invited somewhere not just out of pity, to be someone's choice.

I try to take a drag of my smoke, but it's gone out. He plucks it from my fingers and re-lights it for me. It starts to rain, but the awning keeps us dry—there's a wall of water between us and the rest of the world. He takes a pack of cards out of his pocket and teaches me how to play cribbage. I always pick my cards up as soon as he deals my hand so he knows I'm paying attention, so he knows I'm smart enough to count to six.

∧∧∧

WALKING HOME IN the rain, it seems later than it is because of the dark clouds. I open my mouth but hardly feel any drops. Mom always says I shouldn't drink rainwater. My shirt's soaked through and my shoes are ruined. Tomorrow they'll be dry but different, the canvas stiff and crusted with dirt. I walk slow because it's just water. I used to be scared of thunderstorms. I'd sit in the very middle of my bed and count the seconds between the lightning and thunder, wishing it farther and farther away. Because maybe lightning would strike our house and we'd all be electrocuted or maybe the wind would turn into a tornado.

Thunderstorms are like watching your own death coming slowly. I'd rather it just happen. Snap. Over. Dad always said I should do something to take my mind off the storm, but I couldn't think about anything else. He'd make me sit in front of the TV and watch something with him. When he laughed at the show, I'd want to jump on him and hit him as hard as I could. I never did, though. I just sat there on the edge of the couch, looking out the window and counting the seconds in my head.

As soon as I open the back door, Mom calls to me from the living room. She's on the couch, like she has been every day for the past week. She's lying on her side, facing the wall, and she looks skinnier than I remember her looking even this morning. Maybe she really is sick. I don't know if that would be better or worse. I'm standing over her and she moves her neck so she can see me, turns her body around like it's as hard as making the bed, doing dishes, showering.

"I'm so scared, Katie," she says. "Everything is falling apart." She wraps her arms around my waist and she's so warm. I put my hand on the back of her neck and remember how we used to take baths together, how the water would come right up to the edge of the tub when she lowered herself in, how the water was hot, not just warm; it was like a world where you haven't been born but somehow still exist. I used to think if we were quiet enough, maybe we could hear each other's thoughts.

"The doctors don't know anything," she says. "What if it's a brain tumour?" She starts to cry, really cry, hard. She told me once that I only cry when I want something. I finally get what she means, because this isn't that kind of crying.

"It's okay," I say, because maybe it's not okay and saying anything else will make it worse.

Mom gasps like she's trying to breathe underwater. She's trying so hard to stop crying that she starts to cough. She moves away from me and pushes her fists into her eyes like she's a little kid.

"I'm sorry," she says. "I'm so sorry. I'm okay." Her face is bright red and she swallows big gulps of air. "Will you make me tea?"

"Sure." She used to drink coffee, but it hurts her stomach now.

She moves back into the couch, turns away from me, her body shuddering. She looks small, too small to make the bathwater rise up and envelop us both. It's hot right behind my eyes.

I put water in the kettle and turn on the burner. I stand in the kitchen for a minute and then go downstairs to the computer. I sit and get shocked by the metal chair. I think about calling Lillian—I could ask her to come over. Except she might say no. And I don't know what I'd do if she said no. I stare at her number on the phone screen, trying to imagine what she's doing right now, sending her telepathic messages to call me instead, but then I surprise myself by pushing Call. It rings and rings and when she picks up she sounds out of breath. "Hey!"

"Hey. How's it going?"

"Really good." There's a muffled sound, like she's covering the phone. Then, "Oh my god, stop."

"What?"

"Sorry, not you. Steve's making this face and I can't handle it."

"Oh. I thought you had to help your dad with stuff today."

"Yeah, this morning. Guess what, though?"

"What?"

"I had an interview this week. At that restaurant we applied to, remember?"

"Yeah, but that was forever ago."

"Yeah, I thought it was hopeless because they never called, but apparently the owner, she's this really cool woman named Lindsay, she kept putting it off because interviews stress her out. Anyway, I got the job! I start after school tomorrow."

I swallow a sob that feels three times the size of my throat. "Wow. That's so good. Did you—"

"Steve, stop! Listen, Katie, I have to go. I'll call you tomorrow, 'kay?"

"Sure." The word comes out too high, and I wonder if Lillian noticed, but she's already gone.

I hear the kettle right after I close my phone. It screams for minutes but I just listen until it stops, until Mom must have got up to make tea. I stay downstairs until it's late and when I go up, she's not on the couch anymore.

I have to open the drawer beside my bed really slowly because the wood screeches. My ring box is wrapped up in a long-sleeved shirt. I made thumb holes in the sleeves so they'll stay down over my wrists. It's old and ripped in a few places and Mom thinks I threw it out a long time ago, but it feels safe. It has dried blood all along the arms; I should wash it soon.

I love the colour of blood. I secretly think mine might be better than other people's. It's so pretty; it's the prettiest thing about me. After just a couple lines on my shoulder, I'm floating until I'm not even in the house anymore. I'm made of butterflies.

When I'm about to fall asleep, my phone buzzes under my head. But it's a text from Ivan, not Lil. Maybe he's my new normal, the person I should expect. *U get high?* he says.

I've only smoked pot a few times, and only ever with Lillian— the first time we did it, we swore we'd only ever do it together. Her older brother was always getting stoned and getting in trouble and being an idiot, and she said we'd keep each other from getting addicted. But I'm not going to tell Ivan that—he'll think it's stupid.

Sure, I text back.

Tomorrow. Lunch. Walk.

I tell myself it's not a big deal. I like Ivan. Ivan likes me.

K, I write.

〰〰

SPRING IS THE worst time of the year. Everything smells like garbage and shit, and there's grey snow running along all the curbs. It seems like everyone loves those first weeks where you can walk around without a winter coat on, but I always ruin my shoes. Even once the snow is all gone, you have to wear something light, but with sweaters and a jacket on top because the temperature changes all the time. You never know what it's going to feel like.

Ivan and I walk along Cherry Street, passing a joint back and forth. He's been kicking a rock since the corner, but he loses it when it hits a hole in the pavement and bounces off the sidewalk into the middle of the road.

He's talking about bands he likes, bands I should listen to. He says you can tell who someone is by the music they like. He talks about Eric Clapton and Neil Young and the Rolling Stones. He's wearing a thin long-sleeved sweater with a polo shirt over top. There's a little eagle, wings spread, stitched above his heart.

There's a drugstore down the street where everyone goes to buy juice and candy because it's the cheapest place in town. Ivan stops in front of it. He's still smoking the joint, and when he holds it out to me, I shake my head. I tell him it's because I don't want any more, but it's really because I'm scared someone will see me. I've never smoked pot in public like this before. Every time a car goes by I panic a little, because it could always be the cops. Maybe we'll get arrested. I'm such a pussy sometimes, but I can't help it.

We go in and Ivan buys a bottle of Coke. I see him put a pack of gum into his shirtsleeve while the cashier gets his change.

Back outside, he opens his gum and gives me a piece without asking if I want one. He just knows. While we're walking toward school, I look at the sidewalk and it sparkles, like someone dropped a whole bag of glitter in with the concrete. I wonder if it's real, if

I've just never noticed it before. I wonder if this is the first time I've really been stoned. When Lil and I smoked pot, it always felt more like the world was muted, but this time, everything has a shine. I want to tell Lil about it, and I feel a twinge of guilt when I realize I can't. This is just another thing between us, another thing that's my fault. I wonder what she's doing right now.

Then Ivan stops walking and his face is right in mine. For just a second, I wonder if he's going to kiss me. I think about what his tongue would feel like. I don't think I like him as anything but a friend, but I do like him. It could work. I close my eyes. He smells like peppermint, like winter. I can feel his breath on me and then I can't anymore. He's kicking another rock like nothing ever changes here at all.

six

^^^

The first ad I put up has a couple pictures. It says I'll do anything. It says I'm young. It doesn't say I'm a virgin because I don't know if that's a good thing or not. I read the ad and look over the pictures of myself about ten times before I click Post. After I do, I have to stand and walk around the room because I'm so nervous. It doesn't feel sexy anymore. It feels stupid and embarrassing and gross. Nobody will want me. My body is disgusting.

Someone comments after a couple minutes, and I read the message standing up, shifting from foot to foot. I feel almost like I have to pee. He says he likes the pictures and wants to know more, then he requests a private chat. I make myself breathe. Sometimes when I'm nervous, I hold my breath and forget I'm doing it until I feel sick. It used to happen a lot when I was a kid, enough that Mom took me to the doctor. He said I should look at things in the room, in the real world, remind myself where I am so I remember I need to breathe. I sit down at the computer and open the chat window. It's just words, not webcam. I wouldn't do video because then this guy would see I'm just in my gross basement wearing my Powerpuff Girls pajama pants.

Hey hon . . . I love your pictures

Thanks! How are you?

Good good. How old r u?

18

How much for the white pair?

$15 for 24 hr wear

He's typing for a while before he asks, *What other stuff do you do?*

I feel like I don't have enough information. I wish there was an instructions sheet for this. I wonder what he looks like. His profile picture is an image of an American flag.

I type, *Anything you want*, hit Send. I don't know what I expect him to say. It feels like a circle where neither of us will admit what we want. Maybe we'll just do this forever, talking around sex instead of about it. Even though this isn't really sex.

I bite my fingernail in between my two front teeth. I know that looks sexy because I've done it looking in the mirror before, and I need to know I look sexy right now. Sometimes you think something looks good until you see it. Even if it feels great. In grade three, Alex told me boys like it when you suck on things, like Popsicles or bananas or the end of a pen. One day I noticed Jonah staring at me in class so I put my pencil in my mouth. It tasted like metal and dust. I let my mouth hang open, dragged the pencil along my bottom lip. He looked back at the chalkboard, and I bit the eraser right off and swallowed it. A couple days later, I tried doing it in front of the mirror. It looked horrible.

I decide the guy from the site looks like Nate Murray, but older. Older like he's married, maybe. His hair is black like when you first turn the lights off.

Touching yourself? he says. *If its OK. And a few pictures for me. some wearing the panties . . . something more?* I can almost hear his voice, see him sitting on the couch across from me, so close he could reach out and touch me if I let him.

Is no face OK?

Of course hon :) whatever your comfortable with

$20?

OK

I move two fingers under the elastic of my underpants. I think about how it felt before I gave Nate a blow job, when he wanted me, how I wanted something from him even though I couldn't explain what it was. I think about the sweat-and-mud smell of him when I passed him once in the hallway after he had gym class. I imagine this man has the same smell. I can feel the calluses on his palms against my thighs. When I push fingers from my right hand over top of the left, it feels almost like it's him touching me. Afterward, I wipe my fingers off on the fabric of my pajama pants because I'm just in my basement and he's just words on a screen. He hardly exists.

He gives me his address and sends me the money. I know where he lives—I know a lot about him now and I could do anything I want. He trusts me—my chest fizzes just thinking about it. I put my underwear in a plastic bag and then into an envelope. I lick it and get a paper cut on my tongue. Then I walk to the post office and the underpants are gone. It's the easiest thing in the whole world.

~~~

I LEAVE HOME for school ten minutes later now than I used to—just so I don't accidentally run into Lillian and Steve on the way. Lillian's a stickler for leaving on time.

It's spring-cleaning week and the streets are covered in everybody's junk. Every year, most of it disappears before the garbage trucks go by. Someone else's trash. People are starting to sit outside in the mornings now that it's warmer. There's a guy sitting on his porch steps at one of the houses near the school. He's drinking a beer and rolling a cigarette. His front door is just a screen. His eyes follow me when I pass by. I know he's going to watch me the whole way, until he can't see me anymore. I try to act casual, like I don't care, but it makes my posture a little straighter.

The first time I really noticed men noticing me was because of my mom. We were driving home from my grandma's house and I had to go to the bathroom, so we stopped at a gas station even though we were only a few minutes from home. Mom gave me money to buy a can of ginger ale for me and a box of Smarties for her. When I got back in the car, Mom just stared at me.

"You know those men were watching you?" she asked.

I had no idea what she was talking about, or why men would be watching me. It felt like I'd done something wrong. She pointed at a couple guys leaning up against the building. They were smoking cigarettes and laughing. One had red hair and freckles and a face like a Cabbage Patch doll. The other one was just a regular man.

Mom turned the car on and hot air blew in my face. "You're old enough now," she said. "You can't wear anything you want anymore."

She adjusted the mirror and I looked down at my tank top and jean shorts. My legs looked like sausages because I'd gotten the shorts two years earlier and they didn't really fit anymore. I was wearing my favourite shirt, a red one with spaghetti straps. It had a built-in bra—I didn't have a real bra yet.

I felt bad that I didn't see the men, that I couldn't feel their eyes on me, and that Mom had noticed. That's what it must feel like to be a woman, I thought. Knowing someone's eyes are on you all the time.

∧∧∧

IVAN AND I are sitting behind the grocery store smoking pot at lunch. He works here sometimes, stocking shelves and lifting things. He says they let him choose his own shifts. It might be true. The owner is this young guy who wants to be friends with everyone. Last Thanksgiving they all got drunk and bowled with turkeys down the aisles. They used bottles of salad dressing and paper towel rolls for the pins. It wasn't even after closing.

An older lady comes out the back door of the store with a bag of garbage and stares at us. I hide the joint behind my legs.

"Hey, Martha!" Ivan yells. Way louder than he has to.

She waves at him like she's brushing dust off a table and looks away, throwing the bag of garbage into a bin and then shuffling back to the open door. Before she goes in, she looks up at the sky, holds her hands out like it's the only way to tell if it's raining. Or maybe she just wants to feel something on her bare skin. It's been misting all day and it's starting to get dark and foggy.

Ivan reaches for the joint. "I don't know what her name is."

That makes me laugh really hard. I don't know if it's because I'm stoned or because it's funny. When he gets up, brushing the dirt off his ass, I'm still geeking out.

"Wanna skip the afternoon and go to my place?" he says.

I hardly ever skip school. But I think about walking back by myself and then having nothing to do after school, going home alone again. Lillian still comes to my locker sometimes, but it's usually just to tell me she can't walk home with me. I think that might be worse than if she just didn't show; it's like she's rubbing it in my face that she found someone she likes more than me.

Ivan found me at the beginning of lunch today. I'm not sure what I would've done otherwise—it seems like there are fewer people in the caf every day now that it's warmer outside. Lillian's never around, and even Marcy usually goes out for lunch. All my old friends go places without me. But Ivan acted like we already had plans, like lunch is something we do together now.

"Sure," I say. "Walk?"

"No. It takes forever. I'll double you."

He has his bike because he got drunk at work last night and forgot to bring it home. I sit on the back with my arms around his waist, trying to keep my butt off the metal because every bump hurts. I don't want to tell him it's uncomfortable. I always worry if I don't do things the way he wants, he won't want to hang out with me anymore. When we go over a big pothole, my body bounces and lands hard, and I scream but I'm laughing, too. He slows down and I jump off.

"I might just walk," I say. "I can meet you at your house?"

He steps off the bike and stands beside it, holds it up with one finger on the handlebar. "That's cool. I like walking with you."

He walks slowly because I'm walking slowly. There's so much fog now that it's hard to see the houses. It feels like we're all alone together in the world. We walk in the very middle of the road, but it doesn't feel dangerous. There aren't any cars the whole way.

〰

LILLIAN TEXTED THE other day and said Marcy told her I'd been hanging out with Ivan, and I texted back, *Not really.* Lil wouldn't get it; she'd think he's using me for something. I used to think that, too. It all just seemed too easy. But Ivan is my best friend right now. We show each other our scars. I haven't shown him my arms or any other new cuts, but he's seen the puckered skin on my hand from a fall, the line on my ankle from a cat scratch that comes out bright white when I get a tan. The place on my eyebrow where hair doesn't grow because I split my head open when I was a baby and needed four stitches—the doctor put a towel over my face to quiet my screams. I've seen the skin stretched tight on his thigh from boiling water, the raised jagged line on his palm from broken glass. Tiny pits and craters on his chest and back from scratching chicken pox. This is how we measure where we've been, who we were before we were a *we*, an *us*. Sometimes we go to my old elementary school and sit in the big plastic tube, our knees scrunched up to our chests. It makes the whole world yellow. Lillian and I used to sit in the tube at recess, back when we were small enough that we hardly had to scrunch. The first time Ivan went in there, I couldn't follow him because it felt like betrayal. But everything gets easier with time.

〰

THE FIRST TIME I try coke, it's like going home to a place way better than home. I pay for it because I'm the one who has money, but Ivan goes to pick it up—he makes me stay at his house while he leaves for like an hour—and we do our first line on the dresser in his bedroom. He's done coke a bunch of times. Everyone does it. Everyone says it's fun. What nobody says is that it makes everything okay. It makes you feel like you could do anything and you'd be good at it. It makes you like yourself, like you're finally beautiful.

After we do a couple more lines in Ivan's room, we go to the park. We sit on a bench and drink bottles of Corona. We run into Izzy from school. She's on coke, too, but she's not drinking because she's sure it'll stop her heart. Ivan says that's all just a myth. He says if you're really drunk, doing coke sobers you up right away and it's a better choice than acting like an idiot.

Izzy tells us she wants to buy a magazine because it's been so long since she's read a magazine, but she doesn't have any money. When she walks away, Ivan asks if I've heard she has something wrong with her brain. Her brother is in his grade and he told everyone about it. "She's retarded," Ivan says.

"No, she's not." I feel like I might cry. I want him to take back what he said, to admit he's just joking. "We grew up together and she's not."

I want Ivan to believe me but I don't know why I care. I don't have anything in common with Izzy. A lot of the time just being around her makes me anxious. I can never figure out what she wants—she's not popular, exactly, but she gets invited to parties without even trying. When we were kids, she used to eat her hair. Not just chew on it—like, full-on *eat* her hair. The teacher sprayed stuff on it so it would taste bad—it smelled good actually, like fake apples, sour green—but she still kept pulling it out until you could see bald spots all over her head. Her hair seems fine now, but I wonder if she still eats it in private. Maybe she just learned how to keep things secret. In grade seven, there was this rumour that Eminem died, and Izzy cried at her desk all day. She says "seen" instead of "saw" because her mom's from somewhere else, somewhere even worse than here. I know all that stuff sounds bad, but Izzy's actually really nice. She just never has any money.

"I heard she's a dyke, too," Ivan says.

I heard the same thing. I don't know if it's true or not.

When we leave the park, it's so dark that I can't see Ivan in front of me. *This is what being blind is like*, I think. We go to the corner store to buy cigarettes. We've already gone through a bunch tonight because we've been chain-smoking. Each one makes me feel better than I've ever felt before. It seems impossible that something could just keep getting better after it's already the best, but it does. Ivan makes me ask to use the bathroom so we can do more coke inside, and I wonder if the guy who owns the store knows what we're doing, if he just doesn't care. Maybe this stuff happens all the time.

I don't get home until five in the morning. The clock on the microwave says four because it didn't get changed at daylight savings. It doesn't really matter if it tells us what time it is.

Mom's asleep in her room with the door open. I go to the washroom and look in the mirror. My hair is sweaty because I walked home as fast as I could without running. I look shiny and happy like I imagine I'd look if I'd just had sex. I think about cutting myself so I'm tired enough to sleep, but I also want to stay awake forever because I know when I wake up, everything will be back to normal. I'll just be starting all over again.

I put on a T-shirt that Mom accidentally shrank in the laundry. I like the way it stops above my belly button, and when I lie down, everything is flat. I start taking a video on my phone. I push my underwear down to just below my hip bones so I can see them on the screen.

I found this video online the other day on how to make yourself feel better when you're freaking out. This woman gave tips on how to ground yourself, make yourself calm. She said you should start at the top of your head and brush it with the tips of your fingers, then move down, until everything feels slow and quiet. Like cutting without cutting. She didn't say that part, but that's what it reminded me of. Her voice was whispery and almost made me fall asleep right in front of the computer. I could feel my head getting heavy but every time it dropped I woke myself up.

In my video, I touch my stomach with my fingertips, make circles around my belly button. I rewatch it in the dark a couple times, look at my own tight stomach and long thin fingers and bones and underwear, but I decide not to put it online. It feels private even though it shows hardly anything.

〰️

MY ADS GET lots of replies. I always say I'm eighteen if they ask, but they usually don't. They probably don't want to know, either because they want to think I'm old enough or because they want to think I'm not.

I take pictures wearing all my underwear. I sell at least a couple pairs a week now—not enough money to really do anything with, but it's better than nothing. I mostly get asked to wear them around for a day or two, masturbate in them, sometimes go for a run while I'm wearing them. A man from Vancouver wants a period-stained silk thong, so I tell him I'll send it as early as I can. If you're really desperate, you can fake stuff like period blood and discharge, but if you get found out, people will ruin you on the site with bad reviews and comments. Sometimes they'll even find girls in real life, post their real names and locations for anyone to see. It's not worth it for a few extra dollars. Scheduling is hard sometimes, but it's another kind of fun. You need to know your own body, your cycles, how things move through you. My panties make the men feel close to me—they can smell me, taste me. It's physical. And figuring out how to do what they want, fitting them all in, makes me feel close to myself.

Compared to real life, this is easy. Online, you can say whatever you're thinking about and someone wants to listen. It's not like school, where saying yes or no can end you; online, you can say yes or no or maybe. And it doesn't mean the same thing if someone calls you a slut: the word still hits me in the stomach, but not in the same way. When a boy calls someone a slut in real life, you know the girl messed up, broke the rules. Online, I can call *myself* a slut, because being a slut just means being a woman who knows what she wants. It's a whole other world.

seven

ᐯᐯᐯ

Ivan and I spend all our time together lately. We drink two-fours of Carling and smoke Du Maurier regular regulars. He buys lottery tickets and lets me scratch them because I'm lucky. Lillian and I tried to make plans this week, but she had work Monday and play rehearsals Tuesday, and today I had plans with Ivan. I didn't tell her that, though—I just said I was busy. We finally decided not to decide, to let it work out on its own. That's how we always used to hang out anyway—showing up at each other's doors, sending messages on MSN saying *Tim Hortons NOW!* But back then we only had each other.

The air is filled with dandelion and cottonwood fluff; it always looks like it's snowing, but it's warmer every day. Ivan's parents are in France for their wedding anniversary even though they've almost gotten divorced like three times. Ivan says they hate each other but they're too stubborn to end it. Ivan's mom is usually at home whenever she's not in another country. She always makes us grilled cheese sandwiches and cuts the crusts off. Ivan says she's a terrible cook, but it's hard to fuck up grilled cheese. She never eats with us; she just makes food and stands in the kitchen. It's like she never runs out of dishes to wash.

I've never seen his dad. Sometimes there's another car in the driveway, but I don't know if he's in the house. I feel like I have to walk on tiptoe and whisper any time the car is there. Ivan always acts like a smaller version of himself and we never stick around his house for long. Once he came to school with a black eye and I asked him what happened and he told me it was his dad. But then he burst out laughing, so I don't know if he was being serious or not.

It makes me feel closer to Ivan: his parents who hate each other, his invisible dad. But if that's what it's like when people don't divorce, it seems like marriage is mostly shit.

School finished half an hour ago, so we're sitting on Ivan's back porch. I only tried ecstasy for the first time this week, but it's my new favourite. I'm using my library card to break up a pill on a coffee-table book about birds while Ivan talks about *Schindler's List*, that movie about the Nazis. He talks about *Schindler's List* all the time.

Making lines is one of the best parts of doing drugs. I love taking out all the tools, getting things ready. It feels like making something good happen for yourself, and everyone has to wait for you. I make sure the lines are the same size and then push the book over the picnic table to Ivan. He does the one he thinks is bigger.

He starts talking about the scene in the movie where the Nazi shoots the engineer woman. He's obsessed with that scene. Sometimes he acts it out and laughs. I don't know if he wants people to think he's crazy, or if he actually thinks it's funny.

"I bet I can drink four beers," he says.

"I can drink four beers. That's not even that many."

"No. Now. I bet I can chug four beers now, in less than a minute. Time me."

I time him and he does it no problem. He wipes his face off on the front of his shirt. In that second, I wonder if this is the best it gets, if Ivan is going to be my best friend for the rest of my life, if I'm stuck with him. I don't want to think it, but I know something is missing. I can taste the E and it's horrible—dripping, burning down my throat.

"Can we hang out with my friend Lillian sometime?" I never talk to Ivan about Lil—I doubt he even knows who she is. Sometimes I have to stop myself before telling a story about her. She probably doesn't tell stories about me anymore, either. But I suddenly want to see her so badly, and I want to tell Ivan all of our stories because then maybe he could be part of our story, too, and everything would work. Maybe that's all that's missing. The way I feel right now, I wouldn't even care if Ivan loved Lillian, if they wanted to hang out all the time, as long as I could come, too.

"Is she Jewish?" he asks.

"No," I say. I don't think I know any Jewish people; I wonder how you're supposed to know.

"Good. Because then I'd have to kill her." He makes his fingers into a gun and shoots me in the head.

〰

I'VE BEEN CHATTING with a woman on the site lately. It's nice to talk to her instead of just the men, just the buyers. She's always online, it seems like. Her screen name is MilkBeaut. She sells stuff and makes videos and does cam stuff. She said I can ask her whatever I want because I'm just starting out. She'll be like my mentor, she said. She knows where I'm from and she says she grew up in a small place, too, a place where there were lots of rules.

She's really beautiful; her boobs and nipples are huge. My nipples are tiny, like dimes. It doesn't really matter what you look like online because there's someone who wants anything.

MilkBeaut shows her face in her pictures. Her skin is darker than mine, and she has big lips—*blow job lips*, people at school would say. She says I'm smart not to show my face until I'm sure about it. *You should feel ready*, she says.

How do I know when I'm ready? I ask.

How did you know you were ready to show your body?

I remember the doubt I felt after that first time I posted an ad. How my palms were sweating and I had to remind myself to breathe. Maybe I wasn't ready; maybe I'm not supposed to be here. But then I remember the relief I felt at the first reply, the warmth of someone wanting me just the way I am. I remember how good I am at giving people what they want, taking pictures and making something new with my own fluids and smells and mess.

〰〰

MOM ASKS ME to feel her forehead. She's in her bedroom instead of on the couch; she says she can't watch TV because it gives her a headache. I put the back of my hand against her head like she used to do for me when I was a kid. She actually does feel hot, but then I feel my own forehead and I feel hot, too.

"Did you take your temperature?" I ask.

"The thermometer's broken. It says it's normal."

She asks me to get her two Advil. She never takes more than two at a time because she's worried she'll overdose. Sometimes I take five or six if I'm hungover.

The medicine cabinet is filled with stuff. Not just pills, but hair elastics and creams and face wash and tweezers and toothpaste. Mom never cleans up in here, even when she's cleaning everywhere else. The hair stuff is all on one shelf, which is above all the face stuff. The pills are mixed in with everything and there are bottles on the counter and in the drawers, too, but if I asked her, I know she'd know where everything is.

Once Mom and I got sick at the same time. I had a fever and she stayed in bed with me, spooning me while I shivered. When it got to be five in the morning and I still hadn't slept and she thought something good would finally be on TV, we got out of bed and moved to the couch. She covered me in blankets and made me chicken soup for breakfast. I ate it with saltines covered in butter. It was only another hour or so before I heard her puking in the bathroom. Back then, it was so easy to tell when things were real. She came into the room in her comfiest pajamas and got under the pile of blankets with me. I put my head in her lap and we watched cartoons all day.

〰〰

WHEN I CALLED Lillian to ask if she wanted to hang out, she sounded like she was far away, like the phone line was open to the whole world. She said we should go to Tim Hortons because she hadn't been in weeks. I said sure but she couldn't hear me—she finally took me off speakerphone and I was glad I hadn't told her I missed her. Anyone could have been listening.

Ivan and I are waiting for her at Tim Hortons. When I took my change from Glasses at the counter, my hands were shaking—just a little, but I'm keeping them under the table so Ivan doesn't notice. I don't want him to think I'm nervous because then he'll think this whole thing is stupid.

"How long do we have to hang out with her for?" he asks.

"Can you be nice?" I can feel the sweat on my palms so I rub them on my thighs.

"Does she even smoke weed?"

"Yeah." I remember the promise I made to her and my stomach drops with guilt. I've smoked pot without her so many times now, done so many drugs. Ivan and I snorted E half an hour ago—I can still taste it in the back of my throat. The first time Lil and I smoked pot together was for my birthday in grade eight. Her older brother got it for us. We spent the whole day at her house watching MuchMusic and eating chocolate frosting out of the can.

Lillian walks in and looks from side to side, but her eyes pass over us a couple times. I wave at her and she finally looks right at me. I wonder if maybe she didn't really want to see me, if she was hoping I wasn't here so she could just leave. She looks down at the ground the whole walk over to our table.

She's wearing overalls that she got for Christmas last year. She used to hate them; I guess she likes them all of a sudden. Maybe Steve likes them so she thinks they're cool now. I'm wearing one of the T-shirts we both have—we got them on purpose to match. I guess I was hoping she'd be wearing the same one and we could laugh about how we still dress the same. I just feel stupid now. I wish I had a sweater or something to put over it. I cross my arms over my chest but then uncross them because hiding it just makes it worse.

Once I got really mad at Lillian and popped the head off her favourite Barbie. I regretted it right away and tried to put it back on but it just wouldn't go. Lil wouldn't let me come over for a week. I told Mom we weren't friends anymore and Mom said I needed to get over whatever I was mad about. I couldn't tell her I wasn't mad at all and that's what made it impossible—I couldn't do anything to fix things and I hated myself for it.

Lil sits down at the table, says, "Hey, I'm Lillian," and puts her hand out like she wants to shake Ivan's. I cringe and hope he doesn't say anything. But then he shakes her hand and says, "Ivan," like it's not weird at all. Lillian's nails are painted bright red. It's the only colour she ever paints them. She says red is classic.

And things are like normal for a little while. I ask Lil about the play, and she says it's so much work and she feels like she never leaves the school. Ivan asks if she wants to be an actress and then tells a story about a guy who used to go to our school who was in a bunch of movies with a talking dog. Lillian laughs. Her teeth are whiter than I remember, and I wonder if she's using whitening strips again. She loves them even though they make her teeth hurt. She can't eat soup for months after she goes through a box.

And then her phone rings. I can tell it's Steve from the way she looks at the screen and keeps the phone in her hand. I wish he was calling to break up with her. I wish she wasn't so fucking happy. Once Ivan asked me what my biggest secret was and I told him I didn't know, but I did. Even when I like girls, even when they're my friends, I still want them to fail.

"You should answer it," I say, nodding at the phone in her hand.

She doesn't even have to think about it. "Yeah, I'll be right back," she says, getting up from the table.

When she pushes the door open to go outside, to get privacy from me, the whole world gets so sharp I have to close my eyes for a second. Then I follow her. I know Ivan must be staring at me, wondering what's going on, but I can't see anything but the door. I push it open and she's standing just a few feet away. "Why'd you even come?" I ask.

She spins around to face me. "Steve, can I call you back?" She snaps her phone shut. "What?"

"Why are you here?"

"I wanted to see you."

"Why?"

Her phone rings again and she looks at the screen.

"Just fucking answer it."

"You're the one who made me hang up the first time. Are you on something?"

"I didn't smoke pot. We promised."

"What?" She looks at me hard and I realize she doesn't even know what I'm talking about. She doesn't even care. "Okay, well, you need to chill. I was just answering a phone call."

The anger bubbles in the top of my head. Half the time when I call Lillian, she doesn't pick up. The other half, she's with Steve or on her way to work or busy with something she won't even tell me about. "Fine. Then don't bother calling me anymore. I'm obviously not as important as your loser boyfriend."

Lillian turns red. "It's not my fault I'm busy. Are you jealous? You're with Ivan all the time anyway. I can't believe you invited him. Do you know how fucked that is? Are you dating him or something? Do you know what people say about him?"

"He didn't even know who you were."

She sucks her top lip into her mouth. "What's wrong with you?"

It's the worst question. "Why don't you tell me?"

"What?"

"Tell me what's wrong with me."

"No."

"Tell me."

"No."

"Tell me!"

"You need me too much sometimes! Okay?" There's a moment of silence, like even the birds and the trees are holding their breath. "I want things that are mine."

My head is filled with pins. I know I have to pull back or I'll start to cry. "Okay."

She sighs. "Maybe we need a break. Why don't we just take a break, talk in a few days."

I shrug. "Why? We're not friends anymore, right? We haven't been for a long time."

Lillian's eyebrows get closer together. "I should go," she says.

"Fine. You made your choice."

"There's no *choice*, Katie."

"Yes. There is." I shrug my shoulders like it doesn't matter. "I already said it's fine. You hang out with whoever you want. I'll hang out with who I want."

I spin around and walk back into Tim Hortons, to the table where Ivan is making a pyramid out of creamers. I sit down with my back to the window. The most powerful you can be is when you don't even care.

〰

I TALK TO a guy online who tells me he's married. He says his wife is always talking shit to him and he's tired of it. He's a man, he says. He fantasizes about ripping her clothes off and coming all over her face, in her perfect hair. He wants to come all over her until she's a statue.

He sends me a full-body picture and he's bigger than I thought he would be. Not tall, but wide, like a guy whose back you could ride on for a long time before he got tired. I don't mean that in a sexy way, but I guess that could work for some people, too. His head is shaved bald and I wonder if it's like that because he likes the way it looks or because he was losing all his hair and he had to shave off the bits that were left.

He wants to talk a bit before he buys any panties. He wants me to pretend I'm scared of him. He says he'll pay extra for it. I'd do it for free, but I don't tell him that.

Do you like me? I ask.

Yes, he says.

What do you want? I'll do anything for you. This is one of my regular lines. Sometimes I wonder if it's true.

Want u dirty

How dirty?

On ur knees covered in my cum

I try to imagine him in this room with me. I'm at the computer listening to music, so I don't hear when he comes up behind me. I feel his hands on my shoulders and I start to scream but he puts a palm over my mouth. It tastes like sweat. The door is locked. He throws me onto the ground and I try to crawl away, my knees chafing on the carpet, but his hand is around my neck. He pulls me up to kneel in front of him, pushes his gym shorts down so his cock pops out over the elastic. I know what he wants.

Please don't hurt me. I'll be your slave, I tell him.

So hot

Online, even when I pretend someone else is in charge, I'm actually in control. It's easy. It's fun. Like being an actress. I wonder if this is what it feels like for Lillian when she's onstage in front of a bunch of people, pretending.

I'm sucking your cock to make you come all over me, I say. *Just don't hurt me. Please.*

Call me daddy

Tons of guys love being called daddy. Usually it's the ones you'd never guess, though. The ones who look normal and talk nice. It seems like something for weirdos, but it's pretty regular. I wonder what this guy's house looks like. I think about how it'd be to sit at his kitchen table and tell him about my day.

You taste so good, daddy.

Fuck

What are you going to do to me?

Ur a slut I tell u that til u cry n then I wipe the tears off ur whore face wit my cock n cum all over ur little tits ur tiny fucking tits

I start touching myself, but it feels like work. And he doesn't tell me to come, anyway. I don't think he cares about that. He wants three pairs of panties. Pissed in.

〰

I HEAR AT school that Lillian had sex with Steve. Someone said they did it in the drama closet behind the theatre and one of the grade twelves walked in on them. Lillian was wearing a skirt, but Steve was naked. What a loser. He probably wanted someone to walk in, to see his gross naked body. They've been doing it for weeks now. It feels like I should have known, like she should have looked different when we hung out, but she didn't, obviously.

In grades six and seven, I spent a lot of time wondering if people I saw on the street or in movies or at school had had sex. Every time I saw a TV show, I'd try to figure out if the actors looked like they had. I thought there must be something about a person that changed after they did it, but since I didn't know who'd lost their virginity, I couldn't compare the before and after. Then, in grade seven, after Emma and Russell had sex, I realized she didn't look any different at all.

If they've been doing it for weeks, Lillian and I were still friends when she lost her virginity, and she didn't even tell me. It makes me glad that I left her standing alone in front of Tim Hortons, that I've been strong enough not to call her. She was keeping things from me the whole time.

eight

ᴧᴧ

I get called to the office during first period. The whole walk down the hallway, I feel like I can't breathe. When I ask the secretary why I'm here, she just raises her eyebrows at me like I should know, and motions with her chin for me to sit down. She always looks like she's stuck in the middle of a breath, like she's about to blow a bubble of gum. She has a printed-out map of Spain on the wall beside her desk. I wonder if that's her dream, to go to Spain, or if she took a trip there and just really loved it. It makes me sad either way. I sit in one of the metal chairs across from her desk. I try to keep my chin up, like I know what's going on, like this isn't a big deal, but the secretary can probably hear my heart beating from across the room.

The vice-principal, Miss Ness, comes out of her office and looks above her glasses at me. "Come in," she says. Her eyebrows are so plucked it's like they're just two single long hairs. She waits outside while I walk into the room ahead of her, and then she closes the door behind us.

I've never been in here before. There's a big wooden desk but it has hardly anything on it. No pictures or anything. Just a stack of papers that look really neat and organized, like they're freshly printed off, still warm.

Miss Ness sits down in the swivel chair behind the desk and I sit in a plastic one in front. It's bright orange.

"Mr. Slager told me about your most recent English project."

It was an essay about any book series. We had to read at least two of the books, then compare and contrast them. Most people did Harry Potter. I did the Sleeping Beauty series by Anne Rice—MilkBeaut told me about it and I got the whole thing from the public library.

"He said we could write about whatever we wanted." The room spins and I stare at Miss Ness's stapler to try to make it stop.

She leans forward, resting her elbows on the desk, and pushes her glasses up her nose. "It's pornography. Do you think that's appropriate?"

I swallow what feels like a mouthful of spit. "I don't know." I'm not even trying to be smart—I feel more and more like I don't know what normal is.

"Are you still on the Library Team?"

"Club."

"Oops, Library *Club*. You're still in that?"

"Yeah, kind of. I've been busy with other stuff lately." I haven't been going to meetings, so I haven't had a reshelving shift in a while. And I didn't show up for the club picture last week. I skipped school with Ivan that day, so in the yearbook it'll just say *Katelin Henry (absent)* at the end of the list of names.

"You should reconsider your choice in friends."

I don't say anything, but I know exactly what she's talking about.

"I saw you walking out of school with Ivan Krovopuskov on Monday. I don't think you know what you're doing."

She has a bunch of certificates framed on the wall and I wonder why she works here if she's done so much school.

"I looked at your records. You're a good student. The next couple years are the most important, though. Don't ruin them, okay?"

"Okay," I say. "I'm sorry."

She smiles. "You don't have to be sorry. Just be careful."

I nod. "I will."

On my way out, I see one of her certificates is for going up in a hot-air balloon. What a loser.

〰

I GO TO the back parking lot later to have a smoke. The doors are propped open with rocks because it's sunny and the air is warm. Our school is four floors but we only use two and a half of them. The whole fourth floor is locked up so you can't even get to it. The building is big and brick and old and there are always broken windows. Out back, there's a fence that divides the parking lot from school property, but most people don't pay attention to it. Sometimes teachers come out to yell at us, and anyone who's on the wrong side just jumps over the fence. The music room windows face the parking lot, so when kids are smoking pot, the teacher, Mr. Mudford, sticks his head out and says he's calling the police. But he's joking.

I find Ivan around the corner. When I tell him about Miss Ness, he starts to laugh. "Fucking bitch!" he says. "She has no idea who she's dealing with. I could kill her and rape her fucking dead body and nobody would even care."

I wish someone else was here so I'd know how to respond. I just keep smoking, toeing the grass with my sneaker and staring at the ground.

There's a story everyone knows about Miss Ness. Apparently when she was just a teacher here, she was in love with Mr. Cox, the gym teacher. He's still pretty hot even though he's old now. Miss Ness was obsessed with him and he ended up getting a restraining order against her but then cancelled it when she tried to kill herself. She lives with her mother and people say she's still a virgin. But he's still the gym teacher.

When I get home, there's a message on the answering machine. I know Mom already heard it because the light isn't blinking anymore. It's from Miss Ness. She wants Mom to come in for a talk whenever she has a free hour. I listen to the whole message a second time and then press Delete.

〰

WHEN MILKBEAUT ASKS me why I sell panties, I tell her there are lots of reasons.

I like how open everyone is, I say. *I like hearing what people like. And it feels powerful.*

I don't tell her that I like being wanted, being liked, because it sounds desperate. And I don't tell her that I think I might like it the same way the men do, that it turns me on, because that's worse than desperate. I've already done more than most of the other girls—a lot of them won't do bathroom stuff at all. For them, it's just a job.

Do people know what you do? I ask her.

Yes, she says. *My mom, my boyfriend.*

There's another chat up on my screen with a guy named BIGdickBrit47. He wants me to take pictures with my face in them even though I say on my profile that I won't. There are lots of these guys, ones who are never going to buy anything but want to waste as much of your time as possible. I'm lucky my first buyer was a unicorn—knew what he wanted, paid right away, didn't fuck around. He made it seem easy. If he hadn't, I might have quit my first day. I can spot the time wasters faster now, though. In real life, I'd probably be nice, keep talking, but on here I don't have to. His profile says he's looking for something real—*You ladies are more than this!* When I told him I don't show face, he said, *Aww, babe, but I have to know if Im attracted to you. Lets build a connection and explore together.* I haven't responded to him in a few minutes, so his last two messages are just lines of question marks.

I click back to my chat with MilkBeaut. *Do you talk to your boyfriend about it?* I ask.

Sometimes.

What's he like?

Nice. He's nice. He works in an office. He really likes basketball, he plays a few times a week. I like him a lot.

So why do you still do this stuff?

I like it a lot too.

More messages pop up from BIGdickBrit47. *Skank,* he says. *Bitch . . . Act like you want it but your a liar.* He's still typing. It always ends badly with these guys. They start out saying you're the one and end up calling you a whore. I close the window and he disappears. That's one of the best things about these sites—you can just quit conversations. You can delete people because they're only half real.

∿

MOM'S NEW THERAPIST'S office is in a building almost outside of town. I'm wearing a black dress with a white collar on it that I haven't worn since elementary school because Mom told me I had to dress up. It's too tight on my chest and it doesn't hang the way it's supposed to, but the length is still okay. I didn't realize I hardly ever wear dresses anymore until I looked for one in my closet.

We have to hit a code and get buzzed in. It's just a regular apartment building, but it looks familiar. Mom stands in one corner of the elevator while I stand in another. The elevator clangs and moves slowly, like someone is pulling us up, hand over hand, with a pulley.

There's no waiting room, just a bench outside the door. There's a little chalkboard sign that says, *Thank you for removing your shoes*, so we do. I have a hole in my right sock and I know my feet smell—I've been wearing these socks for a few days so I can sell them. I wonder if I could make more money if I said I walked around a therapist's office in them, if men would pay more to know I'm extra fucked up. There should be something in this for me—it's exams this week, so I didn't even get to miss school.

We don't have time to sit down before the door opens and the therapist is there. "Hello." She holds her hand out to me like she wants me to think she respects me, like she wants me to think she sees me as an adult. "I'm Ellen."

"Katelin." I hold on to her hand hard, because she's doing the same to me. Her hand is soft and papery like an old lady's, but her grip is a man's. I wonder if she practises by shaking her husband's hand before they go to bed at night.

She's really pretty, and I wonder if Mom hates her because of it, or if it makes her want to get better, makes her want to be someone who's healthy again. Ellen looks a little bit like MilkBeaut, but older. And her lips are really thin—when she smiles they disappear.

We follow her through the door. It looks like somebody's living room. I guess I thought there'd be weird paintings or leather couches, but everything seems comfortable like it's been here forever. It reminds me of somewhere I've gotten stoned before, but I can't remember where. There are too many places to sit. I don't know if I should take the spot beside Mom on the couch or not. I choose one of the chairs instead and sit on the very edge, crossing one foot over the other and trying to keep them under the chair so they don't stink up the whole room.

"So. How's the week been?"

Mom looks at me and then back at Ellen. "Good," she says. "I've been keeping the list we talked about."

"Great. Does Katelin know about the list?"

"No."

It's so obvious that Ellen wants her to tell me about the stupid list. But Mom doesn't say anything else and I can hear the clock ticking all the way across the room. A noisy clock seems like a bad choice in a therapist's office. It would drive me crazy, but Ellen must like it. I wonder how much money she makes.

"Do you want to tell her about it?"

Mom clears her throat like she does when she's embarrassed. I don't know why she cares so much. "I write down symptoms I have, and then beside that, I write what I think they mean."

"Okay." I nod once.

Everyone is quiet for a minute. It feels like a trick.

"Since Katie's here, maybe we could talk about how she feels. Katie, how do you feel being here?"

I didn't tell her people call me Katie, and I realize I have no idea how much this stranger knows about me, what Mom has said in this room. It feels like a punch, like I've lost my breath and can't find it. I can't imagine what Mom would even be able to say about me. "I'm fine," I answer.

"Okay." Ellen uncrosses her legs and then crosses them again. I know she's waiting for me to say more, but I don't. "Do you talk to your mom about how she makes you feel?"

"Yeah. We talk all the time."

"That's great. Have things changed in the last little while? Have things gotten better or worse, or just different even?"

I realize why this room is so familiar. Ivan and I came to this building to buy coke once. The dealer wanted us to do K with him, so we hung out for a couple hours and watched *Fight Club*. The walls and doors in this unit are in the same places, but everything else is different.

"I don't know," I say. "I guess worse."

"Why do you think that is?" Ellen looks right at me, like she wants me to think she thinks I'm interesting.

"I don't think about it," I say.

At first, even before Dad left, it was like Mom and I were in it together. I liked it. I would never say that out loud, because I know it makes me a shitty person, but I really liked it. She took me to her doctor's appointments and we talked about her symptoms. She said I was the only one taking care of her. She was like a best friend, a sister, instead of a mom. But nothing was too serious then. She wondered what a mark on her arm was, and she'd laugh it off when I showed her all my little moles and freckles. It felt like we were whispering and giggling under a blanket. It felt like I could make everything better. Now I wonder if it's all my fault, for letting her pretend.

Ellen nods. "What about your dad? His leaving?"

It's like she read my mind, but I try not to look surprised.

"That can be a hard event, especially for someone your age."

An *event*. I don't think of my dad leaving like an event. He was here and then he wasn't. There's a before and an after, but the actual leaving? I didn't even see it happen. I wasn't even home. I shrug and look down at my lap and wait for Ellen to move on.

Mom says the most common symptom this week was dizziness. She thinks it's neurological. Ellen gives her homework. She's supposed to shake her head from side to side, or spin around in a circle for a minute. She's supposed to make herself dizzy and see what it feels like.

〰〰

"KEEP YOUR THUMB on the outside," Ivan says, "or you'll break it."

We're sitting in his basement drinking vodka and playing records on a real record player. I think it's his dad's. He tells me I'm still making my fist wrong, so I hold my hand out for him and he moves my fingers into the right places.

"Now punch me in the arm," he says.

"After I pee."

"You're such a pussy." He makes a fist and punches me in the shoulder. Ivan would never go easy on me; it's one of the things I like best about him. The punch is hard and it hurts but I don't show him that.

When I get inside the bathroom, I rub my arm for a minute. I smell my underpants right up close to my face while I pee. They smell a little like my grandmother's attic when we'd visit her in the summer. I don't know what the smell is, but maybe I inherited it from my grandmother. I get why men like this. I'm wearing this pair for a man who only fucks other men but loves women's underwear. These are pink cotton with pink lace along the top and around the legs. I don't know what he likes to do with them, but he always wants pink ones.

I go back out and Ivan has his sleeve rolled up. "It's your turn. Do it. Punch me."

I walk over and make a fist, wrap my thumb around my curled knuckles, hit him as hard as I can just above the elbow.

"Fuck!" He says it in a short, loud staccato, a yelp like a dog's bark.

For a second, I worry that he's mad, but then he says, "Good one," and I feel so important. "This time, hit higher." So I do.

He passes me the vodka and tells me to drink as much as I can at once, so I swallow and swallow. The next punch doesn't hurt as much, and the one after that makes me laugh because my arm's already numb. We scream and drink until we can't land punches anymore.

The next day I'm blue and purple and not as hungover as I thought I would be. I wear the bruises up and down my arms—proof that I can take someone's worst.

〰️

I'M STANDING IN the bathtub with my legs wide open, looking at myself in the mirror. The first time, I thought it'd be hard, that my brain wouldn't let my body do it, but it's actually the easiest thing in the world. When I start peeing, it's like I'm not wearing underpants at all. I push out my belly so it looks swollen, pregnant. For a lot of the bathroom guys, it's enough just not to wipe well after peeing. But some of them want more—some of them want to know you were soaking wet.

I shake my lower body like a dog after a bath and then take off my underwear before I step out of the tub—they peel off my skin. I put them in the sink for now. They need to dry before I put them in a plastic baggie; if they're still wet, they'll grow mould in the mail. I grab the tweezers from the medicine cabinet and pluck out one of my pubic hairs, nestle it into the crotch of my underwear because I like to think of that as my signature.

Sometimes I sell bras online, but not as many people want them. Once a guy asked me if I could shit in the cups and wrap it up like a present, and I was so surprised he asked that I said no. I think now I'd say yes.

I've sold a couple more pairs of underwear to the bald guy. For one pair, he wanted me to cry and wipe my face off with them before I wore them for a day. Crying is easy.

〰️

MARTY JACKSON HAS the best E right now, blue butterflies, but he takes forever to get a hold of. He set his phone up with no voice mail so nobody can leave messages about drugs, but he also never picks up the phone, so we have to call a million times. He's so paranoid about the police that he won't let anyone come to his house anymore, and there's always some stupid shit he wants you to do to get the drugs.

We meet him at the park even though it seems way worse to meet here than at his house. There are little kids everywhere. He's sitting on a bench with his hood up. We go over and I say hi, but he glares at me and doesn't say anything. Ivan passes him the money and Marty drops a baggie on the ground and then just walks away without saying anything. What a fucking idiot. Ivan bends right down and picks it up.

We sit for a minute watching the kids on the swings. My dad used to bring me to this park. I was obsessed with the slides; he'd help me cover them in pebbles as far up as possible. Then I'd slide down and try to knock them all off, like a bowling ball with a million tiny pins.

We go back to Ivan's house because his mom's out of the country again. We sit in the living room, and I crush the first pill into lines. You can also break it into powder and put it in a little bit of toilet paper and swallow it if you want it to work fast, but I like snorting. It's like something you have to go through to get to the good. It feels more real, like more of a story.

"You know, at one point, you were the youngest person alive," Ivan says. He puts on Soul Coughing because it's what everyone should be listening to, he says. I let him take the first line.

We dance around the living room and I'm laughing so hard my chest hurts. I don't even know where Ivan is. Sometimes my arm hits his chest or his hand brushes my waist, sometimes I see a blur of him, and that's enough of a reminder that he's here with me. I start to feel dizzy like I'm going to throw up, like all my organs are expanding inside me and I might split wide open.

When I stop spinning, Ivan is sitting at the coffee table and there's a game of Monopoly set up even though Ivan knows I hate it. We split another pill and use a fake hundred-dollar bill to snort it.

"You took one. A pill," he says. "Where is it?"

"I didn't."

"Did you do it already?" He looks frantic, too high. His tongue moves over his lips when he's not talking.

"There are two left. We had four. We've each done one full one now," I say.

His music is playing. He always chooses the music. It sounds like a city, out of place in his living room with all of his mother's traditional Russian art. "We didn't do two."

"Are you kidding?" I say.

He smiles at me and it's a smile I've never seen before, like there's something underneath his face. I'm sure his skin is pulsing, that there's something crawling a path under his cheeks. I wonder if I'm dreaming, if he's going to unzip his skin and show me what's underneath. "Get out," he says.

I need him to believe me. I start explaining, telling him what we did, when we took lines and how much I cut up. Everything was fine a minute ago. I try to tell him every detail so he remembers it all, too, but he's yelling now.

"Get the fuck out!"

He's leaning over me, so my body brushes his when I stand. But once I'm across the room, away from him, I feel brave. I feel like I could be done with him forever, burn it all and never have to see him again. "Give me a pill, then," I say.

"Fucking slut." He throws the bag with both pills at me. "If you want it, take it. We're not even friends. A friend would never treat me like this."

I take a pill out and put it in the extra little front pocket of my jeans, which I think was made especially for drugs, then leave the baggie with the last pill on his coffee table. He's still yelling when I leave.

When I get home, I go to my room but I'm crying before I even shut the door. It's the kind of cry that starts out like silent screaming. It doubles me over, curls my stomach with wet heat, and I have to sit right where I was standing, on the floor beside the bed. I pull my pillow over the edge and push my face into it so my gasps are muffled.

"I have no friends, I have no friends, I have no friends," I whisper into the pillow. It feels like casting a spell. Ivan wasn't at school the last day before exams, and the whole time I was eating lunch in the caf, I was the only person sitting alone. Even the real weirdos at school have people they can eat lunch with. Nobody likes me. Nobody wants me. Ivan hates me. Lillian hates me.

Ivan calls me a million times. When I finally answer, he screams at me. During one phone call, he cries and tells me he can't live without me, I'm the only person he has. In the next, he tells me he's the only person I have, too. "Your mother is a pig who's going to die," he says. "If you don't have me, you have nobody." I don't know if he knows how true that might be. He's never met my mom. I snort my last pill of E all in one go and my nose starts to bleed, just enough that I can taste it. The salty blood is a lot better than the powder going down.

In the last voice mail Ivan left, he tells me he just wants us to try, that I owe him that. He says he knows we love each other and he can make me happy. I think about what it would be like to do it, to give him a chance, to be his girlfriend. I want people to like me, to be obsessed with me. It feels so good when someone wants you; it's like walking home after a haircut and feeling new, hoping everyone sees you. I think about kissing him in front of other people and holding his hand.

The last thing he says is that he knows me better than anyone else does, and I realize how badly I want that not to be true. I know I could try with Ivan, start over. I could do anything if I really tried. But I don't want to.

When I finally fall asleep, I have dreams about him, and in the morning when I look in the mirror, the skin around my eyes is swollen and blotchy red like a rash.

nine

ʌʌʌ

The first day of summer vacation isn't even warm. Ivan's having people over because his mom's still in Russia. She goes all the time for weddings, funerals, birthdays. He never goes with her.

I get to his house early because I don't want to show up by myself when everyone's already there. That's something you're not supposed to do. I haven't seen him since he freaked out on me, but we talked on the phone and he told me to come early—he acted like the other night never even happened. We sit around and smoke pot and watch *Law & Order* in the kitchen while we wait for other people to get there. Ivan always says, "Obviously," when they read the verdict. During every episode. Like he knew all along how it would go and he's mad at the imaginary jury for doing exactly what he knew they were going to do. Like he wishes the show would surprise him just once. Every time I hang out with him now, I see more cracks, more things I hate. I wonder if they were invisible before, or if I was just blind.

"Your tits look weird." Ivan moves to poke me in the chest and I hunch my shoulders, cross my arms over myself. He pulls away like I burned him, squints at my boobs hard like he can see right through my arms and my shirt that way. "They're pouchy."

"It's my bra. It just looks like that."

"Whatever."

I look down at my boobs and they do look weird. He's right. It's like they're flat on top and then stick out all at once. They never look exactly the way I want them to. I always wanted boobs, even in grade one and two. When we had swimming lessons at school, we all used to pretend we had them. Sucking in could turn ribs into breasts. Even the boys did it sometimes.

I'll have to stand with my arms crossed under my boobs all night so they look rounder. It's annoying. Maybe if I get drunk I'll forget about it. I think about taking my bra off but that'd look worse. I want to look real but not too real.

I take my beer into the bathroom. I look at myself in the mirror and notice the pimple right above my left eyebrow, the dry skin under my nose. Even when I think I look good, there's always something missing.

I was in grade two when girls started talking about their bodies and all the things they didn't like. It seemed like it happened overnight; suddenly everyone wanted to talk about everything that was wrong with them. I was quiet the first few times it came up—I couldn't think of anything I hated about myself—but then they started leaving me out on purpose. I'd go out for recess and some of the girls would be standing in a circle and they wouldn't even make space for me.

"I hate my nose," I finally said one day at lunch. "It's huge." It was something I'd heard a woman say in a TV show. All the girls reassured me and told me my nose was small and pretty and cute. It felt like they really believed it. It felt good, like that was all I needed to do to be loved. I started finding new things to hate about myself. But for a while, I secretly still loved all the parts of me. I'd talk about how my arms were flabby and then go to the bathroom and lock myself in a stall and kiss both arms all the way up and down. I'd tell my arms I loved them and that I was so glad they could carry things and reach up high and give hugs.

One day I said my eyes were too close together and then looked at myself in the mirror for an hour, until I thought maybe I was right. Maybe they were weirdly close together. I looked like a Muppet, I thought, a caricature. Maybe that's what growing up is: seeing yourself for what you really are. Or maybe saying the words out loud made it all true.

Ivan's first-floor bathroom is next to the front door, so I'll hear when people get here. I have time. I pull my jeans down and sit on the floor against the door. My thong is red; it's just straps, really. The tile is bright blue and cold. I can see the goosebumps, the thin hairs on my thighs reaching straight up, trying to get away.

I take my ring box out of my purse and slice into the fat on my thigh, high up, right where my leg starts. It's too warm for jeans most days now, but shorts cover everything important. It's easy to cut through skin, soft like warm butter. I let myself deflate, all the air leaving my body through my brand-new holes. The blood looks brighter under the sharp light. It runs down to the back of my thigh and gathers there in a drop, hesitates like it's trying its hardest not to leave the warmth of me. I wipe it up right before it drips onto the floor. I hold myself tight for a few minutes, let myself soak into a wad of toilet paper, and then close right up.

The hair on my arms is jumping now, too. Goosebumps happen because of tiny muscles. I learned that in Science. The scars on my arms are just faint white lines now because I haven't been cutting there this week. Under the light, that whole part of my arm looks wrinkled, like it's older than the rest of me. I do my makeup until my face doesn't look dry or oily anywhere and I can't see the pimple at all.

∧∧∧

PEOPLE START SHOWING up around eight and then everyone is here. I've been at Ivan's before when he had people over, but I've never seen his house this full. And I don't really know anyone. I wish someone I know would show up, even someone I don't really like, just so I'd have someone to stand around with. I do circles around the main floor, from the living room to the kitchen to the hallway to the living room.

When I get back to the kitchen, Marcy's coming inside with a couple girls from school. I hold my breath, checking to see if Lillian is with them, but of course she's not. She'd never come here. Marcy's eyes land on me and she looks down at the ground like she's embarrassed to be caught staring. But I was the one staring.

"Hey, what are you doing here?" I ask.

"You know. Party."

The girls she's with motion that they're going to the living room, and she waves them off. I don't even know who they are.

"So, are you and Ivan, like, together now?"

I cringe. "No. I don't know why everyone thinks that."

She raises both eyebrows. "Maybe because you're together all the time?"

I pull my bottle of vodka out of my purse and take a drink before I offer it to Marcy. She accepts.

"Do you ever see Lillian?" The words are out before I think them.

She shrugs. "Of course. Did you see *Annie*?"

Lil's play. They put it on the last week of school, and everyone got an afternoon off classes to watch it for free. Ivan and I ditched after first period. I couldn't go; thinking about seeing her onstage made my head spin. Ever since our fight, anytime I walk down the halls, it's like I'm half out of my body. "No."

"You should've. She was good." Marcy takes a long drink of the vodka, then hands it back. "She worked really hard for that, you know?"

"Sure." It comes out sounding sarcastic, but Lil works harder than anyone.

"I don't know exactly what happened with you guys, so whatever, that's not my business. But I do think you should fix it."

Everyone thinks it's all my fault. I wait for more, for Marcy to tell me I'm a shitty friend, but she acts like that's it. She takes a beer out of her bag and opens it with her keys.

I'm about to push back, but then Alex and Cassie and a guy I don't really know come in. Alex focuses on us right away. "Guys! It's like an elementary school reunion." Her bangs are cut high, to show her whole forehead almost, but it looks good on her.

"Hey, yeah," I say.

"You guys looks so great," Alex says. It feels real, but I can't tell with Alex. Once she told me the best way to make people like you is to compliment something you don't even like about them.

"Hey, Al, I need your card." Cassie's already sitting at the kitchen table—in front of her is a textbook and a baggie of what

I'm pretty sure is coke. I wonder whose book it is, if it's Ivan's or if Cassie's carrying it around to do drugs on.

Alex pulls a student card from her pocket and hands it over. "Katie, Marce," Alex says, "do you know Cassie? And that's Matt."

"I should go find my people. See you later?" Marcy says, already backing out of the room. She turns around before I can even nod.

I feel better once she's gone. *My people*, she said. I used to be one of her people, me and Lil. I'm glad I didn't embarrass myself asking more about Lillian, though. There are things I'm trying so hard to forget. For a second, I feel okay. Then Alex says, "Katie and I used to be best friends. We know all each other's secrets." She winks, and I try not to bite my cheeks. I wonder if she really does know everything about me.

"You want one?" Cassie asks me as she pours a pile of coke onto the textbook. We had Science together last semester. You could hear her laugh from anywhere in the room. Her seat partner was in love with her so he did all the work and she passed even though she missed more school than anyone. My seat partner was Lillian. We made an elbow joint out of wood, elastic bands, and condoms, and only got a B-plus.

"Sure, yeah," I say. "Thanks."

I sit in the worst chair. Its back is broken and splintered, so I have to lean forward. I put my elbows on the table and watch Cassie press on the coke with Alex's student card, right where her face is, until there are no clumps and it's all powder. I take a quick look at Matt, who I've never really met before. I know he used to go to our school and he has a kid now. His mouth is moving fast and he keeps licking his lips. He has his hand on the back of Cassie's chair and he's staring at the lines. She takes hers first and he leans down level with the tabletop so he can see which one she's doing. She pushes the textbook to him and hands him the five-dollar bill she used. As soon as he's done, he pushes his chair back from the table and leaves the room.

"Who the fuck even is he?" Alex whispers.

Cassie just rolls her eyes.

We finish the lines and Alex talks to me about elementary school and it actually doesn't feel so bad. She brings up this kid who used to eat paper constantly. People called him Paper Boy for like six years. He was the first person I ever slow-danced with—it was on a dare during an indoor recess and the song was "I Don't Want to Miss a Thing" by Aerosmith.

Alex tells the stories but she keeps looking to me for confirmation, and it feels like sharing something. But it's also all for Cassie. Every time she laughs it's like we've won. Drug friends are the best friends ever for an hour. When you meet someone new, you have to deal with yourself, see yourself for who you really are, like hearing your own terrible voice on an answering machine—but coke turns that into a good thing.

When I stand up to look for a beer, I see myself in the mirror across the room. My lipstick is gone but I look good anyway. And Ivan was wrong. My boobs look great.

〰〰〰

WE STAY IN the kitchen for a long time, doing more coke and talking to random people who come through. At one point, Ivan sits down next to me. He puts an arm around my shoulder and I shrink away. "Why do you do that?" he says. He leaves his arm there anyway. He's wearing a bandana around his forehead and his pupils are huge.

Cassie changes when he's around. Her voice gets sharper, like she doesn't want him to think he's part of the conversation. Ivan and I hardly ever hang out with other people—this might be the first time I've really seen how someone else looks at him. A girl leaning on the counter just sighs when he tries to make fun of her, and Jonah left without saying bye as soon as Ivan showed up. Now that I've noticed it, I can't stop—everything feels tense around him, like he's a dangerous animal. I don't want Cassie to think he's my boyfriend, so I push him away with my elbow. I feel shame heavy on my body. I want to get as far away from him as I can.

Alex gets up to go to the bathroom. I can feel Ivan staring at me, feel the anger coming off him like a smell. "You know you make me feel like shit?" he whispers.

He gets close again, and I push him with my hands this time. I can feel heat behind my eyes but I know I can't cry. It'd ruin everything. I try to laugh instead, pretend it's a joke, but it feels scary, like someone's hand is coming up through my body and squeezing the right parts to make the sound, like I'm a puppet and someone else's noises are coming out of me.

Cassie lights a cigarette. She keeps her smokes in a metal box and uses matches to light them. It smells like campfire. She smiles at me and then looks at Ivan. "Fuck you," she says. "You're a dick. The only reason anybody's here is to use your fucking house." She does this thing sometimes where she scrunches her nose up really quick, like a wink, and it makes you feel like you're in it together.

Ivan starts laughing. He gets up and leaves but I can hear him laughing all the way outside.

"We should hang out sometime." Cassie's smile looks so genuine. She holds her smoke in between her thumb and pointer finger like it's a joint.

"Cool," I say. I wonder if I had to be friends with Ivan just so this moment would happen—it feels like things might be possible again.

Alex comes back from the bathroom and wants to leave. She says a guy who got obsessed with her after she slept with him once is here. I wonder if maybe they'll invite me along, but Cassie just hugs me and we put our numbers in each other's phones.

When they leave, the whole party changes. It feels like someone turned the lights on or the music off, even though neither of those things happened. I have this moment of panic where I wonder if I'm ever going to have a real friend again. I sit in the kitchen by myself for a bit and just feel so sad. People start to leave, like they can feel the difference, too. I light a cigarette and smoke the whole thing without anyone coming to talk to me. But when I open my phone, Cassie's number is right there at the top of my contacts—she called herself *Cass.

〰〰

IT'S LATE WHEN I make it home. I was planning to stay at Ivan's, but I left without saying bye. I get dizzy going downstairs to the basement and everything goes black, but it only lasts a couple seconds and then I can see again. I go online and end up on MilkBeaut's profile, looking through her pictures. When we first met, I didn't look at her videos because I thought maybe she wouldn't want me to. I feel like I know her now, though, almost like we're friends. I know she has two kids and a boyfriend and lives in Boston. I don't know her real name but she doesn't know mine either and it doesn't matter anyway because we're not our names. Knowing her makes me think it might be exciting to watch her videos. Watching someone I know do something sexy, something dirty.

In the first video, she's just sitting in a chair at a kitchen table. Milk starts to squirt out of her nipples without her even touching them, and she makes little kitten noises. The more milk comes out, the louder she is, and the louder she is the more milk comes out. After a while, there are two puddles on the table in front of her. At the end, she reaches off-screen and pulls out a cloth to clean up the milk. It has her screen name embroidered on it like an advertisement.

In another one, there's music playing in the background. The lyrics are in a different language. She holds her boobs like they belong to her and points her nipples right at her mouth. The milk dribbles down her chin. She gets on her knees and moos like a cow.

The last one I watch, she squirts her milk into a cup of coffee, then drinks it.

∧∧∧

THE NEXT DAY, I get up around noon. Mom has been vacuuming for hours. Usually when I'm hungover I just drink a bunch of water and make myself puke it all up, but I don't think I feel bad enough for that. When I pull my phone from under my pillow, there's a text from Cassie. She wants to know if I'm doing anything today. I take my phone into the bathroom while I pee, and I type out a response a few times before I just text back, *Not really.* I felt so good about her last night—it seemed like she really liked me—but maybe it was just the drugs. Or maybe this is all some big joke. Ivan was so embarrassing last night; I hope Cassie doesn't think I'm anything like him. I think about the other night in my room after fighting with Ivan, snot running down my face from crying so much, feeling like I have no one. I'm back in bed when my phone buzzes. *Let's do something*, Cassie says.

~~~

THE FAIR IS in town for the weekend, so Cassie and I are meeting out front. It comes every year and usually Lil and I go for a couple hours. It's not much of a fair. There's a Ferris wheel and some slides and a teacup ride. There's lots of shitty food. There's a vegetable competition in one building and a craft competition in another. I won a prize when I was seven for a papier-mâché owl I made. Another year I won the colouring contest. My dad used to help me with that stuff. He'd get the brochure every year with all the prize categories for each age group, and he'd pick a couple that looked good. It's not like he did the arts and crafts for me, but he did have the ideas.

Cassie's not here yet, so I sit on the curb and watch people walk past. Mrs. Young, my grade-five teacher, walks by and waves at me, so I wave back. She asks how my mom is and I say she's fine. Lots of people I don't know walk past. Most of them are fat and ugly and their clothes are horrible and I bet this is the most exciting thing that happens to them all year—a stupid fair. This is something I'll never go to as an adult. These are the worst adults.

I see Cassie come over the hill. I stand up but she doesn't walk any faster. She's wearing a crocheted tank top over a bathing suit, and white shorts with flip-flops. They slap on the hot black pavement. We go into the fair without really talking—it costs a dollar and we each get a Tweety Bird stamp on our left hand.

The fair is just a big circle. We don't really see anybody to talk to. I half hope Lillian's here and sees me with Cassie, but I half hope I don't see her ever again. Steve can have her. Cassie passes me a water bottle from her purse. It smells like vodka but I can't tell which flavour. I turn toward the wall to drink some so I can plug my nose without anybody seeing. Then I wipe my tongue on my shirtsleeve to get rid of the taste. It helps a little. Cassie watches me but she doesn't laugh. "I hate the taste, too," she says. We pass the bottle back and forth and by the third time, I don't have to plug my nose at all. I watch my own feet take steps and think, *Remember this, remember this, remember this.*

We walk around and around and every time we see someone from school, Cassie tells me everything she knows about them. She acts like she's whispering—she even puts her hand over her mouth like someone might be able to read her lips—but she has to yell so I can hear her over the music and games and rides. She knows weird shit about everyone.

We find a few clowns hanging out in a small tent, and Cassie asks one with a huge purple wig if she can touch his tiny red nose. I stand behind them and see how close she gets to him, how he touches her waist with his fat pink fingers. Cassie takes the nose right off his face.

We eat cotton candy and Cassie gets french fries and a hot dog. The heat and the vodka and the fullness in my belly make me feel like I might puke, but in a good way, in a light and dizzy way. I get corn on the cob and I can feel the salty butter on my cheeks like a smile.

ten

^^^

At first, it feels horrible to wipe my ass with my underwear. It's uncomfortable—wet and warm and wrong. The first time someone asked me to do it, I felt sick just thinking about it. But after a couple times, things changed. It started to feel good, literally letting go. Afterward, I'm empty.

I'm taller now—I can hold my head higher than everyone else because I know something about myself they don't. I can stretch right up to the trees, to the ceiling, because someone wants me so much they even want the gross parts. Every little bit of me is worth something.

^^^

THE FIRST TIME I go over to Cassie's house, there's a chicken in the oven and classical music is playing through the whole downstairs. Cass lives with her grandma but she stays with her mom or dad or sister once in a while. Her grandma's rich. Antique-furniture rich. Liquor-cabinet rich. Cassie introduces me to her in the kitchen, and she says I can call her Lucy. Cassie tells Lucy my dad is a lawyer—I don't know if Cass knows he doesn't live with us anymore, but she doesn't tell Lucy that part. And Lucy smiles, so I just smile back. She's wearing an apron covered in little red berries. My mom has an apron that says, *I'm still hot. But now it comes in flashes!* It was a present from someone; when she got it a few years ago I laughed with her about how stupid it was even though I didn't get the joke. She's never worn it.

"What have you girls been doing today?"

Cass looks at me. This morning we met up at Wal-Mart because she wanted to buy pot from a guy who works in the garden centre. We stole a bottle of water and some tinfoil and made a pipe and smoked in the delivery area behind the store. Then we walked to Pizza Pizza and got free slices because Alex was working. You're not supposed to have piercings or tattoos if you work there, but Alex told me her boss lets her do whatever she wants. He doesn't even make her cover her piercings up with those little stickers like they have to at Wendy's and McDonald's. He's a devout Jehovah's Witness. She said he watches porn on his computer at work—sometimes he shows it to her—and he only hires girls who are cokeheads or in high school or both. He's always asking them for hugs, but Alex says he's never done anything really wrong.

"Nothing," Cassie says. "We're going upstairs."

"Okay, lovey. I'll call you for dinner."

"We already ate."

"Wait." Lucy turns on the cold water and runs a plastic container of strawberries underneath it. She dumps them into a bowl and passes it to Cassie.

Cass rolls her eyes at me but she must love her grandma. She chooses to stay here even though there are rules and she can't just do whatever she wants like when she's staying with her mom or dad. Cassie's mom showed up in the parking lot the last week of school and went crazy. Later, someone told me she was on crack. She wouldn't stop talking but she didn't make sense. It was like there was something really important she had to say but she kept forgetting what it was. Cassie laughed right in her face.

Stepping into Cassie's room is like getting to know her up close. The air smells like her—Flintstones vitamins and the first few minutes of a thunderstorm. The rest of the house is old and smells like wood and silver polish. My mom would say Cassie's room is festering. You can't see the floor because there are clothes and bags and CDs and textbooks everywhere. All she has for furniture is a bed and a dresser, and neither one of them has any space free. She has a lamp shaped like a gun. It's silver and ugly, but I wish it was mine anyway. I can never tell when things are cool until someone else has them.

Cassie sits on top of a pile of clothes on her bed, so I do the same. She looks at me, all the way up and down, and then goes to her closet, pulls out a bright pink dress that's tight on the bottom and loose on the top. It's sleeveless. "Wear this. It'll look good. You have a really nice ass."

She doesn't tell me to go to the bathroom or anything, so I take off my clothes right in her room, right in front of the mirror she must change in front of all the time. I can see her behind me in the reflection. She starts looking through some of the clothes on her bed while she talks about what we're going to do tonight.

I've never thought about whether Cassie is pretty. She's more than that, maybe. Her nose is a little crooked, but you can only see it when she looks straight at you. She hardly ever shaves her armpits, but in a cool way, like it's a choice. She's skinny like I wish I could be. I used to pray for curves, pray to look like a woman. I was tired of my flat chest and no hips. Boys wanted tits and ass and I had neither. Once I sat on a guy's lap at a party and he told everyone that my face was pretty but my butt hurt his legs. Too bony, he said. Nothing there. I looked in the mirror that night and wished I could stop being a skinny little girl. I pinched myself until I was bruised.

Now I look at magazines where the women are so thin you can picture their skeletons. Cassie looks like that, especially in the last couple months. Every pound matters. Now I wish I could look like Cassie.

She watches me in the mirror for a minute, then grabs makeup off her dresser and holds it out. "You can cover that up if you want." She nods down at my arms.

I look at the deep pink lines. It's not that I forgot to keep them covered, exactly. Maybe I wanted her to see. Maybe I just wanted someone to ask me about them so I could deny it. It's actually really easy to lie about. Most people will believe whatever makes it easiest for them. Once a teacher asked me about some cuts on my shoulder. I told her they were from walking into a bush. She said I should watch where I'm going.

Cassie shrugs. "You don't have to. I don't care. But someone else might ask." But she keeps holding her arm out to me like she knows how important it is to keep secrets.

I take the makeup. It feels like being caught. I hate those moments when I realize how someone else sees me. I'm too embarrassed to put the makeup on in front of her so I go into the bathroom.

When I get back, everything is normal, like nothing happened. Cassie starts to talk about people from school. She's never asked me about Ivan, but I know she will eventually—I'm worried she'll still think we're friends. He still texts me every few hours, and sometimes I respond, but I haven't seen him in days, not since the party. I keep making up excuses not to see him. I bring Ivan up to Cassie instead, tell her about the time he tried to shit-talk a ten-year-old so she'll know I think he's a loser. She laughs, and it makes me feel funny and smart and like people want to hear what I have to say. It makes me feel good enough. We finish getting dressed and eat strawberries until our fingers are stained bright red.

〜〜〜

WEARING CASSIE'S DRESS is like being free. She picked it out for me. I know she'd wear it, so I don't have to worry about whether it's cool or not. I feel like everything is good, like I'm finally happy and not alone and nothing can go wrong. It's like having a best friend again. I feel like I've done coke even though I haven't.

When it gets dark, we go to Cassie's dad's. He's drunk when we show up. He seems way older than Cassie's mom. There are no glasses to drink out of, but Cassie finds a set of measuring cups under the sink. She washes them and we use them as shot glasses. They have long handles and they keep tipping over so we have to hold on to them the whole time. Cassie tears the top off a frozen juice can and we eat it with little spoons. It's so sweet it's almost sour.

A few other girls are supposed to meet us here—Cassie called them earlier—but I don't know most of them. She said her dad likes it when her friends come over; she never has to ask permission. His new girlfriend is only a few years older than us, but she left high school a long time ago.

Alex shows up first. I know she and Cassie are close, maybe best friends. It makes sense. Alex always seems comfortable—she always has—and I think that's how it must feel to be popular. She walks like she knows where she's going. Tonight she's wearing black nail polish, and she has bright silver stars in her dimple piercings. She must have just re-dyed her hair; it's so black it's shiny blue in the fluorescent kitchen light. She asks me to go outside to pee with her, and I don't want to leave Cassie, but I do have to pee, and the bathroom here has no door. There's just a rug pinned over the entrance. It's thick and heavy and doesn't go all the way down to the floor.

Alex starts telling me about how she did acid last night. There's a mirror hanging on the brick wall in the alley and I see a flash of myself when I walk past, but I don't look into it. I crouch behind a bush and move my feet far apart so my shoes don't get wet.

"I actually thought the kitchen was on fire at one point." Alex laughs. "I thought I could put it out with my own body, but obviously it was fine because there wasn't actually a fire."

I can hear her pee hitting the ground because she's going right on the driveway instead of in the grass. I don't know if we're friends again or not. I have to trust her because I have no other choice, but I don't really trust her at all.

"Jonah took care of me instead of doing acid himself. Super cute. Once he did a shit ton of it and ate a pack of smokes. Literally a whole pack. He just sat in the corner, just on the floor in a corner, and ate them one at a time. People were cheering him on and it was like he didn't even see them. I wouldn't tell him this, but it was actually kinda creepy." When she stands up, a motion light goes on behind her and her shape is cut out from the world. Just a silhouette pulling up its pants. "Anyway, I think he's secretly scared to do acid again. So adorable."

After a couple more hours, everyone is drunk. Cassie's sister, Rosie, is here, too. I've never met her before. She's pregnant. She had her first kid when she was still at our school. Someone told me that she and Cassie don't get along most of the time, but they seem fine tonight. We're sitting around the kitchen table, which is covered in little bits of weed and tinfoil and wax.

Cassie's dad is sitting beside me, and when he tries to stand up, the chair slides, screeches loud on the kitchen floor, and he falls into me, his body draped over my arm. One of his arms lands across me and he pushes, grabs my chest. He hits my shoulder with the bottle of beer he's got in his other hand. At first it's like he's trying to catch himself. Maybe he did need some catching, but it lasts too long and he's *drunk* drunk; I can smell his breath, like cigarettes put back in the pack when they're half-smoked, like whisky and vinegar.

"Whoa whoa. Whoa. Sorry, honey." He slurs the words and his hand is still on me. I can feel his whole body up against my back and the pressure of him over my shoulder, a heavy shadow. He squeezes my chest again before he steps away.

At first I think the laughter is about something else, that I can pretend nothing happened, but then I realize everyone is looking at me and Cassie's dad. A guy I don't know hits him on the shoulder. "Dirty old fuck," he says, laughing. Cassie's dad swings his body like he doesn't know what's happening, like he's falling apart.

There's a wet spot on my shoulder where he spilled his beer.

I think I'm going to cry. I can feel the shape of his hand on my chest like he's still touching me. And I can't leave to do anything that might help—like cutting or putting my face in a sink full of cold water—because then everyone will know I'm upset. I dig my thumbnails into my fingers so hard that I know I'll see little red moons on them tomorrow. I want to scratch myself until I bleed, until I can see inside my own body.

Cassie isn't laughing. She just stares like she's looking right through me. Then she turns around and goes upstairs. I don't even know what's up there. It doesn't feel like a house that has bedrooms.

I take a shot from the bottle of vodka on the table. Everyone knows Cassie doesn't need anyone—that's why people want her. I keep looking at the stairs until everyone stops laughing, until they move on. Cassie's dad's girlfriend is asleep in a chair across from me, her chin resting on her own collarbone.

∧∧∧

I'VE ALWAYS BEEN worried about messing up. I've always been worried that I'm disappointing, that people are going to hate me and it'll be all my fault. Lillian always said everyone feels like that sometimes, but she didn't get it. She didn't understand how that's the first thing I think about when I wake up, how I replay every conversation I have because I know I must have done something stupid. She's proof that I can't help ruining things, even things I thought were impossible to mess up—the one friend I thought I'd have forever, no matter what. Now I've ruined things with Cassie, too.

When I was in grade six, I made friends with this girl named Beth. She was a year older than me and she was so cool. She wore shiny denim jeans instead of the leggings all the girls in my grade wore. She brought a Lunchables every day and gave it away to whoever wanted it. She had a trampoline in her backyard.

She'd find me at recess and we'd sit on the hill by the baseball diamond. People in my grade—Lillian, Marcy, all of them—were still playing stupid games, but Beth and I would just talk the whole time. She knew about things because she had a sister who was older, already in high school.

Then Beth moved closer to the school, closer to me, and we could walk home together. It felt like all my wishes were coming true. I usually walked home with Lillian, but I figured she'd understand. She had to. The first time Beth and I walked together, she came over to my house. Mom was nice while Beth was there— the kind of nice where she asked questions she already knew the answers to. But when Beth left, Mom told me I couldn't walk home with her anymore. She said Beth was *too mature* to be my friend, that she was the kind of girl who'd get herself into trouble. Mom could tell just by her attitude.

I sobbed into my pillow that night—at first because I wanted Mom to hear me, but by the end it was real.

I started acting sick after lunch every day so my teacher would call my parents to come pick me up. That way, I wouldn't have to tell Beth I couldn't walk home with her. My mom started taking me to appointments because of all my headaches, to eye doctors and neurologists. But then she took me to a therapist and the next week she wouldn't pick me up at all, even when I spent the whole afternoon with my head down on my desk. She only believes therapists when they're diagnosing somebody else.

I avoided Beth for as long as I could—I hid in the bathroom until the school was basically empty, or I purposely forgot something in my desk so I had to go back at the last minute. But it started getting harder and harder and one day she caught me on my way out. When I told her I wasn't allowed to walk home with her, she didn't look upset. She just shrugged like it was nothing, like I was nothing.

The next day, I said hi to her at recess and she turned her back on me like I wasn't even there. I think if she'd yelled at me, screamed in my face, I would have been okay—I would have been angry but eventually okay. But she acted like I wasn't even enough to acknowledge.

That night, I plucked out my pubic hairs, one by one. They'd just started growing in and they felt like a nuisance I could still control. I didn't cry. I could only finish a tiny section, and it was burning red, but it was also smooth and lovely. The rest of me was an explosion. Once I finished it all, I'd be perfect.

But every time I finished a little bit, more hair grew in. I'd rub my finger on the smooth section and try to ignore the rough bristles around the edges, already coming in since the last time. Eventually I had to give up. But I still do it sometimes when I get really anxious, when I've done something wrong. I pluck and pluck and then rub my tiny spots of perfect skin.

〰〰

I KEEP MY cell phone with me in case Cassie calls. When it vibrates, I feel like I'm holding all the pieces of myself together with my own breath. And then when it's not her, when it's just Ivan, I loosen until my stomach falls over the top of my jeans and my mouth hangs open. I want to pretend I don't care but I care so much. Way too much to be cool, because I'm not cool. I'm a stupid loser who wants everything, and everyone knows.

I don't have anything to do, just waiting around for something that might never happen, so I've been watching a lot of porn. Some of it makes me laugh even though I can feel that bubble getting bigger and bigger inside me. It can be sexy even when it's funny. I always end up watching one where two girls rub up against the same vibrator. It almost looks like they're conjoined twins. They moan together like one heart beating. I think if they were walking somewhere together, they'd take all their steps at the same time.

One of my buyers tells me about a BDSM site. I find a discussion group on it called Sluts/Cunts/Whores, so I join. There are threads like *How many men have you fucked in one day?* and *What's your most whorish fantasy?*

In one of the discussions, people give the women "slut assignments." *Go outside and fuck the first person you see. Give a hand job on a city bus. Keep a peeled hard-boiled egg in your vagina for a day—then eat it.* The women do things and then describe what happened. Some of the posts make it hard to settle exactly right in my chair. I sit on my knees, then cross-legged, then move to the couch and lie down for a minute. I read through the archives until I'm a year back, two years, three. But I don't say I'll do anything.

Eventually, I get bored of being online, so I go upstairs. Mom and I decide to watch *Titanic* in the middle of the day. I like it even though it's old; it's a classic. I was only seven the year it came out. When I was finally allowed to watch it, I had to pinch myself so I didn't laugh at the nude scene. I wanted so badly to prove I was grown up, but I still almost laugh at that scene every time.

I rewind the first tape while Mom makes popcorn. She gets mad at me because I always take the best pieces—the ones that are wet with butter and covered in salt—instead of just grabbing a handful and eating what I get. I don't know what the point of that would be, though. I don't want to eat the worst when I can fill up on the best. We turn off all the lights and shut the blinds so it's like we're in a real theatre. We sit on the couch, legs curled up beside us, under the same blanket.

~~~

I STILL HAVE the dress I borrowed from Cassie. I put it on a couple times every day and look in the mirror. I was sleeping with it beside my pillow, but it doesn't smell like her room anymore. At night I practise talking to her, work out conversations we might have. I don't actually say the words out loud, but I move my lips and I can hear them in my head. I used to do that a lot—practise what I'd say to people, make it perfect so I'd always be ready. I don't think I ever practised talking to Lillian, though.

When I was a kid, I was in bed with my parents once—I think we must have been on vacation or something—and I was practising a conversation. I moved my lips, but I thought I was being so quiet. I felt Mom lean over me and I kept my eyes closed. She said to my dad, "I think she's talking in her sleep," and so I just pretended I was. I was so embarrassed she could see me. It felt like I'd accidentally opened myself up. If she could hear my secret words, maybe she could hear anything.

~~~

THE UNDERPANTS IN my newest ad are nice—I thought about keeping them, but I can always buy another pair if I decide I miss them. The first guy who commented looks young in his picture. Blond hair, wearing a polo shirt. Cute in a regular way, not my type.

He's online now, so I send him a private message. *Hey sexy. I like your pic.*

The message goes unread for a minute, but then he responds. *I like yours.*

Can I do anything special for you?

Do you stuff? he asks.

This is my favourite moment, where I can take things any way I want. I can feel him right on the edge. After letting him think I might say no for a minute, I agree that I'll wear them for a day, stuff for a full hour, and then send him my dirty laundry.

An MSN message pops up from Ivan. *Where have you been?* I've been ignoring him. Last night he called my house phone—I picked up and tried to talk to him, but he was so drunk he kept losing his words. After I hung up, I left the phone off the hook for the night. I still haven't seen him since his party.

I minimize MSN and go back to the panty site. There's a new message from the guy—with his address. And I can't breathe. He lives here. In town. This has never happened before. Buyers live in the province once in a while, sometimes even just a couple hours' drive away. But he could be someone I know, someone from school—a teacher, even.

Where the fuck are you!? Ivan writes, and my head is going to explode. I set my MSN to Appear Offline so he can't interrupt, so I can focus. The house phone rings beside me, and I know it must be Ivan, so I pick up and hang up on him, then leave it off the hook again.

I remind myself to breathe. If I wait too long to respond, the buyer will think something's wrong. I could end it here. I could tell him I'm sorry, that I forgot I sold that pair already. I could block him. But I want to be someone who takes risks—he never has to know.

I tell him that everything is good and I'll send the panties in about a week. I spend the rest of the day imagining what might happen if he found me, and by the time I go to bed, I have a whole new set of fantasies.

∧∧

CASSIE FINALLY CALLS. We end up hanging out in front of the library when we get too stoned to go to her grandmother's. We had seven dollars, but Cassie wanted to buy a *Cosmo* and a bag of M&M's. Now we don't have enough for anything else. She's looking at the magazine and both of us are sitting on the curb, our legs sticking out between two parked cars.

"Do you like your dad?" she asks.

"He's an asshole." Even as I say it, I know it's not the whole truth, but Cassie nods like I said the right thing, like she gets it.

"At least he's not around so you don't have to talk to him."

I didn't tell Cassie that. I wonder if she asked people about me.

"Don't you like your dad?" I thought Cass loved him. He treats her like they're friends. She usually laughs at everything he does, except she didn't laugh when he touched me. I remember his hand on my chest, the burning weight of it like a brand, the stupid drunk smell of his breath on me, everyone else laughing at his bold clumsiness, and I feel my face getting guilty hot.

"Sometimes he's okay." She spits her gum out on the road between us. It's bright pink. "I lived with him when I was little. He'd leave me alone a lot, usually just to go to work for a few hours, or for a day maybe, but one morning I woke up and he was still gone from the night before. The first day was okay—I microwaved Pizza Pops. But then after a couple days I ran out of food. There were boxes of Kraft Dinner, so I dipped the dry noodles in ketchup. When he came back, he brought this tray full of chocolate cupcakes. They had icing on them that looked like *Sesame Street* characters. I still don't know where they came from. They tasted so fucking good. Every time I finished one, he put a new one in front of me, so I kept eating. He sat with me at the table for, like, it must've been hours."

I hold out my hand for Cassie's cigarette. "He came back, though."

"Yeah." She passes the smoke and her fingers shock me with static.

It was never like this with Ivan. I don't know if he ever told me anything true.

"I think my dad got tired of us," I say.

"You and your mom?"

"Yeah."

She tries to take one M&M out of the bag, but she spills the whole thing onto the pavement. She picks up a handful and puts them all in her mouth at once.

"That's disgusting," I say.

"You're disgusting." Cassie's mouth is full of melted chocolate so her teeth are brown and her tongue is slimy, but she always looks good.

eleven

ᴧᴧ

I've been wearing the same pair of underwear for four days. I'm not making much more money for the extra days, but I like thinking about someone wanting to smell me like this. The man who bought them didn't talk to me except to say exactly what he wanted and give me an address.

There's a discount underwear bin at the department store down the street. They sell everything, and it's all cheap. If anyone I knew ever saw me there, I'd pretend I wasn't really looking for underwear, that it was just a joke, that I was better than that. But nobody I know goes there.

Some days I go and stay for a whole hour, just looking through every loose pair for something perfect. I rub the material between my thumb and middle finger, push deep into the pocket of the crotch panel. I wonder if someone will buy these panties and wear them without washing them, if my skin cells will rub off on their bodies. I never wash the ones I get—I know other people have touched them, too, but I don't mind.

Sometimes I steal a couple pairs just because it's easy. It's harder to catch someone stealing if they don't really need to steal. The cashier never even looks at me on my way out.

I have regulars on the panty site now. There's one guy who loves to talk about television shows. He sends me recaps of *Frasier* even though it's in reruns. I read every word because it's weird to see a guy getting so excited about something that's not sex. It feels like having a secret camera in someone's mind. In real life, you're not supposed to get excited about anything. That's one thing I miss about Lillian, I guess. When she got excited, she told me all about it.

There's a guy online who has a fantasy of being swallowed by a massive snake. He can get off just watching nature videos. He says it's not the dying part that turns him on; he just wants to be swallowed.

And then there's the guy who lives in town. There are other orders I had to get done before his, but the whole week felt like waiting. I left his pair on my bedside table as something to look forward to. It was hard to care about what anyone else wanted. But when it was finally his turn, I was ready for it to be over with. I wrote his address on the envelope in perfect cursive, like I learned in elementary school. When I licked the stamp, I gave him part of me. But I probably won't sell to him again—it's too much thinking.

Mom wants me to get a job for the summer because she did when she was fifteen. She sold popcorn at the drive-in and got to see all the movies for free. I say I'm trying, but I wonder what she'd do if I told her I already have a job.

〜〜〜

CASSIE'S GRANDMOTHER IS gone for the weekend. The key to the liquor cabinet is taped to the back of one of the drawers in the kitchen. We open the cabinet and pour a little from each bottle into a mug. It tastes like smelling nail polish remover. The cat meows at us like it knows we're trespassing, but we ignore it.

Cassie's dress is shifted up all the way. She's sitting with both legs under her and I can see the pink of her underpants. I think about what's underneath the fabric. I wonder whether the roots of each hair look like tiny bulbs sprouting wires like mine do.

"I wanna get fucked tonight." Cassie puts her hand around the wrist of her other arm, makes quick bracelets with each finger to her thumb. She can touch each one around her wrist no problem. "Maybe Kyle," she says.

Kyle has dreads. Once they caught on fire while he was lighting a smoke at a party, and Alex put them out with a carton of milk from the fridge. Kyle tells that story all the time.

"He always has such good pot. And his dick is huge. I just wish he didn't smell like BO," she says.

For just a second, I want to defend him. I want to say, *He's a person. People smell*, but I don't even like Kyle. And Cass is the best thing that's ever happened to me—she makes me feel like someone people want. Maybe I always was that person but I needed Cassie to realize it. When Cass pays attention to someone, it's like they suddenly matter. I get invited everywhere. People I didn't even know existed know my name. Sometimes I run into Marce at parties; we usually nod at each other, but we hardly say hello anymore. My heart used to beat a little faster, wondering if we'd have to talk, but I guess anything feels normal after a while. Lillian's never around—we're in two completely different worlds now.

Cassie doesn't have rules when it comes to sex. She's allowed to do anything with anyone she wants. I don't know why it doesn't matter for her the way it does for other girls. When she lost her virginity, the guy told her he was in love with her and she told him he was garbage in bed. Everyone knows that story.

She pulls the cat into her lap and it meows high and screechy. She holds it around the middle and pushes her face into its face. It closes its eyes and stays so still. When she lets it go, it licks itself all over and then stalks out of the room.

Cassie lies down on the floor, balances the mug of liquor on her stomach. "I bet you five dollars you'll lose your virginity tonight."

"Yeah, right. With who?"

"Who cares? That's not the bet. Don't worry about it. I'll make sure it happens."

"Whatever." I pretend I'm not excited, that I haven't been thinking about this constantly. Usually it feels like I'm never going to have sex; I don't even know how it'd happen. I feel like I'm falling behind—I thought all the stuff online would make sex easier in real life, but it hasn't. I should probably wear the right underpants just in case.

Cassie passes me the mug and there's a dark wet ring left on her dress. "I'm so hungry," she says.

I take a drink and lean back against the wood cabinet. *Right now, at this exact moment, I'm fine*, I think. *Everything is fine.*

〰

WE DON'T GO to the party until like eleven. Cass says it's not the kind of place you want to be when there's only a few people there. She heard about it from Izzy, whose brother buys drugs from the guy who owns the house. Everyone says you can always find the drug dealer at a party as long as you can find Izzy. Even when she doesn't know they're a dealer, she somehow sniffs them out. They're just her type.

The railing of the front porch is broken in pieces, lying in the yard, and people are sitting with their legs hanging off, passing a bottle down the line. Russell Daniels has been making vodka in his bathtub and selling big plastic jugs of it for twenty dollars. Everyone has puked at least once from it so far this summer.

There are so many people that it's like a party scene in a stupid movie. You can't even move without pushing through people. It's the kind of party that you have to be there for, that people will remember. Most of the people here are from other schools, but there are lots I recognize. The guy who owns this house was in an episode of *The X-Files*. He died in it. I heard he likes to put it on while he has sex. Cassie says it wasn't really him. She's seen the episode.

We go to a room up two flights of stairs. There are three mattresses on the floor, and a few people are sitting on each one. I'm not friends with anyone, but there are some people I know, mostly stoners. One of them is this guy that everyone calls Asia. I have a couple classes with him even though he's older than me; his real name is Ben. He's the only Chinese person at our school. There are two Black guys at school, too. We call them Shoes and Afro. Everyone else is white.

Ben's smoking out of a huge bong. A guy I don't know asks him, "Can you even fucking see when you're stoned?" He pulls his eyes at the sides so they're just thin slits.

Ben exhales, and then he laughs, so I laugh, too. We all laugh, so it's okay.

Cassie sees Kyle in the corner and she goes over and hits him in the arm, sits beside him up against the wall. He lifts his arm to put it around her shoulder. It looks so easy, but when I think about what I'd have to do, how cool I'd have to be, to make someone touch me like that, it feels impossible. I can see the sweat in the armpit of his T-shirt. Maybe that makes him a man. I wonder if she can smell him, what it's like to smell a boy's armpit right up close.

Someone pokes me in the back of the thigh and I turn and see Andrew, one of Ivan's friends. He was sitting behind where the door opens, like a surprise. He used to go to TCI, so we never went to school together. I've met him a couple times with Ivan. He's older and cooler and hotter than Kyle. I wonder if Cassie would be jealous. Andrew probably smells more like what girls are supposed to want boys to smell like.

I sit beside him when he grabs my wrist and pulls me down, but I look everywhere but at him. Ben makes a joke and I don't know what he said but I laugh anyway. My head feels like it's higher up than usual, like it could touch the ceiling. Andrew fills a pipe with weed and passes it to me. It's blue with white spots all over it, like an animal from someone's dreams.

Andrew lights the bowl while I inhale the smoke, suck it in, and hold it. I won't cough, I tell myself. I can make this look sexy. And when I exhale in a thin line, the smoke disappears and I don't make any noise at all. After Andrew passes the pipe on to someone across the room, he leans back into me, his hand resting on my leg.

Ivan comes in. I knew he was going to be here but I didn't tell him I was coming. I wonder if he's been to the kitchen yet. At parties he licks all the leftovers in the fridge and spits in all the liquids. He looks right at Andrew's hand on my thigh, as bare as it's ever been. Andrew tries to push his hand in between my legs; my thighs are squished tight together and when I move them apart, they unstick, skin separating from skin like slicing raw chicken breast. I keep staring at my legs, at Andrew's hand holding my thigh, and when I look up, Ivan's not there anymore. I feel a rush of guilt, but it melts into anger—he can't tell me what to do. I take off my hoodie and put it over my lap, and Andrew's hand settles between my legs, higher up.

Ben's telling a story about someone's mom. "Every time I go over there she's wearing these tiny shorts and bending over and shit," he says. "You just know she's a nympho." Everyone laughs except for Cassie because she's whispering something into Kyle's ear. And then her tongue is out of her mouth and inside him. He turns his head and kisses her right in front of everyone. I can see their tongues moving in each other's mouths. Then they pull apart and Cass stands, dragging Kyle to follow her out of the room. On her way past, she glances down at my lap, sees Andrew's arm disappearing beneath my sweater. I can see the smile in the corner of her lips.

I close my eyes because Andrew's finger is petting me. It tickles and I close my legs harder around him so he'll do it with more pressure, stay in one place. I feel like a cat getting a chin scratch. Everything else in the room feels far away.

After a few minutes, there's yelling downstairs and someone opens the door to see what's going on. Andrew pulls his hand away and stands up, and other people start getting up off the mattresses and leaving the room, so I follow them. I move with the crowd, a wave of people down the stairs and through the house and out the front door, toward the yells outside.

Ivan is pushing Russell on the front lawn. A girl I don't know tries to get in the middle of them. She grabs on to Russell's arm and when he swings at Ivan, his shirt stretching, she stumbles and falls to the ground. Even in the dark, I can tell her skin is dirty and red from crying, eyeliner all over her face. When she gets up, her knees are stained green. She pushes through the crowd back into the house but no one goes after her. Russell hits Ivan and he's down on the ground and the crowd cheers for a second, but it goes quiet fast because Russell's kicking at Ivan's stomach and another guy is kicking at his back. He rolls himself into a ball with his arms over his face, holding the top of his head, and he's getting kicked in the arms and the head and the shins and everywhere now. A girl behind me says how gross it is and some people look away. Then Andrew and another couple guys are in the middle of it, and suddenly nobody's fighting anymore.

People start moving back inside now that it's over. Someone spits on the ground when they walk past me, a tiny puddle of bubbles beside my bright red Converse. Ivan is still lying on his side on the ground. He's moving his feet like he's on a tiny bicycle, like he's trying to tiptoe away on the air.

A couple guys pull him up by the arms, asking him if he's okay, and then it's just me and Ivan and Andrew and Ben. No one is even on the falling-apart porch anymore.

Ivan's bent over like he can't stand up. There's blood coming out of his nose in bubbles. I used to get really bad nosebleeds and I would pull out huge clots, squish them in my palms while blood ran over my lips, down the back of my throat. Then the doctor stuck something up my nostril and it hurt bad for five seconds and then less bad for a day and then it didn't bleed anymore.

After a while, I missed them, but now I get nosebleeds again sometimes, probably because of drugs.

Andrew says he has a truck and he'll drive to the hospital. It's close enough to walk, but I don't know if Ivan could even make it a block.

"Can I come?" I ask.

Andrew looks at Ivan for a second and then looks at me. He smiles like he wants to say something, and I feel like maybe I'm making a fool of myself. I don't want him to think Ivan is my boyfriend or anything. I don't want him to think it's all about him, either, that I'm desperate.

But he just nods, says, "Sure. Get in the front."

They help Ivan into the back—he's swearing when he moves, and he's bleeding all over but it doesn't seem like Andrew cares about his truck getting dirty. I wonder if he'll even clean up afterward. When he gets in the driver's seat, he reaches across me, opens the glove compartment, and pulls out a half-empty bottle of Jack Daniel's. He drinks right out of the bottle and then passes it to me, so I try to swig it the way he did, like boys do, like girls who sit in cars filled with boys do. I don't want anyone to think I don't belong here. I try to pass it back, but he starts the truck, motions to me to pass it to the back seat. Ben grabs it and takes a drink, then puts it against Ivan's bottom lip. Ivan lifts his head and Ben pours whisky into his mouth.

Ivan doesn't look at me once. There are sirens coming from somewhere.

Andrew's hair is long, curling around his ears, and he doesn't wear the same kind of clothes as Ivan. He wears T-shirts with names of bands I've never heard of, and he dropped out of school last year. He works in a factory; I don't know which one. He lives in an apartment by himself. He looks at me and I look away fast, but I know he caught me. I pretend to be interested in the car door handle, but when I look back, he's smiling. His smile is great. His teeth aren't straight, but it doesn't even matter.

I light a cigarette and take a long drag of it. Ivan reaches between the seats and plucks the smoke right out of my mouth. He takes a drag and then holds it back out to me when we pull up in front of the hospital. Andrew and Ben get out and walk Ivan through the emergency doors. There are red fingerprints on the cigarette, but I smoke the whole thing while I wait in the car for Andrew to come back.

∿∿

WHEN WE GET to his apartment, I sit on the couch and Andrew puts on a movie. The couch is all torn up—because of the dog, he says. He has a German shepherd named Gus that he put outside on a chain as soon as we got to his place. The windows are open and I can hear the chain moving out there, but not the dog.

Andrew doesn't start the movie right at the beginning. It's like he paused it to go to the party and now he's just picking up where he left off. It's not in English but there aren't any subtitles. I think about Ivan's mom, but the words don't sound like any of hers. There's a dinner scene, and naked women are walking around with serving plates. A boy trips one of the women and fucks her while she screams, then he fucks another man. On the screen, other people are watching, laughing, singing.

"What language is that?" I ask.

"Italian," he says. "That's where my grandparents are from."

"Do you speak it?"

He laughs like it's an answer.

We watch for a little while, but I'm not sure what's going on. I can feel the alcohol inside me and I think about French classes in elementary school, whether I learned anything at all.

Andrew's not even touching me. I pull my legs up onto the couch, sit cross-legged and move a little closer to him. My knee hits his leg but it doesn't stay touching. I wonder if we're going to watch the whole movie without doing anything. I wonder if he even likes me.

There's a dead girl on the TV, her throat slit, blood on her face and neck and chest.

And then Andrew's face is blocking the screen and I can't see the girl anymore. He kisses me and I close my eyes because I think it'd be weird if he opened his eyes and I was looking at him.

Andrew's tongue is in my mouth and I'm thinking about Ivan even though I'm trying not to. I'm thinking about his face in the back of the truck, about the way his whole body bent over when he tried to stand up.

Andrew's tongue pushes hard against mine. He tastes like cinnamon gum and I wonder what I taste like to him. Maybe the cinnamon covers it for both of us.

"Your tits are fucking amazing," he says, pushing my bra down and grabbing just the tip of one of my breasts, pinching me. I move myself into his whole palm so he's grabbing the entire thing instead of just the nipple. His hand feels hot like a sick person's forehead.

He moves his hand down to my skirt, playing with the edge of it, and I don't pull away. *This is going to happen*, I think. I know it even though we haven't talked about it. I can feel the calluses on his fingers as they move up my thigh and I don't want to part my legs too fast or he'll think I'm a slut. But maybe he wouldn't mind. Maybe he wouldn't tell anyone. Maybe we could know each other and keep secrets from everyone else. Then he kisses me again, pushing my lips apart hard with his tongue, and as soon as I open my legs, he pulls my underwear to the side with his fingers and puts one inside me. It's dry at first but as soon as he pushes in farther I can feel the slickness, the oil and the rainbows. I'm embarrassed until he makes a sound like a growl; I know that's good without knowing why I know it. He buries his face into my neck, kisses me right under the ear, fucks me with his finger.

He's still inside me when he touches the side of my face. "Shit. I don't think I have any condoms," he says.

"I have one." I've been carrying it around in my purse for a year. Lillian and I bought a pack to see what they were like, and we each took one to keep even though we didn't think we'd ever need them.

I grab my purse off the floor and look through it. There are old receipts and lip gloss and coins covered in lint and so many things, but none of them are what I need.

"It's not here," I say.

Andrew perches on the arm of the couch and looks at me. He's so beautiful, like a picture of a boy in a magazine.

I start to look again, pulling out handfuls of garbage. I know he thinks I lied to him. He looks so much older than me right now, and I feel like such a stupid kid.

"Hold on," he says.

He leaves the apartment and I sit with my purse on my lap, pulling the zipper back and forth.

When he comes back, he shakes a condom packet in front of me while he pulls down his shorts. "Good neighbours," he says. He smiles and I can see all his teeth.

There are children crawling like animals on the screen, begging for food and eating scraps off the floor.

"Lie down," he says. He pushes my skirt up and pulls my underpants down. They're a nice pair, soft and new. I shaved at Cassie's an hour before going to the party, so I'm smooth and clean. I watch while he rolls the condom on. He's inside me before I realize it. I'm wet and the condom is wet and it doesn't really feel like anything. I think about Ivan covering his face while he was lying on the ground, about the sound he made when they kicked him in the stomach. I think about the blood and snot coming out of his nose in a river, flowing over his lip, in through the sides of his mouth. I lick my lips.

Andrew puts his hand around my neck. I've never thought about sex with a guy as something that would make me come. But when his fingers tighten around me, I start to get that feeling under my belly button. I try to move him more into me. I want him to touch the parts of me he's almost touching, but they're just out of reach. It's like being tickled, like being touched with a feather, that relief that's impossible to catch. I try to push my body down the couch, but he moves with me. All I can feel is need, needing, just being empty and wanting to be filled. I raise my hips and he puts one hand under my butt, pulls me so my belly is right up against his. I can feel the hair on his body scratching my skin; I can feel where sweat is sticking us together. His other hand is still around my neck and he squeezes harder. I'm filling up with bees. I open my mouth as wide as I can to let them out.

I remember the way Ivan looked everywhere but at me. *He hates me*, I think, and the feeling deep in my stomach turns to nausea. There's pain down my leg, like my veins are lightning, but Andrew is on top of me and I can't change position. I try to speak but I'm stuck in so many ways. I think about the men online. I think about asking for what I want, saying words that mean something, words I want to hear out loud, but I just let myself hurt until my brain feels numb, until the bees cover every surface, humming.

He finally takes his hand out from under me and moves slightly to the side, and I can bend my leg. It aches like all my muscles have been screaming themselves hoarse. It feels like reaching the other side of a bridge. Andrew's cheek brushes mine, and I push my own into his. It's not sticky like I thought it would be in the heat, but dry, like we both covered our faces in baby powder. It's what I imagine old people's faces feel like, papery. I wonder how we'd look to someone watching.

He lets go of my neck and I swallow air with a hiccup before he pushes the side of my face down into the cushion. It smells like wet wool and concealer and I wonder if part of my face has wiped off onto the fabric, if Andrew is going to sit on my skin cells for months. I can see the television, where a girl is crying. Everyone has dirty faces, dirty mouths.

The dog starts to bark, and Andrew gets up, walks naked to the door. I pull my underwear and skirt back into place. He opens the door and yells, but the dog keeps barking.

Andrew calls me a cab and I go outside to wait for it. I think maybe he's going to kiss me in the driveway, but he just leans down and brushes an eyelash off my cheek, tells me to make a wish. On the drive home, I think about how the cab driver has no idea who

I am now, what an important thing I've just done. I wonder if he can smell me, if I look like a woman to him.

When I get home, I put my underwear into a plastic baggie. I empty my purse and find the old condom. I throw it out my bedroom window so it's like I never had it, and then go sit in the bathtub, where I almost fall asleep.

$\wedge\wedge\wedge$

I CALL CASSIE as soon as I wake up. She asks me if I heard about Ivan and I tell her I saw the whole thing, that I went to the hospital. She says she heard he fingered Russell's girlfriend while she was passed out and Russell walked in on it. She says she can't believe she missed the fight, and she starts telling me about what happened with Kyle, how they went back to his place but he was too stoned to do anything but make out, so I finally just interrupt her.

"Guess what?"

"What?"

"I had sex," I say.

"What! I knew it. You owe me five dollars."

I laugh. "Shut up."

"How was it?" she asks. "With Andrew, right? He's hot."

I'm sitting on the toilet, looking out the bathroom window. There's a raccoon hanging out in the tree right beside the house even though it's light outside. I wonder if it's sick. I hold the phone between my shoulder and ear while I wipe.

"Yeah. It was okay," I say. I don't think I want to tell Cass about the way it felt, about Andrew's hand on my neck. I don't want to tell her about the smell of the couch or the dog barking or the movie or the way Ivan's blood mixed with his snot and turned his teeth a different colour. The raccoon is staring right at me.

"Did he make you pancakes?" she says. She's mostly joking—pancakes are code for a boy who lets you sleep over, a boy who's falling in love with you.

"He kissed me after," I say.

"That's good. That's nice."

We talk for a bit longer but now that I've told her, I don't really know what else to say. She tells me to come over later because Kyle gave her some E and we can do it at her dad's house.

I scroll through my texts and stop on Lillian's—the last message in the thread was weeks ago. When we were little, people used to mistake us for sisters. I wonder when we stopped being the same. Or maybe we never were—maybe it was always superficial. It hits me that I'll probably never be able to tell anyone the truth about what it was like, losing my virginity—just another thing to add to the list. Even if Lil and I were still talking, I don't know if I could tell her. She might not be a virgin anymore, but she's in love. I don't even know Andrew's phone number.

Mom is still in her room, so I have the TV to myself. I turn it to MuchMusic and lie down on the couch. A video of an old Yeah Yeah Yeahs concert comes on. Karen O is wearing a white wifebeater—she's covered in oil and it looks like she has huge nipples, but I know from an interview that she has black duct-tape hearts under her shirt. She makes me sit straight up.

She's definitely had sex. She's a woman. I can feel a smile behind my whole face because I'm just like her now.

〰〰

I SET UP an auction for the underpants I was wearing last night, my loss-of-virginity panties. I've never sold anything in an auction before, but it's an option on the site. With most things, you have to set a price that's not too low and not too high or else the other girls will get mad. But there are exceptions to the rule for special things—things not everyone can do, or things you can only do once. I've never had a good enough reason to do an auction before. I've never had something not normal.

It only takes a few minutes for people to start bidding. It feels weird, like it's a concrete way of seeing what I'm worth, the price someone will pay for part of me. It's scary, but I need to know. I never have to think about what superpower I'd have if I could choose one; I'd want to hear people's thoughts. I always want to know what everyone thinks about me.

I watch the numbers go up until they stop. This is how it works; there are bids at the beginning and there are bids at the end. The ones in the middle are pointless. But even then I keep watching, willing my number higher, thinking about what it'll feel like if I get a number higher than anyone else's. And how everyone on the site will know because they'll see my number, too. They'll see how much I'm worth. If nobody else could see the numbers, would I even care what they were?

∿∿∿

IVAN'S SMOKING AND drinking a beer even though he's on serious medication. His face is all fucked up, and he tells me it feels just as bad as it looks.

"How was the rest of the night?" he asks.

"It was okay."

"You go back to the party?"

"Nope. Ended up at home." It's not a lie but it is a lie.

His eyes are bloodshot and I wonder if it's because of the fight or because he's stoned. We're both sitting on his back porch steps where there's shade. It's so hot out here that it hurts to touch the lawn furniture.

"Cool. That party was shit anyway. I heard the cops showed up." I know he's making a choice to believe me. He's making a choice to keep pretending so we can stay friends.

"Did you do it? To that girl?" I ask.

"People don't know shit."

He goes inside and comes back out with a container of chocolate pudding and a spoon, and I realize I've never seen him eat something with cutlery before. We've spent whole days and nights together, and I can't remember him ever eating anything except with his hands. He sits back down and rips the top off the pudding so fast that it doesn't come off completely. He puts the peel on the glass table beside him, where it sticks because it's covered in pudding. And I know him again because of this, his mess-making, his disregard for things other people will have to clean up.

He puts the spoon back in the pudding and passes the whole cup across the table to me. I eat a spoonful while we look right into each other's eyes.

I let his denial sit between us. I think about that girl's grass-stained knees, how nobody followed her inside. I just need him to tell me the truth for once.

"You did, right? While she was passed out?"

He shrugs. "I didn't know Russell was fucking her."

When I leave, Ivan's mom says something in Russian and clucks her tongue at me. I say goodbye and walk home, sweat right through my underwear.

twelve

⋀⋀

I should have said I was a virgin online earlier. It always made me feel silly to admit it, but it's great for selling. Men are asking me for old pairs of my underwear now, too, ones I wore when I was innocent. One guy calls them pure panties. They ask me if I'm obsessed with cock now that I've had it, how many guys I've fucked, what my favourite positions are. They tell me they can help me figure out what I like. They want both parts of me—the virgin and the slut—maybe so they can see what the differences are. I stare at myself in the mirror, but I can't see any changes.

The guy from town messaged me to say he got the panties, that they were great, and I said I was glad he liked them. Now we talk sometimes. He hasn't ordered anything else, but he doesn't feel like a time waster, either. All we do is talk about our lives— normal, unsexy stuff. I told him I'm in college. He told me he's a doctor. At first I didn't believe him, but he didn't go on about it like it was something I should be impressed by, so now I think it might be true.

The other day, he asked if we could talk on the phone—he just wants to put a voice to the words, he said—but I told him I'd have to think about it. I told him I'm no good on the phone and he said, *Me, neither. But we're low on options.* He's the first buyer in days who hasn't wanted to talk about my virginity.

∧∧∧

I WAS SCARED to have sex for a long time because in grade seven, we watched a video where a scientist said girls can't help but fall in love the first time they do it. They get attached because of science, because of something in their bodies, and they can't let go. "Just wait," he said. "Wait until someone loves you enough to marry you." Now I know that's bullshit. I want everyone to want to fuck me.

It's a lot easier to do something the second time. And the third time and the fourth and the fifth are even easier.

The guy I really want to hook up with is Nate. We've been seeing each other at parties for a couple weeks. At first I tried to avoid him because of what happened last year at the motel. Even being around his friends felt weird; I kept thinking he must have told them. I just hoped Cassie didn't know. But she tried to introduce us the first time she brought me to his place, and he interrupted her and said we're already friends. He said it like he really meant it, too—not sarcastic at all, just nice. I could feel my face going red when Cass looked at me, but she acted like she didn't notice. That's one of the things I love most about Cass—she makes me feel like I'm not as stupid or embarrassing as I think I am.

Tonight we're at Dan's place. His whole family is on vacation. Since it's summer, we just go to whoever's house doesn't have parents. There's always somewhere. It's impossible to remember what day of the week it is because they all feel the same.

It's late and a lot of people have already gone somewhere else with someone else. Cass isn't even here anymore. It's not like when I was friends with Lillian, when we'd promise to leave everywhere together. Cassie knows I can take care of myself. Everyone who's left is sitting outside on the porch. Nate's foot pushes up against mine under the picnic table, and at first I don't move because I'm worried it's just an accident. I've been trying to move closer to him all night, so focused on him that I can't even follow what people are talking about. I've hardly said anything. I can never figure out why I like some people and not others—but I want Nate to like me.

I don't look at him, but I push back against his foot. When he hooks his over mine, it sends waves through my whole body. After a minute of pretending to ignore him, I get up and say I have to pee. I go down to the bathroom in the basement, but I wait outside in the hallway. It only takes like thirty seconds before he shows up. He grabs my hand and pulls me into the room across the hall. It has no windows, so when he closes the door, I can't see anything at all. It makes me laugh for some reason. Maybe because I'm nervous.

"Where are we?" I move my arm out to feel for something, but the wall is way closer than I thought it would be and I hit my funny bone. I bite down on my own lip to move the pain somewhere I can control it.

"Dan's little sister's room."

Nate runs into me and I laugh and he laughs and we listen to the laughter to find each other's mouths. High school boys see me with their hands, their lips. It's always dark and the lights are never on. Nate kisses me, slow at first and then licking me a little, opening my mouth with his and biting my lips, sucking my tongue.

I don't know what makes someone a good kisser, but he is. He tastes like pineapple, but his spit is thick. It could be my spit, too; I don't know. I always think I know my body but then something happens and I realize I don't at all.

Once we're on the bed, he thrusts himself onto me over and over, like he thinks if he just keeps trying, his dick will find a hole. I can feel him poking me in the thigh, then up a little higher, under my hip bone where my leg is bent. He keeps hitting me there and I wonder if he thinks he's found the right spot. He's wearing a woolly sweater even though it's not cold outside, and it scratches my belly when he moves. I put my hand between us to grab his dick and move it to the right place, but before I can touch it he pulls away, sits up on his knees between my legs, and stops moving completely, like he's run out of batteries.

For a second I think he's coming already and I feel so good about myself. I can make boys come with only a bent leg. I wonder if he's always wanted to do this with me, if he's been waiting for this to happen forever. Maybe it wasn't me who fucked up the first time we fooled around—maybe he had to leave because he was so overwhelmed. Maybe everyone knew he was into me and whispered about it whenever he left the room. Maybe he knew I'd break his heart.

And then I hear him gagging. I don't see the puke but I hear it hit the floor beside us. I stay still because he's leaning over me and I don't want him to think I'm mad or grossed out.

"I'm sorry," he says. "I'm so, so sorry."

I prop myself up on my elbows and try to see his face in the dark.

"Wait here?" he says. "I'll go find some mouthwash and come back."

But I know how to do this. I grab the back of his neck and pull myself up to him and push my mouth right into his. It tastes sour and sharp and stings a little bit, like pouring hydrogen peroxide into tiny cuts. He kisses me back and after a minute, it's like I've always tasted that taste, like I've never known anything else. I can get used to anything.

"You're so hot," he says. My whole body is on fire and I wonder if this is how Cassie feels all the time. Then Nate sticks his tongue right in my ear. The electricity hits me in my belly button.

〰

I TOOK A pregnancy test last week. It was negative, but I looked up information on abortions just in case. I'd have to go to the city. Cassie would go with me. Sometimes I think about what the day would be like. We'd leave early, take the bus. We'd sit in the back and Cassie would bring a twenty-sixer of Smirnoff in her purse and we'd take turns sipping from the bottle. She'd sit in the waiting room while I went in for the appointment and then afterward, we'd stay at a motel for the night and I'd tell her all about it. I'd lean my head against the bus window on the way home and we'd pass lots of billboards with pictures of children and Cassie would ask if I was okay. She'd fall asleep with her head against my shoulder.

〰

THERE AREN'T ANY stalls in the bathroom at Tim Hortons—it's just one big room. That's the best kind of public bathroom. Cassie's wearing a romper so she has to take her entire outfit off to use the toilet. She's wearing glitter, and her chest sparkles in the bright fluorescent light. She has tan lines drawn all over from different outfits; it's like her body is a paint swatch sheet of beiges and browns. I wash my hands and then put them right up to my face, smell them. They remind me of someone's house, like laundry or dish soap. My eyes are bloodshot, so I drop in some Visine. We carry our own pharmacies around with us. Drugs, obviously, but also Visine, Orajel, Blistex, Clearasil.

Alex is putting on mascara in front of the mirror. She flinches and blinks hard and there are tiny black lines under her eyes. "Fuck," she says. There's no paper towel in the dispenser, so Cassie passes her a wad of toilet paper.

I put two tiny pink caffeine pills on the counter and break them into bits with my library card, crush them until they're powder smooth. Caffeine pills hurt like fuck going down. They burn your throat and stick in your nostrils so your snot runs bright pink all night. But we've been waiting on E for hours, and we're bored.

Cassie's eating an apple fritter on the toilet. She finishes it and wipes her hands off on her thighs. When she puts her romper back on, she does up each one of the buttons on the front slowly. Her boobs are tiny, so she doesn't have to wear a bra. She says she hates it, but I think she secretly loves them. I see her boobs all the time. She never covers them when she's changing or getting out of the shower. Sometimes she just sits around with her shirt off.

Alex takes the first line. Because they're just caffeine pills, nobody cares about getting the biggest one. It's only enough to get you going, wake you up a little bit to everything.

Cassie takes a line and then looks at herself in the mirror. Her mirror face is different from her normal face. I wonder if that's how she thinks she actually looks, and if I have a mirror face, too, if I know what I really look like.

Once when I was a kid, some older girls made fun of me because I peed for too long in the bathroom at school. "That was the longest piss I've ever heard," they said. "Is something wrong with you?" I started only peeing little bits at a time if there were people who could hear. I remember hearing someone have diarrhea once in a mall bathroom and wishing I could be like them and just go, but also hating them because they were weak. Boys talk about their shit and everyone laughs. But that's not what I want either. I don't want to make fun of things that come out of me.

Now sometimes I think being with other girls in a bathroom is the happiest I'll ever be. I can pee for however long it takes; I can even talk about it if I want. It's like a break from the rules. It feels like belonging. Cassie took a shit while I was in the shower yesterday and we talked the whole time. There's only one thing Cassie won't do in front of me in a bathroom. I've heard her, but she always closes the door. I've seen her puke in fields and outside bars, but never in a bathroom.

While I'm taking my line, someone starts banging on the door. Alex tells them to fuck off and I start to laugh while I'm inhaling. It feels like when you cough while you're drinking pop and you get it up high in your nose. I turn on the tap and put my fingers under the cold water, tilt my head back and suck the drips up so there's no more pink dust around the nostril.

There's more banging on the door, so we throw some water on the counter, wipe our hands on our clothes, and leave the bathroom. The woman who's waiting is pregnant and she looks at us like we're filthy, like she knows who we're going to become.

On the way out to the street, Cassie slaps my ass and tells me I'm beautiful.

We walk around for a few more hours, and then Alex goes to Jonah's for the night. His parents let her sleep over whenever she wants. Cassie and I can't think of what else to do, so we just start walking toward her grandmother's.

There are some guys sitting in a front yard and it's so dark I can't see their faces. When we get closer, one of them calls out to us, asks how we're doing. I move to cross the street away from them—half of being a girl is just learning what to avoid—but Cassie grabs me and pulls me close, hooks her arm around mine.

"Hey," she yells to the guys.

The one who called us over stands up from his lawn chair. He's bald and has a gold earring. He's not tall, but he's big, wide. He looks like someone who talks about going to the gym. We walk over until we're standing on their grass, and he looks at Cassie's body in such an obvious way that I want to roll my eyes, but I don't. I can feel her beside me pushing her tiny boobs right out in front for him to look at.

He reaches into a plastic bag hanging behind his chair and takes out a couple mini-bottles of alcohol and passes one to each of us. It's peppermint schnapps. We don't really care what it is, though. He grabs two more lawn chairs from the house, and we sit for a few minutes. The other guy's kind of quiet. They don't seem so bad, and I really have to pee, so I ask if I can go to the bathroom. Wide Guy tells me I'll be able to find it. I know he wants to make out with Cassie but I don't think she will. It's dark inside and I bump against a table before my eyes adjust. I pass by a couch, and there's a little girl, maybe three or four years old, sleeping on it. She has her thumb in her mouth. There's a blanket over part of her body, but I can see that she's just wearing a big T-shirt that goes down to her knees like a nightgown. I go to the bathroom fast; there's no lock on the door and I'm worried the whole time I'm pissing that one of the guys is going to come in the house, but they don't. I leave the bathroom light on because I don't want the little girl to wake up in the dark.

Cassie and I stay for about an hour. I talk to the quiet guy; his name's Joey. His brother went to elementary school with me. Joey went to our school, too, but he's a lot older so I don't remember him. He's cute in the way guys are when they care too much about how they look. He smells like hair gel. I don't know if I really want to fuck him, but I could.

Cassie gets a call from her grandmother. She was supposed to be home hours ago. "I have to go. She's pissed," she says. "Wanna sleep over?"

I love seeing Cassie when she first wakes up. Her eye makeup is always smeared across her face because she never takes it off before she goes to bed. She blinks a lot and never has eye gunk the way I do. Her lips look smaller in the mornings, and then they grow like flowers coming out with the sun. Her voice always cracks first thing, like she's a high school boy, like maybe she's getting a cold. Part of me hopes her voice will stay like that longer and longer every day until finally that's just who she is. Another part, maybe the same part, wishes that nobody else would ever hear her morning voice.

I look at the guys and at the brand-new bottle of beer I'm drinking. I know there are more bottles of everything. "I'll just walk home in a bit." I don't have a curfew right now. I didn't even tell Mom I was going out. The other day some of my blood came through my pajama pants from a cut on my thigh. Mom noticed it before I did. All she said was, "You're bleeding," like she wasn't surprised. I went to the bathroom and put on a bandage and then we watched a movie together. I didn't even change my pants.

"Okay." Cassie kisses me right behind my ear and whispers, "Good sleeps," before she runs away down the street.

We keep sitting outside and now I'm talking to Wide Guy because Joey's on his phone. Maybe he has a girlfriend. Wide Guy gets a McCain cake from his kitchen and we pass it back and forth, taking bites with plastic forks. Joey doesn't want any.

After a bit, I say I have to go. I have that fullness in my head and throat like I have to throw up. It's after four in the morning. I stand up and so does Wide Guy.

He puts his arm around my waist and pulls me into a hug, looks right into my eyes. He's exactly the same height as me. "You're actually pretty cute, too," he says. "Stay over."

I look at Joey but he's passed out in his lawn chair. I think about the little girl on the couch. I'll tell Cassie I left because they were gross; the truth is, I'd probably stay if I felt better. But I know I'm going to puke and I need to get out of here before I do.

"I have to go." I pull away from him and walk as fast as I can, my heart a rhythm in my neck. I think about how we all have just a finite number of heartbeats, and we could be a million or a thousand or one away from the last. At the corner, I turn to make sure neither of the guys is following me, and then I puke chocolate and vanilla icing between two parked cars.

⌃⌃⌃

BEFORE I GO HOME, I pass by the doctor's apartment building. It's only a few blocks. I don't know which apartment window is his, but

I wonder if I'd be brave enough to walk in and find out. I could stand right in front of his door, knock, even. I dare myself to move and my feet tingle in their spot on the sidewalk. It feels like the pavement is burning a hole through my rubber soles, like I'm melted and stuck. And then the front door to the apartment building opens and my breath is gone and my body is full and bloated with fear. But it's not him. He doesn't know my face, anyway—the pictures I send to men are always cut off at the neck. I still feel like he might recognize me, though, sense me like a dog smells a body.

The sun is coming up by the time I get home. There are a few people on the panty site, but not many. I send the doctor a message. *Hey. I can't give out my number, but I can call you sometime if you want.*

〜〜〜

AT FIRST, I thought sex might be an answer, but even when I like it, it's not enough. The part I do like isn't even the sex. It's lifting my hips off beds so boys can take off my jeans. It's the way their spit dries on my neck and tightens my skin. Heavy breaths that make my stomach drop with want. The way my clothes smell afterward. Spiderwebs of hickeys. Big anxious swallows. I love the way other girls look at me when they know someone wants to fuck me, like they wish they could break the rules, too. But the actual sex hardly feels like anything.

Online, I've found words for so many things. I know how to talk about what I want. Even if it's really weird. Sometimes I even freak myself out. But I can't say those words in real life. When I have real sex, it's always the same, so I'm the same. Online, I'm different, new, with every single person.

thirteen

⋀⋀

I tell MilkBeaut I just finished cutting. I tell her I've been doing it every day for the last few days, adding extra lines every time—first four, then five, then eight, then eleven. I always tell myself to do more, to go higher. I feel like I can talk to MilkBeaut about anything and she won't be weirded out. She won't tell me to stop.

Why do you do it? she asks.

I just like the way it feels

You like blood?

Once I accidentally cut my leg so deep it bled for days. I could see the fat under the skin. I could see the textures I'm made of. It looked almost like brains. I think about the colours of blood, how it looks nice against anything—I love scenes in movies or comic books where red is the only colour on black and white, the only thing you can't help but pay attention to. When I'm looking at my own blood, I feel like a ghost keeping watch on my body. People always think of blood like a bad thing, a scary thing, but sometimes it just means you're alive.

I love blood, I say.

You use a cup?

What?

A menstrual cup.

I don't want to admit I don't know what that is, so I search for it online. It's this plastic cup you stick in your vagina when you're on your period. It catches all the blood and you pour it into the toilet or the sink and then put it back in. Mom would hate it.

Where do you get one?

Health store. Anywhere hippie-ish. Or order one online. You'll love it.

There's a store in town that sells vitamins and expensive health food. Everyone makes fun of it. I call them to see if they sell menstrual cups, and the woman says she can put one aside for me. I tell her I'll think about it.

∿∿∿

"WHAT ARE WE doing tonight?" There's a breeze and Cassie smells like Vicks VapoRub.

"I don't know. I have to get changed if we're going out, though." We're sitting outside the 7-Eleven, sucking juice from a ten-pack of freezies. I need to take off my underwear and change into a new pair because I know I'm getting my period soon and these are for someone who wants them just regular—nothing weird, he said.

"Can I come to your house? Alex doesn't want to go out tonight," Cassie says. "She did Oxys the last couple days. She's shitting piss right now."

Cassie's never been to my house. But Mom's been okay for a little while. We ate dinner together last night. She ordered Chinese, which she hasn't done in forever because of the MSG and because she gets worried about talking to people with accents over the phone. She told me she's looking for a job again.

It was so easy with Lillian because she knew Mom forever. There were so many times I wished Lil would ask me about Mom, when it seemed like she just didn't care, but now I wonder if she didn't really see the weirdness—we never talked about it. Maybe she was too close to notice when things changed. I think about pretending things are fine with Cassie, acting like home is normal. But she shared that stuff about her dad with me, and I saw what her mom was like outside school last year.

"You can come over. I need to tell you something, though."

"Yeah?"

"My mom's sick."

"With what?"

"The doctors don't really know yet," I say.

Cass just nods.

Sometimes I think about what it would be like if all the diseases got cured, if people found ways to fix everything bad that could happen to a body. Nobody would get sick and nobody would ever die, so Mom wouldn't have to think about it. I'm not stupid— I know that's not really the problem. She'd find something else to worry about, something even more ridiculous. But it's hard to fix the thing underneath when there's something huge right in front of your face.

〰〰

THE OTHER DAY I came home and the computer wasn't on. It only gets turned off when there's something wrong with it. I tried to remember how I left it the last time I was online. Mom hadn't been downstairs in forever, so I hadn't been deleting my internet history every time I finished using it. And there were a couple times where she'd called me or I'd had to run upstairs for something and I just left the windows minimized until I came back. I had this feeling—like static in my brain—that I'd left something up on the screen, that I'd been in a hurry.

Later Mom asked me if I noticed anything weird about the computer. She asked if things ever pop up when I'm online. I said, yeah, sometimes. I said I just close it and it goes away. Sometimes people want so badly to believe something that they'll give you an answer, tell you what to say. It was hardly even a lie.

∧∧∧

I FEEL LIKE I'm vibrating the whole walk to my house with Cassie, like every time I talk my voice is really, really high. When we get to my front porch, I ask her to hang out in the hallway for a minute. I want to see what Mom's doing first. Cassie sits in the rocking chair that used to be my great-grandmother's and picks at the electric-blue polish on her fingernails. I love when she has chipped nail polish.

I can hear Mom in the kitchen, so I go in. She's dressed for the daytime, in shorts and a loose tank top, which is a good sign.

"Cassie's here?" I don't know why I say it like it's a question; I guess because it feels like one. Mom gets to decide what the answer is.

And she smiles at me like nothing's ever been wrong. Maybe it hasn't. "I'm so glad. I made enough dinner for ten."

I call Cassie and she comes in and my mom hugs her and tells her she's heard so much about her, and it feels like the elastics that were holding everything tight inside me are snapping. All my muscles have been running and running for days and I'm finally lying down. It feels like cutting myself wide open and watching my body bleed. I try to remember what I've told my mom about Cassie, but I can't—maybe she was just being nice.

Cass eats three plates of food and doesn't even leave to go to the bathroom right after. Mom sits with us, and Cassie and her joke around. Sometimes it's worse when Mom's nice. Because it feels like a trick. Because even though I know it'll eventually fall apart, I always hope maybe it won't.

After dinner, we go to my room. Cassie starts painting her toenails black. She thinks Goth is hot, but says all the Goth guys are gay so it's pointless.

"So what's really up with your mom?"

"What?"

"You said she was sick."

"Oh. Yeah, she's not always like this," I say.

"I thought you meant she had cancer or something."

Even when Mom is doing great, she manages to disappoint me. "She might."

"She's nuts, right?"

My mouth feels so full of teeth. "No."

Cassie laughs. "Come on, Katie. You know I don't care about shit like that. Have you met my family?"

I wish I could be more like Cassie and not worry about stuff. I try to think about what Mom did that might have seemed crazy. I thought things looked so normal—maybe I don't know what that is anymore. Or maybe I'm too close to see the problems.

"Anyway, people who have perfect parents are boring." Cassie blows on her toes and puts on a pair of my dirty socks.

⋀⋀

I'M HAPPY ALEX isn't here—every minute I get Cass all to myself is like being a movie star. By the time we go to sleep, I feel like she loves me back. My bed is just a twin, and she pushes her butt into me until we're spooning. I think about how easy it would be to start touching her body. I'm so tuned in to Cassie that I can feel the moment she loses consciousness. After a few minutes, she starts to shake up against me, almost like she wants to be closer, too. But I know her now; I know she constantly moves in her sleep.

The first thing I'd do is trace her hip bones with my middle finger. Cass loves her hip bones. She says if she ever gets fat enough that she can't see them, she'll kill herself. All her favourite body parts are bones. If I put my hand farther down, maybe she'd start to move against it, try to push herself against my fingers. Her legs would straighten, get tight, her body a stretched elastic band. She'd clamp her thighs together, try to keep all the feelings in one place.

I imagine she turns toward me, tight movements in the small space of the bed. She grinds against my thigh, and I can feel her leg pushing against me, feel my underpants getting wet. She puts her tongue in my ear the way I watched her do to Kyle, and there are little fires around my belly button. I lick that little space in her neck, the place right in the middle, above her collarbone. She loves her collarbone. She makes that noise I've heard her make with guys before, the noise I've only heard from the next room, or across the room, never close up. Her hand snakes down, but I don't want even a finger between us—I want our bodies sewn together until eventually we start to grow into one person. She pushes past the elastic of my underpants, so I grind against her hand. I can feel her pushing against her own hand, too, both of us trying to hit exactly the right spot, the spot boys never try to find. I push my nose up under her chin, fitting myself into her. *We could fit,* I think.

I imagine so many things until I'm so wound up I'm scared I'm really going to touch her. I can't have any of the things I want in real life. I think about the guilt with Alex, the weight of it. Sex can trap people. But we were just kids—we didn't know what we were doing. There are days when I wake up and think it never happened at all.

I move my hips a little up against Cass, hope maybe she's awake and her shaking is on purpose and she's thinking about exactly the same things I am. But she doesn't push back. I move away from her. She's making whimpering sounds like she's half dreaming—she sounds like a hurt baby animal, like something that should be put in a shoebox and kept warm until everything is safe again.

I think about us pushing against one another, about the smell of her when it's hot outside, the way she looks at boys. I try to be as still as possible, quiet, pretend I'm dreaming. I go to the bathroom, and there are pubic hairs stuck to my sticky fingers. I pull them off and drop them into the toilet, watch them swirl in circles when I flush, but I don't wash my hands.

⋀⋀⋀

WHEN I WAS YOUNGER, I thought I was gay. I thought I had to be because of what I'd done with Alex, because of the way I liked it, even though it was never about liking Alex. I don't worry about it as much now, though, especially since I started using the site. Lots of women do stuff together—MilkBeaut even has it listed on her profile that she's bi, like it's a good thing—and it's not like I don't like guys. But back then, I could feel in my body that I'd done something wrong, that I'd be punished. In grade two, I was sure I was pregnant. And then when my belly stayed the same after a few months, I thought I must have AIDS instead. I asked my dad what that was and he said you get it through needles. I knew that wasn't the whole truth.

I worried about it all the time. Once in a while, I'd be having fun doing something and forget, and then it would come back and I'd be so thankful for just that minute of forgetting, wondering if I'd ever feel that free again. Every night lying in bed I'd swear to myself that I was going to get up and go to my parents' room and tell them. At school, the teachers always told us to tell the truth, to get things off our chests, and that's all I wanted, to get rid of the weight of guilt and worry and shame that was killing me. But I never made it out from under the covers.

Mom and I used to watch Dad play hockey every week. We'd go to the warm part of the arena, where we could watch through a window. She'd buy a tea and get me a hot chocolate. We both brought books because we got bored watching the men skate around and shoot pucks at each other. I remember once looking up from my book and realizing how much I loved her, how much I loved it that we could just hang out in this little room and read our books together. And then I realized that once I told her who I really was, this would never happen again. She'd hate me. So I stopped worrying about telling her and started worrying about keeping it a secret.

〰〰

WHEN I START using the menstrual cup, it's like getting my period for the first time all over again, like finding out something brand-new about my body. It's like realizing you can feel your own heart, hear it deep in your head, with just a finger on your neck.

The blood is always a different colour than I think it's going to be, and the texture changes all the time: thick and dark and clotted on the second day; bright and thin like mucus on the third; dotted with tiny clumps like wet paper on the fourth. I feel like I've lost so much using tampons and pads, soaking up my blood until I don't even know what it looks like. I want to bleed every day.

I'm sitting on the toilet and staring at the quarter-full cup—the liquid smells like the deepest form of me, like how I imagine I'd smell if I lived outside and didn't shower, and I wonder what other parts of my insides smell like. I wonder how my liver and my heart smell. If someone held my own rib, stripped of flesh, right under my nose, would I know it was mine? I want to smell all my parts after they've been cooking in the heat of me.

fourteen

⋀⋀

I don't make enough money to save any. Sometimes I use it to buy drugs—coke or E or pot. Raspberry vodka. I buy Lip Smackers and CDs and copies of *Cosmo* and *NYLON*.

Sometimes I take the money straight from my work account to buy more underwear online. That way I can get pairs from La Senza—I don't charge more for those, but they feel better, newer, than underwear from the stores in town. They get delivered right to my house. Mom leaves the packages on the table by the front door.

Sometimes I spend my money on pizza pockets or Subway. Sometimes I buy candy. I go to the corner store and fill a whole bag with sour keys and marshmallow strawberries and Swedish Fish.

When I was a kid, I used to put my allowance in a jar that I called my college fund. Mom thought that was cute. But I always ended up spending it. Now I don't even think about saving. If I was saving, someone might notice, but nobody asks how you found money to buy candy or pizza or drugs.

‿‿

WHEN I SEE Nate's name on my caller ID, I'm so surprised I almost don't answer. None of the boys I've fooled around with have ever called me. I answer even though it feels like my veins might pop right out of my skin.

"Hello?"

"It's Nate. What's up." That's what he says instead of hi. I think of all the things I could say. *Not much*, or *I've been thinking about the taste of your come*, or *I just talked to a guy whose biggest fantasy is being wrapped up in a rug and suffocated.*

"Oh, hey." I panic every time I'm on the phone.

"Come over?"

"Like, now? I don't know if I can?" I want to. I really want to. But I also don't want to. I don't know how other people always know what they're feeling when it seems like I always feel everything at the same time. I chew on the nail on my pinkie finger. A piece of polish flakes onto my tongue and I swallow it without even trying to take it out of my mouth.

"I'll buy you flowers. We'll get a cake, like a celebration."

I wonder what he's doing right now, if he's with anyone else, maybe Dresler, if this is some kind of joke. I open the fridge door and put my whole head inside. It feels great. "Okay," I say.

We've fucked a few times now. He never wears cologne and always smells like himself. The last time we were together, at a party, he licked my armpit. I tried it myself when I went to the bathroom, poking at it with the tip of my tongue, but it just tasted like deodorant.

Today I don't wear deodorant. I go straight to his house. It's way nicer than mine. His dad owns a sporting goods store, and his mom is a psychiatrist. After Dad left, my mom talked to Nate's mom for therapy once a week. Not for long, maybe a couple months. She put Mom on medication but it didn't really seem like it changed anything. Nate's mom's office is here, in another part of the house. I wonder if Nate knows my mom has been here.

In his room, he turns on A Flock of Seagulls because he only listens to '80s music. Everyone knows that about him. We fuck and then I give him a blow job. He gets come in my eye and it hurts like a bitch. It burns. But after it happens he kisses my face. We've both tasted ourselves on each other's bodies. His cheeks get red and his dick gets hard almost right away. I pretend I don't notice how serious he is, and then we both laugh about it because it was a stupid accident. He jokes that I like it in the eye and kisses me on the side of the head. I wonder if he'll tell his friends another version of this story.

He leaves the room, covering his dick with his hand. While he's gone, I pick his underpants up off the floor and put them in my purse. He comes back wearing a towel around his waist, and he doesn't say anything about his underwear disappearing. He just puts on a pair from his top drawer. I'm not sure boys notice that kind of thing. All their underwear looks the same.

Afterward, we go down to the kitchen and he takes out a bag of chips and a plastic container of salsa. It's from the deli section at the grocery store. He takes huge scoops of salsa with the chips, puts them whole into his mouth. He eats differently than I do. I always break each chip into pieces, dip them sideways; just enough flavour that I taste it. Just enough that I want more. I don't eat any now, though, because I don't know if I should.

In elementary school, people used to ask if you wanted to be boyfriend and girlfriend. But I don't think that happens anymore.

Now it's like you're just supposed to know. I can tell people I'm friends with Cassie because I know we are. We share clothes and sleep in each other's beds. But I don't know if I'm supposed to mention Nate to anyone, if we're even friends. I don't know if he tells anyone about me.

When the chips are gone, we go out to the garage to get stoned. I want to be able to kiss Nate in front of anybody. I want to touch him whenever I feel like it. I want to know what he smells like after he plays sports, what shade of red his blood is, if he tastes different depending on what he eats. I want him to walk down the street with me and grab my hand and pull me into him so everyone knows I'm his.

∧∧∧

I GET HOME pretty late. I don't feel high, but I do feel happy. I leave my shoes on the carpet because Mom doesn't care about that right now. She leaves stuff everywhere, too. I pass by the living room and she's standing in the doorway.

"Come here," she says. Her voice is different. I can't explain why—it just isn't right. Her eyes are red like she's been crying, but she's smiling at me. I follow her to the couch and sit down. I don't know if I'm in trouble or not. I can never tell anymore. I shouldn't have left my shoes on the carpet. Everything changes so fast.

She sits, puts a blanket on her lap, and smooths it down over her legs. She's definitely lost weight. That's real. I know because I can see it.

"I made you," she says.

"I know." I pull my legs up under me and she passes me the blanket she was clearly using as a pillow.

"No." She shakes her head. "I made you who you are. When I was pregnant, I talked to you. I looked down at you through my own skin and I could see you growing."

"Okay."

"You were born on the hottest day of the year you were born."

I've heard this story before, but usually only on my birthday. It can't be true—I wasn't even born in the summer—but I always used to like hearing it. I rest my head on the back of the couch.

"I thought you were never coming." She strokes the blanket like she has a cat on her lap. "I was a mess, sweaty all the time. I hardly moved the whole week. It was supposed to be cooling down but we had one last big heat wave."

I feel like my tongue is concrete, like it's stuck in place.

"When my water broke, I was all alone. I had to call the neighbour down the street and she said she'd pick me up in front of the house. I ran outside and stood on the driveway in my bare feet because I forgot my shoes. By the time I got in the car, the bottoms of my feet were burned, but I was already in so much pain and so worried about you that I didn't notice.

"They had to strap ice packs onto my feet in the hospital." She puts a hand on my knee and shakes it a little. "That's what being a mom is like." Her face is thin and she has wrinkles I've never noticed. "I don't think I've ever been as scared as when you came out a girl."

I don't know if I want to think about what she means, so I just nod. "I'm not a boy," I say.

She starts to cry without making any noise. I can see the tears running down her face and I want to know what they taste like. I wonder if they taste just like mine.

"I'm going to leave you alone when I die," she says.

"No, you're not." She's right and she's wrong. She is going to die eventually, but I'm already alone. It's true for everyone. I just realized it earlier than most people.

Before I go to bed, I go to the bathroom. My eye is red from getting Nate's come in it, but I think also because I keep rubbing it. I think about the look on his face when he tasted his own come, the way he focused—he was so serious it was like he'd never smile again. It didn't give me the same feeling as the stuff online, but that's what it reminded me of. I wonder if Nate knows about the underwear site, about BDSM, about the men who drink people down in every way possible. I think he might like some of it. I think I know what kind of person he is, but I don't know if I'm ready to tell him who I am yet.

I check the cabinet above the sink and there's a new prescription bottle. It's half-filled with Oxys. I pour some out and put them in my pocket. It's enough that Mom will definitely notice— I wonder if she'll say anything.

〰〰〰

I USED TO wish I'd find some evidence that I'd been adopted, or even kidnapped. Something to make my story less boring. I'd look through Mom's room for anything that might hold a secret, the same way she looks through mine—seeing only what I wanted to see. I gave meaning to old pictures of people I didn't know, single earrings lost in drawers, documents I couldn't figure out the meaning of. Once I told Lil my real mother died saving her evil twin, and that's who was raising me now. Lil said she didn't believe me, but she looked down at the floor whenever she was in the same room with my mom for weeks after that.

I spent a lot of time thinking about what it'd be like to be kidnapped. I always thought I'd be a really good kidnapping victim. A man would see me walking home from school and he'd know right away I was special. At first I'd fight, but it'd just make him like me more. Sometimes I'd imagine getting tied to a chair, or being locked up in a basement. Being given nothing to eat but bread and butter once a day. And then he'd rape me. He'd be so good, make me feel so good, that I'd fall in love with him right back. I'd beg him to do it again. I'd be the best kind of girl.

〰〰

I USE *67 to block my number when I call the doctor. I'm so nervous that I have to do coke first—not much, just enough that I don't feel embarrassing. When I try to type in the numbers, my hands are shaking, and I have to close the phone and tell myself to breathe. I think about how this isn't real, how it's acting. Lillian once told me that whenever she's nervous, she gets into character. If the thing she's worried about is something her character would do, there's no reason to freak out.

The person I am online is good at this. She talks to men all the time. She's confident and knows exactly what to say. She has an answer for everything.

I think about where she lives. She'd be calling the doctor from her bedroom, in her apartment where she lives by herself. She has old wood furniture and heavy blankets and too many pillows. She's a person who said yes to this. She wanted it. She wants it.

I type the numbers in fast while I still feel like her, the online me. The doctor and I arranged this time, and he picks up after the first ring. The relief at the thought he was looking at his phone, waiting for me to call, flushes the last bits of anxiety away. I've been practising this conversation for days already.

At first, we just talk—about how we feel about summer, the heat. He says where he is, the humidity feels like a burden. I tell him it's like that where I am, too. His voice is so familiar, but I can't figure out who it reminds me of. It's a good voice, a good memory. It makes me trust him, as if people with the same voices are all somehow the same.

"Can I ask you something?" His voice hits a high pitch, like he's nervous all of a sudden. It's sweet. I wonder if this is where the sex starts.

"Sure."

"I don't want you to be offended."

"Okay." I thought this was going well.

"How old are you?"

"Oh. Eighteen." I can feel his pause, so I add, "Almost nineteen."

He finally responds. "Okay. Good."

"It's on my profile."

"I know. You just sound young."

"What?"

"Sorry. Your voice. Not you. I mean, not that you're not young." He laughs. "Sorry."

"How old are you?"

"Thirty-two. Is that okay?"

"Mmm, I guess it's not too old," I say.

When he laughs, it feels like settling into a steaming bath.

"If I was there right now, what would you do to me?"

There's a long pause and I worry I fucked up. But then he says he'd position me face down on the bed. He'd tie my hands to his bedposts. He talks about the marks left by belts, canes, paddles, crops.

MilkBeaut told me the best phone-sex advice is to remember the senses. "What do I smell like?" I ask.

He talks about my vagina like it's real, and I remember he's already smelled me.

It's my first orgasm that's ever felt like it's not just me.

After we hang up, I figure out who he sounds like. There was this TV show I liked last year about two teenage girls who were in love with each other. The characters' names were Spencer and Ashley, so their relationship name was Spashley. The doctor sounds just like the dad from that show.

I check my messages on the site and there's one from him.

Would you ever send me a face pic? Nothing sexual. I'd just like to know who I'm talking to, he says. *Put a face to the voice.*

When he first told me he was a doctor, I wondered if he'd met my mom, if he'd recognize me—a lot of people say we look the same. But when I send him a picture of my face, he just says *Wow*.

〰〰〰

I PUT ON a CD I burned, one by the Cure, and stand in front of the mirror wearing Nate's underpants. Listening to this kind of music is almost like being with him. It makes me feel like I know him, and like maybe he could know me—all the good parts, but all the bad parts, too.

His underwear sticks out at the front where there's room for a dick and balls. I cup a hand over it, lift the empty material like I have something to grab. Imagine having something there. Imagine having something to hold on to. Something you can use on other people instead of just waiting for someone to do something to you.

I touch myself over top of the underwear. When I take them off, it looks like red in an egg. I sell them for forty dollars to someone in Tennessee.

fifteen

⋀⋀

I used to be the neighbourhood babysitter, but I hardly ever do it anymore. There's a family across the street with fourteen-year-old twin daughters, and they get all the jobs now. They're away at camp this week, though, so today Mrs. Hamilton from the house on the corner asked me to babysit her daughter, Myrna.

Myrna's seven. You can tell she's spoiled; she thinks she's brilliant. She's allowed to swear and she wears whatever she wants. She says she could go to school naked if she wanted to, but she wouldn't because that'd be gross. I don't tell her she can't do that because, first of all, I don't know, maybe she can, and second, it would definitely make her want to do it. She's that kind of kid.

We're watching a reality show about teenagers in California because it's her favourite. She knows all the people's names and tries to explain to me what's going on with them, but then stops midsentence and stares at the screen with her mouth open. There's a little bit of drool at the corner of her lips but she keeps slurping it back in.

She pushes into my side and puts her head on my shoulder while we watch, and after a while I think she's asleep. I close my eyes because the couch is comfortable and it makes me sleepy to have another human so close, so warm against my body. When I open them, Myrna is close to my face, staring into my eyes. It's not as surprising as it seems like it might be.

"Can I kiss you?" she asks in the littlest voice. She sounds like someone who's watched a lot of television.

"No," I say. It feels like there are cotton balls in my mouth, like my brain is filled with fluff. Maybe I fell asleep. Maybe I'm still asleep. I try to sit up and move away from Myrna.

"Please?" she says.

Maybe her mom doesn't love her. Maybe she doesn't show affection. Or maybe she shows too much.

"Okay. On the cheek. Just once," I say, and turn to the side.

She ducks around and tries to kiss me on the lips. Her tongue is out and she licks the side of my mouth when I turn away.

"Don't do that," I say. "You can't kiss like that until you're older."

"You're older," she says.

"I am."

"Do you kiss people?"

"Sometimes," I say.

"Do you fuck people?"

I stand up and she falls to the side of the couch. She crosses her legs like she's an adult.

"Sometimes."

"What's it like?" she asks.

I don't know if I should even answer. She'll just keep asking if I don't, though. I don't know how truthful I should be—I always feel like kids might be able to tell better than adults when people are lying. "It's not the worst," I say, "but it's not the best, either."

She bobs her head like she gets it.

I go to the kitchen and find some giant freezies. She has a choice of red or blue and she chooses red. I take the blue for myself and cut them both open with a knife from the drawer. I want to tell Myrna there are secret things, things you're not supposed to talk about, but she wouldn't understand. She's just a kid. She doesn't know anything.

Another episode of the show comes on because it's a Saturday marathon. She stares at the TV and licks freezie off the back of her hand.

〰〰

EVEN THOUGH I have regular buyers now, I still put up ads once in a while so I can read the comments. They're usually nice. It used to be exciting but that's not how it feels anymore. Now it feels more like I'm a professional. I still like it but I want people to ask me for new things. I want them to be more like the doctor, to tell me who they are and why they want me and ask me questions about my real life so that maybe I can feel like they're part of it. I guess everything gets boring after a while.

The worst is when guys stop buying from me but don't tell me why. It feels like being dumped. I wish I could believe they got caught by their wives, or even that they died. But they probably just found someone better than me.

I'm reading new comments on my ads when MilkBeaut comes online, so I thank her for telling me about the menstrual cup. *You were right. I love it.*

Fun, right?

Yeah. I feel like my vagina is a whole separate person now, and she's my best friend haha.

She says I should use the word *cunt* instead of *vagina*.

Vagina is a word for what men can get from our bodies, she says. *It's a tunnel for them to put their cocks in. It's a passage for their babies to travel down.*

What about the word pussy? I ask.

Overused and boring, she says. *Every guy thinks he wants pussy. Pussy is for porn. It's not real. I'm not a fucking animal and if I want to act like one, that's my choice. I don't beg for food and shit in a box. Show them you've got a cunt. They can't own that, so they'll beg you for it.*

It sounds a little like she's stoned, but I like it. It sounds like she knows something about what she's talking about. It sounds good. There aren't enough words for the pieces of us.

And you should know your cunt. You know what ends up on those panties you sell? Touch it while it's still inside you. Look at it. Smell it. Taste it. It's part of your body. You should know why they want it so bad.

When I think about doing that, my insides tighten and pucker. It feels like having my future read from my hand.

Cunts aren't nice, she says. *But what's so great about being nice?*

〰

I LOVE THE word *cunt.* I find excuses to use it online; it's easy. I start to use it in secret in real life, too. *Cunt,* I whisper to myself while I'm in the shower and walking to meet Cassie and sitting at the computer. I touch myself and draw the word out for a whole orgasm. *I have a cunt. I am a cunt.*

Now when I have showers, I put my middle finger up my cunt and see what's there. It's like a secret way into seeing myself the way the men do. They want to drown in me. I only feel bad when I think about how many people I let see me before I ever saw myself.

〰〰〰

IT'S SO FUCKING HOT. Sometimes the last days of summer are the worst ones, like the season is trying extra hard to stick around. Mom hates the heat. She says it kills more people than guns do. She drinks a lot of water because she constantly thinks she's dehydrated. We don't have air conditioning so she has a lot of cold showers.

Cass and I are wearing bathing suits and lying on beach chairs in Lucy's backyard. Cassie has her legs wide open and propped up on another chair. Her arms are out to the sides so she looks like a starfish. I can already smell my own armpits even though I put on deodorant a couple hours ago.

My bikini is white—I got it at Wal-Mart for twelve dollars. The top ties around my neck and makes me feel like Marilyn Monroe. It makes me feel like a goddess. When it's this hot, you can wear a bikini top with short shorts anywhere you want. We both have towels draped over the backs of our chairs even though there's no pool. Cassie's towel is Sailor Moon and mine is Care Bears. Cassie's had hers since she was a kid, but I bought mine this summer. That kind of stuff is cool for some reason.

We're meeting up with Alex tonight to pre-drink for a party in the middle of the woods. The cops usually break these parties up early, but we heard Kyle found a really good place this time. Cassie goes inside and comes back out with a bowl of cherries. They're dotted with shiny drops of water. We eat the flesh and spit the pits back into the bowl. The cherries bleed onto our fingers, into the pads so we can see our fingerprints.

"Why do you do it?" Cassie rubs a spot of juice on her chest and licks it off her palm.

"Do what?"

"You know. Your arms, your legs. Your hip." She reaches over and touches my underwear line, the place where the scabbed star is hiding under my bikini bottoms. I didn't even know she knew about that one. "The cuts."

"I just like it." I close my eyes and I can feel the sun on my eyelids, the tissue-paper skin. I wonder how fast they'll burn.

"Yeah, but why?"

"It makes everything stop. Kind of like drugs."

"It doesn't hurt?"

"No. It just empties me out. It makes me feel clean."

Cassie's lips move like she's sucking on a hard candy. "That's how I feel when I throw up sometimes."

We all make ourselves puke, but not like Cass. She eats and eats and pukes after everything.

"For a while I thought nobody knew. Now, sometimes, I think everyone knows and just doesn't care," Cassie says.

"I care."

"Yeah." She sits up and crosses her legs. There's a patch of hair right above her knee that she missed shaving. "Do you ever want to stop? Maybe we could both stop."

When Lil saw the cuts on my arm, she made me promise not to do it anymore. She didn't get how unfair that was, to make me stop without giving anything up herself. I guess she couldn't see how I'd be losing something if I quit. She couldn't understand how much I love cutting. But Cassie knows what it's like to give something up.

"Okay," I say.

"Deal." She gives me her pinkie and we swear like little kids.

I think about telling Cass everything, about the underwear and the doctor and all the things I think I want, because for the first time in a long time, it feels like someone is listening, but then a car alarm goes off somewhere, and there's a man yelling far away, and the moment breaks like a crack of thunder.

Since we're going out to the middle of nowhere, we have to buy smokes before we leave. Cassie calls her sister, Rosie, who sends her boyfriend to pick us up. We get in his car without putting anything over our swimsuits—we have to come back to get dressed for the party anyway. Cassie gets in the front and Rosie's boyfriend acts like he's annoyed but his head stays turned toward her even while he's driving. She sticks her tongue out at him but he doesn't laugh. I say her name but she's not paying any attention to me. When I touch her shoulder, it's hot like a burn and she flinches a little, like she forgot I was here.

There's a drive-through corner store on the east side of town where you can buy cigarettes with no ID as long as you don't go in. The guy who owns it also owns a strip club outside of town. You need an ID to work there, but a couple girls at school have fakes and work there on the weekends.

We buy two packs each—Cassie smokes Pall Malls because that's what her whole family smokes, and I still smoke Du Mauriers.

Rosie's boyfriend drops us off at the end of Lucy's street even though we're not wearing shoes. The pavement feels like needles and we hop from foot to foot. The air is hot even in the shade. People walking down the street don't look at us, but they see us.

We could take all our clothes off and people would still pretend we're invisible.

∧∧∧

AFTER DARK, we meet up with Alex near the edge of town. We have to walk down a path through the woods and then follow construction-paper signs to get to the bush party. It doesn't take that long, but Cass complains the whole way. We bought an eight ball just for tonight.

Alex has been texting while we walk so she's mostly been quiet—I think she's fighting with Jonah—but when we get close to the party, she says, "I wish I could get a hysterectomy."

"That's idiotic. What if you want kids?" Cassie asks.

"I don't. Ever. Kids are the worst. I hate worrying about being pregnant. I'm always worried about it. I'd get a hysterectomy right now."

She's only worried about getting pregnant because it might not be Jonah's. Everyone knows he'd be a great dad.

"If you changed your mind, you could always adopt," I say.

Alex nods hard. "Right? See? Katie gets it." She looks at Cassie like she's a dog, like she's waiting for a pat on the head, and I wonder if I do that, too. If I'm that obvious in my love for her. A rock in my stomach tells me yes. But I think about pinkie swearing earlier, how she told me something important, how she listened, and I can't help thinking that we're special, that maybe I'm Cass's best friend now.

"I'd love a little baby." Cassie just keeps looking straight ahead. "Babies have to love you," she says.

The party's okay. Alex finds Jonah and they go off together. Cassie makes out with a guy from the country. I spend most of the night walking in and out of the woods and sharing my drugs with people I've never met before.

I look for Nate, but I can't find him anywhere. I end up making out with some other guy. He has curly hair and smells like a fire and is cuter than a lot of people are. "You're so lucky," I tell him. "Yesterday someone paid me for my spit. You get it for free." And then I kiss him again before he can ask what I mean.

When it starts to get light outside, I find Cassie in a tent with Kyle. She can't stand up. I tell her we have to get a cab, but she looks right through me. Kyle helps me get her out of the tent. "She smoked something like a half hour ago," he says. "Not weed." I want to ask what he was doing in the tent with her if she's been like this for a half hour already, but there's no point.

Cass's body is hot and vibrating. My phone is dead, and I realize Cass isn't holding her bag, so I drape her arms around Kyle's shoulders and go back inside the tent to look for it. I did my last line maybe ten minutes ago. I look from one side of the tent to the other—everything is sharp and quick, like my vision is one second ahead of my movement. Cassie's bag isn't here, so I crawl back out.

Kyle doesn't have a phone, and he wants to go smoke a joint with Brandon Vickey, so I tell him we're fine. I can hardly walk with Cassie—she feels like dead weight, her feet dragging on the ground—and nobody I ask has a working phone. Then I remember how we got here, realize I'll have to find a way to get Cass out of the woods before we can even get into a cab. A guy I don't know says that we can stay in his tent, but he says it like it's a joke, and I almost start to cry because it all feels so hopeless and I just want to not be here anymore. I remember Cass sometimes keeps her phone in her back pocket, but when I shuffle her body so I can check, she starts to scream. Not at me, really. Just a high-pitched shriek, like a siren. And then she starts to push me away and I can't hold her up anymore. She keeps screaming and by the time she's on the ground, she's kicking at me.

People start to pay attention, a crowd gathers, and someone asks me if she's all right, but I don't know how to answer. I don't know if she's all right. My heartbeat is in my eyeballs, and I can see everything just a second too long after I look away, like pictures burned into my vision. Cass smells wrong, like burning rubber, underneath her sunscreen and cigarette smoke.

I can feel the panic building in my body, everything tensing and filling. Cassie's screams are inside my head. If other people weren't here, I might think this was all my imagination, a hallucination, a dream. Everyone must think she's screaming because of me. The pain behind my eyes is so sharp, like the tears are there but can't come out, and I think maybe I've done so much coke that nothing can come out anymore. Maybe I fucked myself up. I only notice I've backed away from Cass when my shoulder bumps someone's chest.

And then Alex is on the ground beside Cassie. She shakes her and she pulls Cassie's head into her chest and she whispers, "It's okay. You're okay." And Cassie's screams turn into sobs. It's like Alex knew exactly what to do, like she wasn't scared at all. Alex gets Cassie to stand, and she starts to walk with her to the trail, to escape. Her eyes catch mine and there's a split second where I think there's anger in her face, but maybe it's actually surprise, because she says, "I thought you left already. You coming?"

When we get to the street, the taxi Alex called on our way out of the woods is already waiting. She gets in the back and promises the driver that Cass won't puke. Cass crawls in, lies down across the seat, and puts her head in Alex's lap. I sit in the front, and none of us talk the whole way to Cassie's grandma's house.

The worst part is I should have known what to do, because I know that feeling so bad, wanting someone to hold you and keep you from falling apart. But it's also hard to think that you're exactly the same as other people, that you need exactly the same things as everyone else, that you're not really special at all.

sixteen

ʌʌ

Nate acts like he's teaching me something every time we have sex, and I act like he is, too. I know the sex is good because he always comes, and he always kisses me on the forehead before he pulls out. He's never given me an orgasm—I don't know if he's tried.

It makes me think about the doctor, how he knew exactly the right things to say on the phone, like he could tell by the depth and speed of my breath when to push me, when to be hard or soft. I thought it was good, but he must have hated it. He sent me a message the other day. *Hey, what happened on the phone . . . I don't think it should happen again.*

You don't want to talk on the phone again? I asked.

No, talking was nice. That's not what I mean. It's not really a sex thing for me, though. Do you know what I'm saying?

I hadn't even been self-conscious when I'd come on the phone because I thought he wanted me to, but now I felt embarrassed, stupid. The shame felt like that moment after jumping off a diving board, scrambling in air, when it feels like you might never land. I realized he was breaking up with me.

I'm not explaining myself properly. I mean I don't want to have sex.

That's the same thing, I think? I said.

The sex part doesn't do it for me. I like the play, the BDSM. Talking about that on the phone was good. But the sex aspect, it doesn't feel right.

I didn't know you could have the second without the first. I couldn't help thinking that he didn't want me, that it was just an excuse. All of a sudden, something that used to seem so straight-forward felt like a game.

With Nate, I know he wants me, at least when it comes to sex. With the other stuff, though, I'm not so sure even he knows what he wants. Last week he asked me if he could spit in my mouth. He acted like he was joking, but when I said okay he got serious. I lay down with my mouth as open as I could make it, my lips curling over my teeth and my cheeks stretched until my jaw pulsed with aching. I was very still; I imagined I wasn't a person but an object—a bucket, a trash can—and it turned me on so much I could feel my heart in my cunt. My eyes were closed because I didn't want to know exactly what he was going to do. I stopped feeling the cold air on my thighs from the floor fan, the way the bottom of my shirt kept blowing up a little and then settling back on my belly. I stopped smelling the peanut-butter-and-wet-dog scent of Nate's pillow and hearing the beep of the truck backing up outside the window. I almost wasn't there at all until his spit hit the back of my throat. It went straight down like I was a drain. The second time, he missed and some of it hit the side of my mouth. I felt it slide down my face until it was under my chin.

I wondered if he could see how turned on I was, if he could smell my need. I tried to be quiet and completely still so I wouldn't ruin it, but I couldn't help pressing my legs together tighter, pushing my butt down into the mattress so the folds of me would rub together and give me just a little relief. I opened my eyes when I heard his door open and close. I was alone in his bedroom. When he came back a few minutes later, he got on top of me, sucking my neck. He'd never done it so hard before and I wondered if he wanted it to last, if he wanted people to see the marks and know it was him.

I wonder if I'll ever be able to tell anyone in real life who I am. The doctor knows but he doesn't want me, and with Nate, I'm not sure he'll ever be able to accept it all—the real me, the real him. But I don't think I'm misreading things. Once Nate came all over my boobs. He pretended it was just another thing to do, but it felt special, different, like we had a secret, like we could really see each other. I went to the bathroom like I was going to wash it off, but I just rubbed it into my skin and walked around like that for the whole day. Usually, with Nate, I have to try so hard; sometimes it seems like if I wasn't standing right in front of him, he wouldn't even remember I exist. But that day, we hung out after and it was so easy, like we were actual friends. A wall had broken. He kept sniffing the air and whispering to me about how much I smelled like sex. It felt like magic.

Sometimes I want him to ask me out on dates, kiss me on the forehead, blush when he talks about how much he likes me. But other times I want his hands around my throat. I have dreams that he licks me with a cat's tongue, rough and barbed, and keeps licking while I bleed.

∧∧∧

THE BDSM SITE has a forum for people who have murder fantasies. Some people want to kill and others want to be killed. It's all pretend, I think. They talk about cannibalism, how it'd be the ultimate intimacy—you can't get closer to someone than that.

MilkBeaut says she understands it, but she still can't get into any of that stuff. It feels like a step over a line to her; it doesn't matter that the line's imaginary. She tells me she tried needle play once, though, and that it wasn't as scary as she thought it'd be.

Who'd you do that with? I ask.

A guy who does it a lot. He teaches classes and everything.

So . . . a professional?

Yes, literally! He even used to be a nurse. It's dangerous if you don't find the right person. I mean, they're putting needles under your skin so . . .

How did you find him? I ask.

I already knew him really well.

I have maybe a weird question . . .

I just told you I let someone put needles in my arms . . . for fun.

Haha, true. OK. Is it possible for someone to like you but not want sex?

Sure. Why?

This guy I've been talking to.

Did he say what he does want?

Yeah. BDSM stuff.

Well, yeah, that doesn't have to be sexual. Lots of the time it isn't. But what do YOU want? If you're gonna do something with him, you should make sure you're on the same page. And be careful, k? You have to really trust someone, like REALLY trust them for that kind of thing.

I know she's right, but I wonder how you're supposed to know who you can really trust.

⋀⋀⋀

MOM WANTS TO talk to me about something. She sounded serious on the phone when she asked me to be home for dinner, but most things sound serious until you know what they are.

It takes her forever to get dinner ready but finally we're sitting together at a clean table. There's a steak right in the middle of each of our plates. Mom always cooks them until they're almost burnt, grey right through.

"I'm seeing a new doctor," she says.

"All right." I get up to look through the fridge for Becel. It's in the very back, behind brown bags filled with vegetables that look like they're from the farmers' market. I sit down again and scoop margarine onto my beets. It hardly melts at all.

"And?" I say.

Mom isn't eating. She looks down at her food. When she raises her head, I can see tears in her eyes and even though I know what this is, I feel like I have heartburn.

"He said it's MS."

A piece of beet drops off my fork and lands in my lap, in the meeting of my thighs. I pick it up with my fingers and then wipe the juice with my palm, lick it.

"How does he know that?"

"I told him everything." She talks to me like I'm six, like I haven't changed a bit in ten years.

"Don't you always tell the doctors everything?"

"I've never gotten it right before. I said it right this time. I must have, because he knew right away. I told him about how things are blurry sometimes, how it's so hard to get out of bed. You know how I have to pee all the time? He said that's part of it. It all makes sense."

We both finish everything on our plates but don't take any more.

"It's almost a relief, right?" she says. "Just knowing?"

"Okay." I don't know if I'm supposed to believe her or not. I don't know what's best. "So you're not seeing Ellen anymore?"

"Of course not. Imagine I kept listening to her? I could've gone months without real treatment. She would've let me die. Psychologists are liars."

I knew it. Ellen seemed kind of nice, and not like a liar, exactly, but I'd never tell Mom that. "It'll be okay," I say.

I go online and find out all about MS. It says it's genetic, and my chest starts to feel tight. But then I remember this is Mom, and I feel like a stupid fucking idiot for taking anything she said seriously. I won't be able to stop thinking about it now, even though I know it's not true because it's never true. But I don't really know for sure, and that's all her fault.

⌃⌃⌃

I PULL MY lip down and cut a line across the inside, where it already looks disgusting, where it looks like the inside of a body. I do it because I know it's going to hurt, and because I know it'll keep hurting for a long time. I'll feel the cut every time the inside of my lip touches my teeth, and nobody else will know it's there. Not Mom, not Cassie. So it doesn't count. It'll keep bleeding, but when it stops bleeding I'll be better. I'm giving myself exactly that much time to get my shit together and then everything will be good again. I bare my teeth and I look like a fighter. I spit blood in the sink and leave it there for someone else to find.

‸‸‸

IT FEELS LIKE Mom is always looking over my shoulder lately—she finds all kinds of excuses to come down to the basement—so the computer at home isn't safe like it used to be, even though I always delete the internet history. I go to the library a lot now to check in and message buyers. It's busy for a weekday, so I sit and look through magazines while I wait for a computer. My favourites are the wedding magazines even though I don't want to get married.

There's a couple using the computer across from me to check the lottery numbers. My computer's right in the back, so nobody can see my screen. The computers at school have blocks on all kinds of stuff, but the library ones don't. I've never tried looking up actual porn, though. That seems like too much.

I sign on to the panty site, and the doctor says hello. We talk for a few minutes, but it feels like something is missing now, and I want to scream at him, fill up the space. I want to tell him about the dream I always have, over and over again, about someone who has a million hands. They touch me until I'm surrounded, until I'm completely filled up—their fingers turn to liquid and come in through my ears and nose and pores. They travel all the way up my cunt and fill in the spaces between my organs, between my cells. It's like having a mould made of my entire body. And in the dream it never matters that I can't see the person's face or hear their voice or know what they think about anything or even know if they're a person at all. It's only once I wake up that I wonder about those things.

I want to tell him about Andrew's barking dog and Nate's semen in my eye and how sometimes I picture Lillian and Steve in the drama closet when I'm masturbating. I want to tell him I bailed on Cassie right when she needed me, and if Alex hadn't showed up, I would have kept backing away. I want to tell him it's my own fault I don't have any friends, that I thought the only way I could feel strong was if I only cared about myself, but now I'm not sure that's true.

I want to tell him I've tried, that sometimes I put Nate's hands where I want them, but he's always moving just when things seem perfect. I want to tell the doctor what I'm doing isn't working, so maybe I can try it his way instead.

I need to tell you something

You okay?

I lied

About?

Where I live

I wish I could see his face. The bar along the bottom of the window says he's typing for a long time, but his response is short. *Where do you live?*

Right after I tell him the truth, I get a pop-up saying he's left the chat. If the best part of being online is being able to close conversations, delete people from your world, the worst part is that anyone else can do the exact same thing to you.

I spend a little more time online because I'm afraid if I get up too quickly, I'll fold in on myself like a crushed can of soda. There's a woman selling dirty diapers on the site. She has a lot of people who follow her. She says she'll take any requests. *ANY* is in all caps. I sign off and go home. The couple across from me didn't win the lottery.

〰〰〰

MARCY INVITED ME to her birthday party with a text message. I told her I'd come, then spent the whole week thinking I wouldn't really. I'm sure Lillian's going, but it's not fair that she got all our friends. When it's almost too late, I walk over to Marcy's. It's a girls-only party, and there are about ten of us, some girls I've known since kindergarten and others I've never met. Marcy's mom made a cake shaped like a heart and covered it in purple icing. We all eat a piece. Lil and I end up having to sit next to each other at the table, and even though I manage not to look her in the eye, I can't follow what anyone is saying.

Marcy lives behind the elementary school, so we decide to go hang out on the play equipment there. Someone brought pot, but nobody has rolling papers, so Marce rips out a page from the Bible her parents got her for her first communion and rolls a couple joints with that. She's already used up the pages with no writing on them, so now she's using the table of contents. We climb to the top of the beehive and pass the pot around.

Marcy almost falls when she leans over to pass me the joint. "So, Katie"—she looks at Lil with this smile on her face—"how big is Nate Murray's dick?"

The girls in Nate's gym class last year used to talk about how they could see his huge dick through his shorts. My mouth is full of spit all of a sudden. I don't know why I feel so weird—the whole night I've felt like I can't swallow because everyone will hear it.

"Marce." There's a warning in Lil's voice.

I don't know how she knew I was uncomfortable, but it makes me mad. It feels embarrassing for her to protect me now, when I've done so much more than she could possibly know. I swallow, then take a long drag and pass on the joint. "It's not the biggest one I've seen."

It is, actually. I guess I'd call it *heavy*, or *thick*. It must feel like a weight to carry around.

"No way. Gretchen Poole said it's like a monster. Is it disgusting?"

I don't know how you're supposed to know if a dick is disgusting, or nice, or a monster. Some of the women online get paid to rate dick pics; I'd be horrible at that. Nate's dick is okay looking. The skin on his penis is a different colour from the rest of his skin, darker, with some pink patches. His pubic hair is always sticking to his thighs, and the skin there looks puckered, goosebumps where his legs meet. It always feels wrong to want to see it. Like I'm not supposed to want to. I haven't had sex with anyone else enough times to really see what their penises look like. A lot of the time I don't see their dicks at all.

I came here feeling like I knew more than these girls, but I'm just a fake. I look at Lillian but it's dark now and she's far enough away that I can only see the shape of her face.

"It's definitely a monster," I say.

I hear Lil suck her teeth, tsking at me, and it's like all the hair on my body stands on end. "What?"

"Nothing," Lil says. "Just, do you even like him?"

The other girls' conversations get quieter, like they can feel electricity in the air.

"Why? Would that make me a slut?"

She sighs. "I mean, a little, yeah. It just seems sad, I guess."

She says it so casually, like we hardly know each other. But I can hear the sound of her breathing out in the dark, heavy like she's trying too hard.

When Marcy says, "Let's flash the school," a couple of the girls laugh, but nobody moves. *This is something I can do*, I think. I climb down to the pavement, lift my shirt over my head, and throw it at

Marcy. Fireworks start going off across the field. People here take any reason to celebrate.

I run away from the beehive, closing my eyes and screaming, and when I look back, everyone is coming down, even Lillian, all of us in it together. I'm out of breath. The other girls run around the playground, lifting their shirts and laughing. Every time the fireworks go off, the entire schoolyard lights up—red and yellow and blue—and the girls run in circles, screaming for their lives.

seventeen

∧∧

There are parties everywhere the last weekend before school starts, but none of them are any good. Cassie's been on the phone with people all over town. We end up going to Nate's. It's just him and Dresler and a couple older guys I don't know.

Nate asks me to go outside for a smoke and we sit sideways on the same deck chair by the pool. He takes drags and blows the smoke right into my mouth. He closes his eyes while he does it, but I keep mine open. I don't know if he's ever actually looked at me. I wish I knew how he sees me, what he thinks when he thinks about me, what kind of feeling I give him. When I think about people, I always get a certain feeling—not even feelings I can explain. My Nate feeling has changed; it used to be this staticky kind of brain fuzz, but lately it's sort of a drop, like stepping off a moving floor, like waking yourself up from a dream fall.

I move to get up, but Nate grabs my hand, pulls me down onto his lap. "Let's sit a minute."

"Okay."

"Okay. Okay, okay, okay," he says in a high-pitched girlie voice, mocking.

"What?" I tighten, and he pulls me closer.

"Just working on my Katie-isms," he whispers in my ear, turning it sweet and making my stomach melt. He grips my side with one hand, and I take the other and put his pinkie finger in my mouth, sucking hard. I can feel his gasp through my whole body. Then I move his hand to my neck. It's something he'll recognize, something we've seen in porn together. When his fingers tighten around me, it's a rush like we're back at the beginning. But then he moves his hand back to my lap.

When we go inside, Nate ignores me and sits on the couch with Cassie, showing her something on his phone. She talks to guys like they're just normal people, and that's something I can't copy outside the internet even when I try. She knows how to laugh. She catches me looking but I don't look away because that'd be worse. She scrunches her nose at me and I just keep looking. Her sweater has slipped off her shoulder and her collarbone sticks out sharp like it could break right through her skin.

No matter where I am, I always try to figure out if I'm the prettiest girl there. Sometimes, in my head, I just say, *I am the prettiest girl in this room. I am the prettiest girl on this floor of this house. I am the prettiest girl at this party, in this classroom, in this park. I am the prettiest girl here.* When I'm with Cassie, I'm not the best, but I'm better than I'd be without her, and that's something.

Someone turns on the TV and the music video for "Beautiful" is playing. Nate goes to change the channel but Cass tells him to leave it. "I love Christina Aguilera," she says.

When the gay guys start kissing in the video, Dresler takes the remote from Nate and changes it to Adult Swim. Cassie starts to tell him off, but he talks over her, says, "No way. That shit makes me puke."

Jonah shows up without Alex. I didn't even know he was friends with these guys, but he sells pot so he's probably friends with everyone. He comes to sit next to me on the couch. He's wearing his shoes inside—the same skater shoes the guys all wear, except his look used.

Jonah and I went to elementary school together so we've known each other forever. In grade one, he had a huge crush on me and I used to wish every day that he'd just like someone else, that things would go back to normal and we could be friends again. I always think I want someone, anyone, to like me, but then when they do, I hate it. But then Jonah started liking Emma, and it was horrible, like someone had taken away the best thing that ever happened to me.

After a minute, Cassie and Nate go upstairs together. They don't even look at me on the way out. I can't focus at all on what Jonah's saying. I just keep nodding at him, trying to look concerned the way he does. He always thinks Alex is going to break up with him. I don't know if he's right or not this time. All I can think about is not being with Cassie and Nate, wondering what they're doing, if they'll talk about me, what they'll say. I feel so fucking stupid. I know the only reason I care is because I don't want to be left out—and I don't want to be anyone's second choice—but knowing that doesn't help me care any less.

"Has she said anything to you about last weekend?" Jonah asks.

I know Alex fucks around on him because I've seen it. I've seen her sitting on other guys' laps and going into bedrooms at parties. He's asked me about it before; I don't tell him anything, but I don't lie either. This time, I'm just tired.

"Honestly, Jonah? Why do you even like her?"

"What?" He has a look on his face like I just appeared out of nowhere, like he's been talking to himself this whole time and didn't expect anyone to answer.

"I'm serious. What is it that makes you like Alex?"

"Why? Did she say something to you?"

"Do you even know why you like her?" I realize I want him to answer. Really answer. I want to know how other people point to reasons so I can do the same. I want to be able to look at something and decide why I feel the way I do, why I want some things and not others.

"I mean, I just love her. You know."

Except I don't. Everything is always changing and I don't know how anyone feels just one thing at a time.

Cassie comes back alone. She sits down in the space between me and Jonah and grabs me around my waist. She whispers to me to ask Jonah to leave, but obviously he hears her so he just gets up. I mouth *I'm sorry*, but I'm not.

Cassie keeps whispering, not quite in my ear but up close to my cheek. It feels like her breath is condensing on my skin in little droplets. She's not making any sense, but I let her talk because it feels nice. It makes me feel like I might fall asleep.

When she puts her hands on my cheeks, I wonder if she's going to kiss me, but then she starts laughing. An alarm goes off in my head. "What the fuck, Cass? What's wrong with you?" I hit at her arms with my fists. Her hands are irons on my skin—I slap at them, spin a tornado at my face and hair. When I realize she's not touching me anymore, I put my own palms on my cheeks, which feel bright red.

Cassie looks like she's asleep with her eyes open. She's blank. And all my anger turns into fear that everything could break if I move one pinkie.

"What'd you do, Cass?" I ask. "Did you smoke something weird?"

She keeps looking at something I can't see. "Once I read a thing in a magazine where someone said they picked up Christina Aguilera and it was super easy because she was ninety pounds, so I decided if I ever went over ninety pounds I'd kill myself." And then she just giggles. She sounds like someone else.

"Cass. You're freaking me out. What'd you do?"

She touches my nose with the tip of her finger and then puts her head on my shoulder. "Don't worry. I can hear everything right now," she whispers.

Once Ivan and I tried to smoke crack in the bathroom at his house. We mixed some coke with baking soda and water in a spoon. I held the spoon while he kept a lighter going underneath. My face was close enough that I could feel the heat. The water bubbled and the whole bathroom smelled like plastic, like black pavement marks from car tires. We smoked it out of a can of Diet Pepsi.

Ivan acted like he was super high but I didn't feel like I thought I would. Then we realized Ivan's mom kept the baking soda and salt in identical containers and I'd grabbed the wrong one, so we'd just smoked salt with some coke mixed into it. Ivan said he wasn't faking it, but he lied all the time.

〰〰

ON SUNDAY, I get a message from the doctor. *Can you call me?*

Not right now. Mom has been downstairs to check on me twice already. She pretends she's just looking for something, but the only things down here are old records Dad didn't take with him and that box of DVDs Lillian and I used to watch.

Sorry I left the last time we talked. I shouldn't have.

Why did you?

I freaked out. Needed a few days.

I'm sorry I lied

Don't be. Really. You had to be safe. I just thought I was different.

The word *different* sends a hard knot of guilt all the way up my throat. Because I know what it's like to find out you're not different, special.

You are different, I say. *That's why I told you the truth.*

Would you ever want to meet up?

Like for coffee? I need him to say it, say what he wants.

Sure, I'd like that. But also more than that. I want you to come to my place. The things I like? I think I'd like them with you.

People in real life like boring things and I'm tired of being bored. I'm tired of everyone telling me what I should want when nobody can tell me why. I'm tired of waiting for someone to do something just so I know I can do it, too. The doctor knows what he wants and he's not scared to talk about it. We already know each other better than I know anyone in real life.

Yeah, I say. *That sounds good.*

The cut on the inside of my lip still hasn't healed all the way, and I split it open with my tongue. I can always taste blood now.

〰

THE FIRST DAY back at school feels like being in a movie. Like I can watch everything happening, but it's only half real. When I say hi to people in the hallway, it's like there should be music playing to fit the scene. It's like somebody is watching. Sometimes I want to be invisible and also for everyone to see me all at the same time.

Nate isn't at school anymore—he graduated—but that's okay. I'd rather not see him because then I don't have to worry about how to act with him in front of other people, figure out what's secret and what's not.

Cassie and I have Foods class together first thing in the morning. The teacher says to choose partners, and Cass hooks my middle finger with hers. We're making cookies today. When the teacher's on the other side of the room, we do coke off a cutting board. People see but they don't say anything, either because it is a big deal or because it isn't. Coke only ever feels good for a few minutes now. Sometimes I get a glimpse, just a bit of time, where everything is okay again, though.

Cassie fills a mug with icing sugar and we eat it with tiny spoons. It's so dry it's almost like eating nothing, and when it dissolves on my tongue it feels like breathing cold air. We made sugar cookies, but we're too high to eat anything we have to chew.

I run into Lillian after second period. Her locker's only a few down from mine. I'm so focused on making my movements seem real that everything feels exaggerated. I assumed she'd ignore me, so when she says hi, I almost drop my binder.

"Oh, hey. You scared me."

"You didn't see me?"

At first I think about lying, but I'm pretty sure she'd know. "No. I did. Just, you surprised me. Never mind."

I finish putting my books away, then take a deep breath when I hear Lil click her lock shut. "You staying for lunch?" I ask before she can walk away.

"Going home. My mom has Tuesdays off work."

I bite my cheeks. "Nice."

"Yeah. Are you joining any clubs this year?" she asks.

"Oh, sure," I say sarcastically.

Lillian tilts her head and I realize she was serious. I'm so used to spending time with people who think everything is dumb. But Lillian's a joiner. She never worries about what other people think. She goes home for lunch just to spend time with her mom. I can taste metal.

I saw the librarian in the hallway this morning, but I looked down at the floor when I passed her—I was worried she'd either try to talk to me about Library Club or she wouldn't. I don't know which would be worse.

"I mean, maybe. I don't know yet. Are you?"

She shrugs. "I might try orchestra this year."

I don't know what else to say, so I just nod.

"Okay, well, I should go. My mom's making egg salad." That's Lillian's favourite. I don't have anything for lunch today, but I can always buy fries if I get hungry.

She walks away, and I run my tongue over the broken skin on the inside of my cheek. My eyelids feel heavy like I could fall asleep standing in the hallway.

〰〰

THE DOCTOR SAYS we should talk more before we meet, about other things we do, other things we like. We tell each other so much that I wonder if we're both too excited to finally have someone to be honest with—so excited that we're accidentally breaking rules. He buys me a subscription for a site where you can watch live BDSM. The first time I try it, there's no livestream, but there are lots of videos, girls saying no but not saying their safe words.

There's a girl being told to turn around and show her bruises to the camera. She moves like she's in slow motion, like she's on K or Valium or something—but the voice behind the camera asks her if she's on any drugs and she says no. There are red and purple and blue-green lines all down her legs, from the top of her ass to her knees. She traces them with the tips of her fingers, feels the hard knots and lumps under her skin. Someone asks her why she likes the marks. She looks over her shoulder and the camera zooms in on her face. "When you think you can't do something, when you think you're done, and then you do more? That's the best ending," she says.

︿︿

THE LAST TIME I saw Nate, we were in his bedroom. It was late and he wasn't wearing any clothes. I kept waiting for him to do something, but he just kept talking.

"Have you ever felt like people don't get you?" He had a towel wrapped around his waist. It was falling off at the side—I could see his right hip bone and the trail of hair under his belly button.

I didn't know how to tell him I feel that way all the time. "Sure," I said.

He scratched his nose. Some of his nails were so short there was no white left. "Like nobody really knows you?"

I wondered for a second if he was about to tell me what I thought I wanted to hear.

My jeans were unzipped and he put his hand down the front of them. I touched his chest with my palm. I can never touch Nate until he's already touching me. "What don't they know?" I ask.

He looked at my lips. I thought about how strange it is to always be able to tell what part of your body someone is looking at, but how hard it is to remember that when you're looking at someone else.

"Never mind," he said. He started to move his fingers and I pulled my hand from his skin, cradled it against my own chest like an injured limb. I realized even if he told me something, I could never tell him the truth back.

"Do you like that?" he asked.

"Mm-hmm," I said.

"Do you like me?" He whispered the question down my neck, then mumbled so I could hardly hear him, "I like you."

Nothing ever feels the way it's supposed to. This should have been good—it means I've done everything right. But there was pressure on my chest like someone was sitting there.

"Yeah," I said. "I like you." It's always easiest to say something emotional when it's not completely true.

He took off the towel and pushed himself against my leg. I was still wearing jeans, but he didn't try to take them off. He put his hand back down my underwear and hooked two fingers inside me.

I closed my eyes and thought about the doctor. If he tried to put his hands on me, would they go right through my body like one of us was a ghost? But he's real—he could be real. His hands might be cool, his fingers would leave goosebumps. That spot under my belly button started to burn, sending flames all over. Thinking about him feels like going on a school trip and begging the bus driver to go full speed down a hill with lots of bumps. You hope and you hope at the same time as you hope not.

Nate's fingers wiggled inside me, and it started to feel like nothing really. So I pushed down on his wrist with my palms, kept him in one place and moved myself against his thumb bone. I hoped he wouldn't talk to me and he didn't, and I thought about the doctor and teetered at the very top of the hill. I want to be able to do whatever I want and then stop, not have it mean anything to anyone. I want to be able to change my mind.

Nate left come on my jeans—a spot that shone once it dried, like frost on a window in February—but that's not the part I minded. Afterward, he smiled at me because he knew something was different—he just didn't know what. It felt pitiful, embarrassing. He kissed me like he was saying *you're welcome*.

〰〰

THE DOCTOR AND I talked about rules a couple days ago. He wants to hit me, and I said that was okay. He called it *playing*. He's done it a couple times before, but not since he moved here last year. I agreed to no sex, but I can't help thinking he might change his mind once we're together. He made me tell him what he couldn't do. He said that part was really important. At first I said it didn't matter but he told me it's good to have limits because it means you know what you want. It's better not to do enough than to do too much. I don't tell him I'm scared nothing will ever be enough.

He sent me a list of things to make choices about—yeses, nos, maybes. There were some things I'd never even heard of before, things I had to look up on the internet. The first couple times I crossed things off the list, it felt like failing, but it got easier every time I said yes. Even my maybes felt good by the end.

The doctor wanted to talk about every step, every movement, every slap beforehand. *Especially the first time, there shouldn't be any surprises*, he says. And he gave me rules, too. Once we're together, I'm not supposed to do anything except what he tells me to do. I try to imagine if everything was like that—if I could just hand my whole life over to someone else and have them tell me what to do and where and when.

∧∧∧

A FEW YEARS AGO, I was pet-sitting for a neighbour and their cat started acting really weird. She was moving in circles and it was like she couldn't bend her back legs, like they were stuck straight. And when I tried to pet her, she'd just push her butt toward me. She pushed herself into everything—furniture and the floor and the walls. I ran home and told Mom that I thought something was wrong with her, that we should take her to the vet. Mom came over with me, and when she saw the cat she said, "Oh, she's just in heat." She acted like it was obvious. I had to ask someone at school what "in heat" meant. And I was so embarrassed when I found out, not just that I didn't know what was going on, but because it was such a physical display of desperation.

Usually I feel like I want too much, like my own need is embarrassing and desperate and gross. But maybe I've found places where I won't have to hide it, where I can be a cat in heat, rubbing against anything I want.

eighteen

ᰰ

The doctor's bathroom doesn't feel like what I thought a man's bathroom would feel like. It's big and painted blue. There are light bulbs around the mirror like in some Hollywood dressing room. There's a striped shower curtain and a closet filled with towels that feel soft, like from the dryer. When I was a kid, Mom always dried the laundry outside—she said it smelled best—but it made the towels scratchy and stiff. I hated seeing them on the line, blowing in the wind, the rusty pulleys creaking from the weight of the wet laundry.

While I'm peeing, I move the shower curtain to the side. My heart feels higher up than it should. I don't know what I thought I'd find: another girl, a dead body, a tub full of blood. The bath is clean.

Beside the sink, there are two toothbrushes. One is the kind you get from the dentist after a checkup. The other is smaller and covered in Disney princesses. *Maybe he has a niece*, I think. I tell myself it's not my business.

When I go back out, he's sitting on the couch. I sit down on the other side; I can see him out of the corner of my eye. He looks so much like his picture that I'm still not sure he's completely real. Blond, blue eyes, preppy—the kind of guy I always say I don't like. He's dressed like he's going to a business meeting, except his shirt-sleeves are rolled up. The hair on his arms looks almost white. He's more handsome than attractive. Every time I swallow, I swear the sound fills the whole room. He's looking in the direction of my legs, so I stretch them out, try to imagine they're long and thin so they'll look longer and thinner. My most recent scars are pink like bubble gum because the skin is fresh like a baby's. I wonder if that's what he's looking at, my newest skin.

I try to see myself the way he does. My makeup isn't great because I got hot walking here. My mascara's running because it always is. And my hair's sticking to my forehead. I tried to fix it in the bathroom, but there was only so much I could do without getting it wet and making it obvious. I want him to like me, but I have no idea what he's thinking, if he's thinking anything at all. This isn't like being with boys from school. But it is real—I have to keep reminding myself he's real.

I wonder if I'm doing it wrong, if I'm supposed to say something or touch him to start things off, but I don't want to break the rules. We just sit like that for a while, staring at the TV, which isn't even on.

Finally, he stands and tells me to get up, and it's like walking out of church into a Sunday. He tells me to take off my clothes and go to the window. He leaves the room and I undress, but I don't know where to put my clothes, so I hang them on the arm of the couch. I put my underwear in the pocket of my jeans. He comes back with a fluffy dark blue towel. He folds it once, a soft square, and drops it onto the floor.

"Stand on it," he says. "Put your palms flat against the window."

I do what he says.

"Farther back. Bend over." I bend at the waist and put my forehead against the window, look down. This apartment would have a nice view if we were somewhere else.

I hear him undoing his belt behind me, and I close my eyes, waiting for his hands on my body. Instead, there's hot liquid pouring down the back of my leg, hitting me right under the ass. The stream moves to my other leg and I feel like an idiot. My face is hot deep under my skin. I want to leave. This isn't what I thought it would be like. I thought it would feel sexy like a movie, or like porn, but instead it just feels stupid.

He tells me to turn around and kneel on the towel. I see his body, his skin, for the first time. His dick is out of his pants. I know what else he wants to do, it's all planned, but I don't know if I want it anymore. There's a way out—a safe word—it's up to me how much I can take.

Once when I was a kid, I put a snail in my mouth because it was really beautiful, with bright stripes, and I thought that meant it must taste nice. I was older than I should have been, old enough that I remember the whole thing. My mom saw me do it and she started screaming. She was so loud and scared me so much that I swallowed the snail whole. I remember the feeling of it going down my throat. Mom cried and cried, but nothing bad happened.

I lean forward and put my mouth on him. I want to lick him clean, swallow everything. I gag almost right away and something comes up, but I swallow it. It tastes like sour candy. I can feel his wetness under my knees. He pulls me off with my hair and slaps me so hard it makes a sound.

"You won't do that again," he says. "Tell me you understand." I nod and he slaps me again. "Tell me you understand."

"I understand." The words are survivors, fighting their way through a throat that feels closed, crushed. My face stings as it comes back to life.

Then he puts his hand on my swollen cheek, holds me steady. He zips up his pants like that part of the night is over, like I failed a test. He makes me stand by picking me up under the armpits. I feel like a rag doll. He sits and tells me to bend over his lap, to lie across him. So I do. He hits me first with his hand, slaps me hard on the bottom of my ass. I want to tell him to do it again but I feel high, like I've done a bunch of drugs, like I've done ketamine, and my tongue is numb and my mouth hangs open. After he hits me the second time, he comes back right where he slapped, grabs my flesh, kneading into it like he's searching for something just by touch. My sob is so deep that I can't hear it. I'm so full and it's leaking.

After everything, he carries me to the shower, and then to bed. I let him take care of me. I put my arm over his body and he hums a song I don't know. It feels like being rocked to sleep.

〰

IN THE MORNING, I want him to touch me, but he gets out of bed and gets dressed. I pretend I'm still asleep. I can hear him moving around. I wait for a few minutes to see if he'll come back, but he doesn't. I look at my reflection in the window and even though I can't see details, I know my hair looks messy sexy because it wasn't dry when I fell asleep. When I walk into the main room naked, he says, "Your clothes are in the bedroom."

I stand there for a second, leaning up against the door frame, my hip pushed out, but he hardly looks at me. He's reading the paper. I haven't seen anyone read a paper since my dad left.

I get dressed and go to the bathroom. There's a red blur along my cheekbone where he slapped me, but it's not as noticeable as I thought it would be. I want my body marked, bruised; I want proof someone was there.

When I finish getting ready, there's toast and coffee on the table at the place across from where he's sitting. The toast is buttered and salty and hot. He puts a sugar bowl and a spoon in the middle of the table, but I leave the coffee bitter.

I have to get to first period on time today because Cass and I have a presentation, but I don't want to tell him that because he'll think I'm just a kid. I look at the clock on his microwave. I still have a bit of time.

"Do you like being a doctor?"

"Most of the time." He's looking at his phone. Everything from last night is cleaned up already, like it never happened.

"Do you want to hang out again?" I take a bite of toast, and chew and chew and chew. It feels like there's acid running down the back of my throat. It's really hard to be sure what you want—almost impossible most of the time, I think—but here, right now, at this exact moment, I know. I stop waiting for him to answer me. "I want to do it again," I say.

He looks at me like he's not sure I'm really there. When he says, "Yes, let's do it again," the world feels suddenly bigger—the room stretches out for miles.

〰

THE NEXT TIME I go to the doctor's house, he doesn't take any of his clothes off, not even to sleep. He tells me to bend over the back of the couch. He ties my hands in front of me with shoelaces and he shows me different implements, makes me choose between them. He trails the wooden paddle all the way down my spine before he spanks me with it.

This time, I leave with bruises.

nineteen

᭨

I t's amazing how fast something can take over your life.
How fast you can stop caring about everything else. When
the doctor tells me about some of his favourite albums,
I burn them onto CDs and listen to them on the walk to
school and in Math class. I buy the same toothpaste he has in his
bathroom—it's not minty like the one I usually use. I lick my teeth
and imagine I'm tasting him. The last time I slept over, one of his
kitchen cupboards was open and I saw a box of cereal. On my way
home, I got the same brand and the next day I ate it for breakfast,
lunch, and dinner.

I've been avoiding Nate, and I don't care. I have more than
pretending now, more than stupid baby steps. I don't even go out
after school anymore. It feels like I'm floating through the days
just to go online and talk to the doctor again. I haven't done drugs
in weeks. It always feels like I'm on fire, like something is burning
under my skin. Today Cass asked me to come smoke pot at Nate's,
but I told her Mom's being crazy and won't let me go out. She

didn't believe me, but she thinks I'm lying because of Nate, because I'm avoiding him.

When I got home today, the doctor wasn't online, so I went to a BDSM subgroup I use sometimes for chat. There aren't many people on because it's not the right time of day, but I find one guy I've talked to before. He's a dominant. A lot of guys I meet are submissives. Everything has a word, a name. If Cassie did this, she'd probably be a brat—she'd talk back, talk shit about people just to get hit harder. Lillian probably wouldn't be a sub at all. I wish I was good at being a brat, but I hate it. When I try, I just feel like a disappointment.

I open a new message window with the dom guy. *Hey*, I say. *How's it going?*

Good good, how's life for you?

Good. Wanna chat?

Cyber?

Yeah. Can you make me feel bad?

Like talk shit about your body, like you're a whore?

It's easier here to find the words that'll give me what I want. *More like I'm not a person*, I say.

Limits?

Nothing about family. And don't say cunt.

Once I talked to someone who asked me if I'd ever fuck my own mom. I didn't even answer him, but I could hardly sleep for days after that. I felt so guilty, like I'd done the worst thing. And *cunt* is my word.

What do your tits look like? he asks.

34C

Touch the nipples, tell me about them

I put my hand down my shirt, brush my thumb just on the tip of my nipple. I can feel the tiny bumps on the areola as it gets tighter, puckered, wrinkled. *They're hard. Cold. They stick out.*

Stop touching them, they're mine now

What am I doing?

Just lying there, I don't want you to touch yourself now, you're mine

What are you doing to me?

Looking

I think about the doctor's eyes on my neck. I lift my head, stretch out a little, breathe in and hold it in my chest, as if to let him see more of me. He still hasn't touched me the way I thought he might, the way I'd hoped. But I know it'll happen eventually. Sometimes talking to other people like this feels wrong, like cheating, but it's just until the doctor realizes what he's missing.

You're an orifice, you're nothing but a collection of orifices for me to use, you're no good for anything but fucking

I can feel my pulse in my cunt now. *Am I good at fucking?*

No, you're just a body, just holes

Sometimes I wish I could be unconscious for sex, just hear about it later, how good I was. The doctor could do whatever he wanted to me and I'd have to learn about it from my own body afterward, from sore spots and bruises and blood. I'd follow a map on my own skin.

^^^

THE OTHER DAY I got a pair of underwear ready to mail. I put them in a plastic baggie and then into an envelope. It was already addressed to a guy in South Dakota. You have to write the address before you put something soft inside, or it ends up looking horrible, unprofessional. The underpants were plain white cotton with little pink flowers, almost exactly the kind I used to wear when I was a kid. They had a line of brown running down the back—not a lot, just enough that you'd notice.

I meant to bring the envelope to school to mail on my way home, but I think I forgot it on my bedside table. When I got home, it was gone. I looked everywhere—in my backpack, my purse, under my bed, in all my drawers—but it wasn't anywhere.

That night, Mom put laundry on my bed and the underpants were right in the middle of the pile. I avoided her for the whole next day, but when I saw her, she acted normal, even better than usual. She went to the grocery store and cooked dinner that night and then wanted to watch a movie together. And after she made microwave popcorn, she gave me the bag to lick even though she thinks it's disgusting.

Maybe she didn't see the name or the address. Sometimes I wish I could convince myself of things the way Mom can—it's like she closes off part of her brain, picks at strings to prove the most unlikely reason for everything. It was the first pair of my underwear she's washed in years.

⋀⋀⋀

I GO TO school most days just to avoid Mom. It feels pointless now, though. I guess I could drop out; I don't know what the rules are. Most of school is people telling you what to do and when to do it. But then as soon as you leave, they expect you to know how to make all the right choices on your own.

Lillian ended up switching schedules and moving into my Communications Tech class before lunch. Not because of me.

I heard her telling someone physics wasn't her thing—I could have told her that and saved her a bunch of time. I thought it'd get less awkward seeing her every day, that I'd be able to ignore her after a while, but she's still always there, right in the corner of my eye, breathing the same air as me. Going to class feels more and more like a chore. Every time I step out of the classroom, it's like losing a hundred pounds. Being around Lillian makes me feel like I'm way ahead and falling behind all at the same time.

I'm trying to sneak out of school early on Friday when I hear Cass calling my name down the hallway. I keep walking but slow down to let her catch up outside the back doors.

"You skipping?" she asks. She fishes a half cigarette out of her purse—the tobacco is all unpacked at the end, wiry. She lights it and a few of the strands catch fire.

"Yeah. I can't handle Algebra today."

"Where are you going?"

"Just home. Might take a nap." I have plans to go to the doctor's. I'm sleeping there tonight.

"Want to come to my dad's later? I have shrooms. Or I could come with you—we could nap together and then find somewhere to go?"

It makes me feel good to be asked, but I also just want Cass to disappear. I always thought she was better than me, but now I wonder if that was ever true.

"I can't. Maybe I'll show up later, though. I can call you."

"'Kay." Cass looks at me hard but I'm not worried; I know she can't see me. She tries to take a drag but her cigarette's gone out. When she lights it again, I can tell it's too close to her face and her lips must be burning, but she doesn't even flinch. She just pretends she doesn't feel anything. And for that moment, I want to drop everything and just be with her—I want to smoke pot in the alley behind the school and laugh about stupid shit, like that time we were stoned at Jonah's and he kept thinking he heard his parents coming home. We laughed ourselves right into each other's laps. I want to do E with Cass and talk about how much we love each other, make up stories about the things we'll do together when we're older—I want to rub my cheek against the very top of her shoulder, where the skin is softer than a cat's belly.

But I can't say any of those things. I can say them when I'm high, but I haven't done drugs in weeks and the words are just tiny bubbles in my throat.

"Fuck it," Cassie says, taking the cigarette out of her mouth. There's a daytime moon and she throws her unlit smoke at it. "See you later, maybe."

〰〰

THE DOCTOR TELLS me not to clean myself afterward, to just get into bed. When he runs his fingers through my hair, grazing his nails against my scalp, it's like lightning hits me right in the chest. It feels like cutting my skin and sewing myself back together. The best part of pain is that it turns everything else from just okay to amazing.

I fall asleep on my stomach and dream that I can breathe underwater.

I wake up to the sound of the shower. When the doctor steps back into the room, he's wearing a T-shirt and jeans that have a rip in the knee—it's like seeing your math teacher at the grocery store, realizing they have a whole life you've never even thought about.

I prop myself up on one elbow so he knows I'm paying attention.

"You can shower now," he says. "There's shampoo and soap on the rack."

"Do I have to?" I ask.

"Yes." His serious tone breaks in a smile and I wonder if he's actually two different people, if each knows the other exists. He looks younger than he did a minute ago. "Do you need anything else in there?"

I want to say something like, "Just you," but I know that's not what he means, and it's a corny joke, so I shake my head.

"What about breakfast? Any requests?"

"Umm . . ." I'm scared to say what I really want in case he says no, but he's looking at me like he'd be okay with anything. "Maybe pancakes?" I say.

There's a pause and I'm on the edge of a cliff, and then he says, "I've been craving those all week."

〰

I KNOW SOMETHING is wrong when I get home because Mom's sitting on the front porch smoking a cigarette. Lately all she does is bother me about where I'm going and what I'm doing and whether I'm coming home. I hardly ever know the answers to those questions. If I say I'm coming home at midnight, she'll get mad if I don't, so I'd rather just not tell her at all. It won't last, anyway. She'll get SARS or malaria and get distracted.

I stayed later at the doctor's than I meant to because he wasn't asking me to leave. He made pancakes—he put chocolate chips and apple in them even though I didn't ask him for anything extra—and I sat at his wood table with my knees pulled up to my chest and watched him at the stove. I wondered how much of the air I was breathing was the same air he'd breathed out.

"You can't stay out all night," Mom says. She's wearing a pair of my old pajama pants.

"I was at Cassie's."

She looks like she might cry, but she cries all the time.

"What?" I put my hands up like I don't understand what's going on, like she's being unreasonable and crazy.

"Don't pretend you don't know what I'm talking about." The worst thing about being a daughter is your mom can read all your movements because they were her movements first. She knows you deep down in her blood because she gave you pieces of her. But you gave her pieces of you, too, and sometimes she'll choose to believe you when you lie.

"I called Cassie. She said you weren't with her." I forgot Mom had Cassie's number. I gave it to her once when my phone wasn't working. "What's the point of you having a cell phone if you're not going to answer it?"

"I pay for it. I shouldn't have to answer it when I don't feel like it," I say. I try to brush past her on the stairs and she grabs my arm, holds me tight.

"How do you pay for it?" she asks.

I know she's probably terrified I'll tell her the truth—I wonder how long she's been working up to asking me that. "I babysit. Cass's grandma pays us to clean her yard. How would you know anything about what I do?" I pull away from her and go up another step. "You treat me like I'm a kid."

"You *are* a fucking kid."

"Not when I'm taking care of *you*. Not when you need me all the time. It's always about you."

"Stop it!" Now she's yelling. "It's always about me? It's always about *you*. Don't you get it?" she says. "What's going to happen to you without me?"

The neighbours are probably peeking out from behind their curtains; people love to look at someone else's mess.

"You can't talk to me like this anymore." She sounds like a balloon with no air in it. I wonder if I'll ever be as old as she is right now.

"Why? Because you're my mother? Because you do so much for me? You're fucking crazy." I say it even though I don't want to. Lately I feel like I'm not the person speaking when I speak. Like I'm in a movie and I'm just saying my lines. The worst is when I know exactly what I'm going to say and I still can't help myself. "It's bullshit. The MS. Every single thing you've had—none of it's real. You're insane. It's embarrassing."

She doesn't respond right away, and my heart beats fast like I'm walking past a barking dog. I've wished so many times she'd ask me about everything just so I'd have the option of telling the truth.

"You think *I'm* embarrassing? You think I don't see what *you* are?" She smiles like it's all a bad joke. She turns away from me and sits back down on the porch step and keeps smoking. I wonder at what point it was she stopped being able to convince herself—the ring box, the computer, the fucking envelope.

"I want you out of my house by noon," she says. "You want to be an adult? Get your shit and get out. I can't take care of both of us right now."

I slam the front door behind me and go straight to my room to pack. I can tell right away that something's different. The top drawer of my dresser isn't closed properly—there's a piece of cloth sticking just out of the top. It's the shirt I told Mom I threw out, the one with stains all up and down the sleeves. I'd never leave it like that; I'm careful.

I'm so angry sometimes. It feels like that moment before you drop on a roller coaster, like everything is building up to something and even though your brain knows what's going to happen, your body doesn't. I take my ring box out of the drawer and bring it to my bed. The razor blade inside has dried blood on one end of it, so I drag the other end along my wrist, right in the middle this time, and bits of blood pop up like tiny globes. I'm calm almost right away. I make five more cuts. The corner of the razor disappears clean into my skin and it's the prettiest thing I've ever seen in my whole life.

I sit for a bit and watch myself bleed. I lick my wrist because I've never done that before, and the blood smears across my arm, sits there like jewellery. I think about my mom and I feel like garbage. I don't deserve anything.

I have a rush through my head like I've never had before. I just want the blood to keep coming until I'm empty, so I can fill myself up with good things, things I get to choose. I go to the bathroom and turn on the hot water tap at the sink. I think about everyone's faces—my mom's, Cassie's, Nate's, Lillian's—when I do something wrong, disappoint them, say something stupid, mess things up. What would Mom do if I went out there right now, if I told her I needed her, if I walked up to her and showed her my insides?

I only remember my promise to Cassie, my pinkie promise not to cut, after my arms are under the hot water. I've been cutting in places where it's easy to hide. I'll have to wear long sleeves for weeks now, keep more secrets. I pull my arms out of the water—the blood is like watercolours. I turn on the cold tap and wipe my arms with a face towel. I hold the cold on my skin. I take care of myself.

∧∧∧

I BUZZ AT the doctor's building, but he doesn't answer. It's starting to rain and I have a backpack and a shoulder bag and a purse and I'm tired and just want to be inside. So I wait until I see someone coming through the lobby and pretend I'm looking through my purse for my keys.

The rain is really coming now, thwacking the sidewalk like paint pellets. At first you can see every splotch on the pavement, but then all of a sudden it's covered, dark.

The woman pauses in the doorway, and I put on my best fake smile. "Oh, amazing. I can't find my key."

She looks at my wet sneakers. I don't know when I started looking like somebody who can't be trusted.

"My uncle lives here," I say.

The woman steps outside. She keeps just the tip of her finger on the door.

"I have to feed his cat," I say.

Her finger slips off the door, but she stops it with her hip and steps to the side to let me through.

I go up to his apartment and knock, but he's obviously not home, or he's ignoring me, but I don't know how he'd even know it's me. We didn't make any plans before I left this morning; I'm not supposed to be here. I think about the way he asked me what I wanted for breakfast, the rough way he holds my wrists together, with one hand. The sharp pain of a whip and his fingers in my hair. I lean my forehead against his door and close my eyes and think about how nice it was for him to wonder what else I might need in the shower.

"K?" I don't even open my eyes at his voice. *K.* That's who I am to him. I always thought it made things more special, having secret names, like it gave us permission to be who we really are, but now it feels like pretending.

I lift my head off the door and he reaches in front of me to put his key in the lock. Once we're in the entryway and the door is closed behind us, he just waits.

"I got kicked out," I say.

"Of what?"

I don't know if he's being funny or being an idiot. "My house."

"By your landlord? Can't you find another place?"

It hits me suddenly how little I know—it all seems so overwhelming. I don't actually know how to do anything, how to live like an adult. I don't know how to rent an apartment or pay taxes or cook. "I need somewhere to go."

He clears his throat.

"I don't know where to go. I'm fifteen years old. I'm only fifteen." A sharp heat pinches my eyes. "I need you to tell me what to do."

He's looking down at the ground even though there's nothing to look at. I know he's mad. I know he wanted me to keep pretending.

"I can't be that person for you. Not like that," he says.

"Because of your daughter?" I can feel the sass on my lips. Maybe I could be a brat.

He doesn't react like I thought he would. He doesn't seem surprised. This whole time I thought I knew something he wouldn't have told me.

"Partly," he says.

"I want to stay here."

"You don't know what you want."

My throat gets tight like I'm choking. I wish everything could be like the first time forever. He's still not looking at me, so I move past him down the hallway and close the bathroom door behind me on my own sob. That's the only noise I let myself make, and then I splash cold water on my face. *Get your shit together*, I tell myself, looking into his mirror with his Hollywood lights that aren't turned on. This is all a performance for him, something he can pick up for a few hours, keep separate from his life. I'm just part of a game, and the game is just a tiny part of a whole.

I use the toilet, and when I'm done pissing, I step out of my wet underpants and put them in his top drawer.

twenty

ᴧᴧᴧ

I didn't know where to go after the doctor's, so I sat at the elementary school in the rain and smoked cigarettes—I lit each new one off the end of the last. I thought maybe Ivan would show up because the school equipment used to be our place, but I don't think I actually wanted him to. I made a list in my head of the places I could go, but it was short. I thought about going to Lillian's, but I imagined how she might look at me, that same disappointment I saw at the motel with Nate, that pity. I thought about Nate's, but he probably hates me now for ignoring his texts, and I don't want to look desperate in front of him.

I was soaked by the time I showed up at Cassie's. The pause before she let me in felt like hours. I hoped she hadn't noticed the distance growing between us. Maybe she'd been high the whole time. It still felt comfortable to change into her clothes and dry my hair with her beach towel. Comfortable like stepping back from something scary, knowing what you're moving toward is the safer choice because you were there before and you survived.

﹋

I'M SITTING AT the kitchen island while Cassie looks for food. She makes herself two slices of white bread covered in Miracle Whip right to the crusts. Then she reaches up to the top of the fridge, feels around, and throws me a mini Snickers. They're my favourite. Her grandmother Lucy keeps a box of Halloween chocolate bars above the fridge. I don't think she knows Cassie knows it's there.

"Has Hot Doc called you yet?"

"Not yet."

I told Cassie I've been sleeping with a doctor I met online. She thinks I just met him on Myspace or whatever. She made me promise not to lie to her ever again. She said she wasn't mad at me—she just wants me to trust her. She thinks that's why I came here, because I trust her. I'd never tell her I had nowhere else to go.

Mom never would have found out anything if I'd had Cass covering for me. That's what Cass says, anyway—she might be right.

"He's probably busy. Saving lives and stuff."

"Yeah. Probably." I try to smile, but Cassie knows me. I used to like that it was harder to hide things from her, but now I'm not sure.

"What's wrong? Did he text you or something?"

"No. Nothing."

"It's okay. He probably is actually busy. I mean, he has a real job."

"True," I say. I'd rather she thinks I'm just worried about him calling than have to tell her the truth, that he won't. That I feel like I'm drowning and all I want is someone to pull me out.

Cass finishes her bread and licks each one of her fingers all the way to the tip, pops them out of her mouth like they're suckers. "I'm such a cow today. You know, sometimes I want to move away just so I can't afford to buy food."

"What about drugs?"

"There's always ways to get free drugs." Cassie gets up to go to the bathroom and closes the door behind her. I guess neither of us is good at keeping promises.

〰

MOM CALLED TODAY, but I couldn't answer. I just let the phone ring in my palm until my voice mail picked up. My hand was still vibrating even after the phone stopped. I'll call her early in the morning tomorrow, when she won't be up yet, and leave a message about Cassie's. I know she's probably feeling bad—but I can't help worrying that maybe she wanted to tell me to never come back, that she finally feels free now.

She always needs me eventually. Every diagnosis falls apart and she's left with the way people look at her. She hates the way people talk to her when they think she's a liar. Once someone looks at you, talks to you, like that, there's no convincing them of anything. That seems like hell to me.

Sometimes I fantasize about funerals. It's not that I want anyone to die; I just like to think about what would happen if they did. Like if the doctor died and I found out, I wonder what I'd wear to the service. I wonder if his parents are still alive, if he has an identical twin I could introduce myself to—maybe he'd want to know more about me because of my mysterious connection to his brother. Maybe we'd fall in love and I'd have to tell him the truth the night before our wedding. He'd hold me and we'd cry together, and then he'd get custody of the doctor's kid and we'd end up in our own little family.

If Cassie died, maybe I'd get to sit at the front of the church with Lucy. I wonder if Cassie's mom and dad and sister would come, if they'd even care. I might be the person everyone felt the worst for. My relationship with Cass would be whatever I said it was, and everyone would have to believe me.

If Mom died, I don't know who'd come to the funeral. And if I never go home, would anyone even know she'd died? If I never go back, at least she could always be alive.

∧∧∧

WE GO TO Cassie's sister's to buy some coke. Rosie's boyfriend is a dealer now. But he's not home. Rosie is so pregnant she waddles. Her shirt doesn't even cover her whole belly.

When Cass tells her what we want, she lets us in and we go up to the attic because that's where her boyfriend keeps his drugs. We follow her and every stair creaks on the way.

Rosie reaches behind a mattress leaning up against the wall and pulls out a plastic pencil case. It's full of dime bags, already measured out into what looks like grams. She passes one to Cassie and puts everything away again.

"You can do a line here if you want," Rosie says.

"We should go." Cass looks at me.

I want to do one now, though. I want to be high all the time. "Just one?" I say.

Cass sits on one of the white plastic chairs and pours some coke onto the round coffee table in the middle of the room. Me and Rosie sit down in the other chairs.

She starts cutting it up, and Rosie says, "Can I have a little? Just a bump?"

Cass doesn't even answer her—she just pushes the ends of each line into a tiny pile. While Cass and I do our lines, Rosie keeps talking about how she's not a bad person, how we shouldn't hate her. *New worst things*, I think.

I'm glad when we're done and we can finally leave. On our way out, I look at Cass to see if her face will tell me anything. Before I can talk, she says, "She'd just do it anyway, but she'd have to steal it from her boyfriend." She spits her gum out on the ground. "He's an asshole. He could do anything if he was pissed."

⋀⋀⋀

THE NEXT MORNING, Cassie and I go to the beach instead of school. We pack a whole bag full of food from Lucy's pantry. The lake is close enough to walk. It doesn't smell too bad today. It's bright—no clouds at all—and we look right at the sun. We bury our feet until there's sand stuck between our toes. It feels good, like peeling off a whole layer of skin at once. *If I could stay here forever, exactly like this, it could be enough*, I tell myself. Cassie will be my family. I think about how she hardened yesterday, how she knew she had to make an excuse for her sister. Maybe she needs someone as much as I do. I'll be a better friend from now on—the kind of friend she can count on.

When we walk out into the water, Cass grabs my hand and we swing our arms between us. I realize for the first time ever that she's shorter than me. I wonder if that's always been true. Back on the sand, we shiver in towels. We eat chips and lick the salt off our fingers. We bite into apples and leave our blood behind.

When we get back to Lucy's, I go up to the bathroom. I sit on the toilet and punch myself in the thigh until I'm numb.

∧∧∧

THE DAYS BLUR together at the same time as they feel static and harsh. Sometimes I don't know if it's a weekday or the weekend. I can picture a part of the previous day so clearly, but it's never a part that gives the right clues. Things move around. Sometimes Cass and I end up in the school parking lot while the building is locked, or we spend a whole Tuesday or Wednesday or Thursday in someone's basement. Every day is like walking out of a matinee into the sun. One morning I go to school and it's a new month, and I realize my birthday came and went. I'm sixteen now.

I try to take my mind off the doctor, off the websites and the people I used to talk to. I don't miss selling, exactly. It's strange, though, to take a pair of underwear off after wearing them all day, put them in with Cassie's laundry, and get them back smelling like detergent. It seems like a waste.

The first few days I was at Lucy's, I tried not to change in front of Cass, but one morning we were in a hurry and I just did it. I thought the bruises on the backs of my thighs, on my ass, were faded enough, but she stopped putting her hair into a ponytail and stared at me. "Holy shit," she said.

We looked at each other in the mirror. "How the fuck did you do that?" she asked. "Did you fall or something?"

They always give you the right answer.

"Yeah," I said. "Down the stairs."

"Fuck," she said, pulling a pink mesh sweater over her tank top.

◇

I ONLY REMEMBER I have a math test after I've done two lines of coke off my algebra textbook. The first thing I see when I look up is the calendar on Cassie's grandmother's wall, and it hits me—Friday, Algebra. It's my last period of the day, but I still hardly make it. Halfway through class, the intercom buzzes and I get called to the office. Everyone oohs and aahs and laughs. Mrs. Walsh calls the office and asks the secretary if I can come when I finish my test—they decide on my afternoon plans without me.

There's nobody else in the office when I get there. Miss Ness's door is open and the secretary tells me to go right in. The room is the same as it was the last time I was here. Miss Ness points at the orange chair in front of her desk. "Katelin. Have a seat."

I wear this sweater because it makes me feel invisible, like I'm wrapped in a blanket. It has thumb holes I cut into it so it stays down over my wrists. The sleeves are long enough that you can barely see my fingers.

She gathers some papers, straightens them by tapping them on the desk. Once they're evenly rectangled up and in a perfect pile, she looks at me over the rims of her glasses.

"You weren't here this morning, or this afternoon."

"I wasn't feeling well."

"So why are you here now?"

"I had a test."

"You couldn't have been that sick, then."

I shrug.

"Cassidy isn't in school today either," she says.

I've never heard anyone call Cass that before. I didn't even know that was her real name, and for a second I think I might cry.

"I don't know," I say. I start pulling at a hangnail on my middle finger. Every time I brush over it with my thumb, it's like getting shocked by a doorknob.

"She's hardly been in school yet this year."

I imagine the principal and vice-principal and secretary and teachers all have meetings about us, talk about all the kids they don't like, look for ways to get rid of us. And everyone always wants to talk about Cassie. She has permission to act like a slut, to get fucked up, because bad things have happened to her. Sometimes I wish bad things had happened to me, that I had an excuse like Cassie does. I wish I could point to something and say, *This is why.*

"I know you're friends," she says.

"I think she's sick." The bell rings and I stand up. "I don't know anything."

"Okay. And you weren't here"—she looks down at a paper on her desk—"yesterday. And Tuesday you missed the whole morning again."

I try to remember Tuesday.

"Sit," she says. So I do. "I've called your house twice this week and there was no answer either time." She looks down at her paper again—I think she thinks it's intimidating, like she has my life on paper, but someone's life can't be on paper. "It's only your mom at home?"

"Yeah."

"When's the best time to reach her?"

"She works a lot." My hangnail finally rips; it feels like getting lemon juice in a cut, but I don't flinch.

"Are you okay?"

I'm so surprised that I just say yes. And sometimes I really am okay.

Miss Ness takes her glasses off and drops them on top of her perfect pile of papers, the papers with my name on them. She leans back in her chair and stares at me. "You attract strays."

I'm not sure if she's complimenting me or if I'm in trouble.

"You can't give up because your friends do," she says. "Your grades are way down from last year. And if your attendance doesn't improve, your teachers can't pass you anyway."

When I stand up again, she adds, "Things can get better."

People say the stupidest shit when they're trying to help. She doesn't get it at all. She thinks Cass is broken, she thinks Ivan is trouble, but she doesn't know any of us.

I go to my locker on the way out. The halls are mostly empty. There's a message from Cassie on my phone but it's just background noise. My phone is full of voice mail messages because I can't delete them. I try, but I always hang up before pressing the button, locking Mom's and Cassie's voices inside. There are no more messages from Lillian or Dad; it's been so long that they deleted themselves.

I try calling Cass back, but there's no answer. I don't leave a message because I know she won't listen to it. She hates voice messages. I grab her raincoat from my locker. I don't know how it ended up in there. Cassie leaves her shit everywhere. Once we spent three hours retracing our steps to find her cell phone. It wasn't in any of the places she remembered having it last. We ended up finding it when we went back to her house to sleep. It was under her pillow.

∿∿∿

CASS AND I smoke pot before we go to school, when we go to school. It feels like the whole world is covered in a layer of plastic. We walk around town, sit in people's basements, buy more pot.

At night Cassie wraps an arm around my waist and puts a leg over my thigh. But I can't sleep. I don't even know when I'm tired anymore. I never see it coming. The other day I fell asleep on the bus while Cassie was talking to me. Another time we were in the park and I got so sleepy that I had to lie down in the grass. I can sleep in the middle of the day no problem. But most nights I hardly sleep at all.

Sometimes, if I'm lying in Cassie's bed and can't fall asleep, I think about my body like I'm just made of pieces, like I'm not one whole thing but a bunch of things. Like my head is one part, and my feet are another, separate, piece. My left hand is one part, but so are each one of my fingers. I imagine myself broken down into bones and all the stuff in between. I picture my body like a skeleton taken apart and laid out in the right order, like a dinosaur at the museum, a collection of bones all sewn together. I'm made of such small parts and each one has a purpose.

Sometimes I wait until Cassie's snoring, then I peel her off my skin and go into the bathroom with my ring box. Once I woke up on the floor—the sun was just coming up and my arm was stuck to the tile with blood. The bathroom door wasn't closed all the way, but I don't think Cass knew I wasn't in bed all night.

I used to never want to sleep because I was always scared I'd miss something. Now I just want to sleep when I'm supposed to.

twenty-one

ᴧᴧᴧ

We're eating Smartfood and cookie dough and four different kinds of chips and watching movies we rented from the corner store. Lucy's away for the night. She doesn't know yet how much school Cass is missing. She probably will soon. The other day she asked me why I've been around so much—not in a mean way, but like she was actually curious. I told her my mom's away for work and I don't like staying home by myself. She just nodded, but I could see the beginnings of new questions; I could feel the string holding everything together pulling taut.

We're watching my movie pick first—*Sixteen Candles*. I've never seen it before, but everyone loves John Hughes movies. There's a scene where the main character, Sam, gives her panties to a nerd, and then the nerd charges people to look at them.

"You know, there are people who do that for real." I don't know if I say it as a test or if I'm really about to tell.

"Do what?"

Or maybe I just want to shock her. "Sell their underwear."

Cassie's laugh gives me that feeling like still being out when the sun comes up, where all you want is to get somewhere. "Imagine being that fucking desperate," she says.

It doesn't even hurt my feelings. *Desperate for what?* I think. Money? Power? Aren't those the things people are supposed to want?

The other day I met Alex and Cass after school and they were in the middle of a conversation about Russell Daniels's mom. She had a house-cleaning service, but apparently she used to do it naked for extra money. Everyone found out because one of the grade tens went home sick from school last week and walked in on her dad watching Russell's mom mop the kitchen floor. She'd been cleaning their house for years.

"Apparently she was wearing nothing except a sports bra," Alex said.

"So?" I asked.

"It's creepy. Imagine walking around butt naked but with a bra on? I honestly don't think I've ever done that even by myself."

"But why do you care?"

Alex raised one eyebrow. "She's basically a prostitute, Katie."

"Katie's more *open* than we are, Al. Right, K?" But before she turned to smile at me, Cass winked at Alex.

I couldn't respond; I couldn't talk at all. Heat washed through my body and my fingers felt numb. I thought about that wink for hours. I kept waiting for them to say something more, to make fun of me for something—I wanted to leave but I also wanted to be there in case I missed something they said. Sometimes it's worse when you don't hear it. I kept missing things, though. And suddenly I realized it was almost dark and I hadn't heard anything they'd said for a long time.

Cass nudged me with her elbow. "You wanna head home?"

For a second I thought she meant I should go to my house, back to Mom, and I felt the bubble of a sob in my throat. But she added, "We should make chicken fingers"—*we, we, we*—and I swallowed the sob, turned it into a cough, and Alex and Cass laughed about how bad I am at breathing.

Every time Cass hurts me, she does something to make me think it was just a mistake. All some silly misunderstanding. Maybe it was. And the rush of relief cools the heat in my stomach just enough so I can keep holding on, keep acting like everything's fine and not on fire.

When I think about what would happen if they found out the truth about the doctor, I can't catch my breath, and I end up gasping, crouched with my head between my knees. That happens a lot now. There was a point a few months ago where I probably could have told someone about selling my underwear and made it seem like a joke. I could have treated it like some ridiculous experiment or just a way to make money and maybe then it wouldn't have mattered so much. But maybe not. Maybe even thinking about it was already too much.

Cassie's phone rings and she gets up and goes to the kitchen. I pause *Sixteen Candles*. I hear the door opening and closing, and she comes back with Alex. Cass and I are both in pajamas. Alex is wearing her Pizza Pizza uniform, but without the hat; none of the girls wear them at work even though they're supposed to. Alex said the owner yells at them about it once in a while, but nothing ever changes. I can see her bra through her shirt—it's sparkly with little fake diamonds. It's too big on her. I can hear bottles clinking when she moves her purse around. I act like I'm happy to see her. Once Cass told me friendships work better with three—she said that way if two of us are fighting, the other one can fix it. Cass loves being in the middle; she loves being the one everyone else needs.

She runs up the stairs and comes back a minute later wearing jeans. "We have to go."

"What do you mean?"

"We just have to do something." She's already pulling on a sweater and stuffing a bag of chips into her purse.

I start to get up off the couch. "Should I put on other clothes?"

Cassie glances at Alex and they share this look, like they knew this would happen; I just don't know what *this* is.

"Depends where you're going, I guess? Al and I have to do something, but you can do whatever."

"Can I come with you guys?" I know I'm not supposed to ask. My head feels swollen and tight, like my brain is going to crack my skull right open.

Alex's smile is lopsided and her hair is greasy where it's falling over her eyes. She looks away, like I'm too pathetic to even bother with. I want to kill her. I want to hit her until her body turns purple and blue and she stops moving. I try to keep breathing normally.

"I can't bring anyone else," Cassie says.

"The movie's not even over."

"Well, you can stay here if you want."

Alex just keeps smiling. When they leave, she puts her hand on Cassie's neck and pulls her close to whisper in her ear. Her finger brushes against the thin hairs that never stay in Cass's ponytails. I watch Cassie's face relax, like Alex's fingers are a comfort, like she can finally be herself. The intimacy of it clouds my vision. I think about maggots crawling in through Alex's stupid smile and eating her brain.

I can stay if I want, I think. But this is just a place I'm hanging out, a place where I watch movies and eat Frosted Flakes and have sleepovers. It isn't home.

∿∿∿

ONCE I HEARD Mom and Dad having sex. They were on the couch, in the room right next to my bedroom. I heard the couch squeaking like when I'd jump on it. I crawled to my open door and listened. They went to bed afterward and I was up all night thinking about how I'd never be able to sit on the couch again. It'd be off-limits. I didn't get until later what it was that made me so mad—it was the first time I realized they had this relationship that could never include me, a relationship that was only theirs where I meant nothing. In the morning, they looked the same as always. *Liars*, I thought.

∿∿∿

I DON'T LOCK the door when I leave Cassie's grandma's—I might have to come right back. I pick up the bike that Cass borrowed from someone at a party last weekend, and I take all the quiet streets. It's late, more like early morning, but there are still some people out on porches, kids drinking as they walk down the street. I don't see anyone I know.

At home, I lean the bike up against the brick wall. After I turn the key in the lock, I wait for a full minute without moving. But everything is quiet and dark. The back door screams like a person if you open it slowly, but it's fine as long as you pull up on the doorknob and open it all the way fast. I know all this house's secrets.

When I was a kid, I thought it was haunted; I thought the scratches on my window at night were from a skeleton's fingers. But there's a boring explanation for everything.

I leave the door open and go down to the basement. Everything is the same. Smelly couch and stained carpet and wood desk covered in pens and ripped scraps of paper. The computer's on like I left it.

Nobody wants me, not even Cassie. My body feels heavier every single day, every single time I wake up. I imagine the extra weight filling me, filling my veins—my blood must be syrup thick by now.

I want to get high. I want to get fucked up. I want to fuck *myself* up.

I empty my purse and find everything I've ever kept weed in. I clear off the desk and scrape out a metal candy container, a film canister. I roll the shake up into a joint and stand on the couch, blow smoke out the window. I go upstairs, walking slow so the wood doesn't creak. I find a bag of Mom's cigarettes in the freezer; of course she's been smoking. And I pour a glass of half Baileys and half vodka from the back of the cabinet above the kitchen sink. It's warm. I want to drink everything that's here, everything that's everywhere else.

Sometimes I wonder if I'm crazy, if I'm a psychopath. Sometimes I wonder if I care about other people at all. Lillian used to talk about her brother Dougie. He had cancer when we were kids. He's fine now, but for a year or so all she could talk about was how he cried all the time, how he was always in pain, and not because she was annoyed but because she felt so bad for him. I can't do that for Mom, so something must be wrong with me.

I know where to find things on the computer now. But I end up in places I've never been, sites I've never looked at. There's a video where a woman says no over and over again. She cries it out loud like it's not just a word. I find pictures of women who are bleeding. Women who've been stabbed or hit in the face. Women who look like they drowned, who are so white they must be covered in paint. It looks real but I know it's not.

I find a stream of a girl with a rope tied around her neck. She's wearing a leather mask tight on her head, with only small holes for her nostrils. She's standing on a block of ice, but the more she struggles to stay on her toes, the more the ice melts from the heat of her body. When a man comes up and takes the mask off her face, she has black eye makeup and red lipstick smeared across her skin. Sweat sticks hair to her forehead and she sucks her bottom lip between her teeth when she whimpers. Her toes slip on the melting ice.

There's a live chat feed. *Slap her in the face*, someone says, so the man in the video does. Someone else says, *I like her eyes, hit her again . . . ask her if she's scared.* The man hits her again and she gags, chokes as she loses her footing.

wat a mess . . .
Use the cane!
tel her she butiful
I hope she dies
I don't say anything at all.

The woman tries to speak, but she can't get the words out. Drool leaks from the corner of her mouth and drips down her face.

She's real, I think. But is she? If I did what she's doing, would I still be real? Would I still be me?

I freeze when I hear footsteps, but it sounds like they're walking away. I close all the windows on the computer and wait for a full minute.

I go on to my site. There's a message from him, from the doctor. I don't open it but I don't delete it either. Bad decisions always seem like good ones until after you've made them, until you can't take them back.

MilkBeaut is online—she says hi before I do.

I can't stop thinking about Cassie and Alex—how Alex's thumb grazed her earlobe, the goosebumps on Cass's forearm, how embarrassing it all felt. I wonder how much Alex has told her about that party, the time I almost left her, if she's been trying to turn Cassie against me. When we were little, she'd try to do that to me and Lillian, but it never worked—Lil and I always saw the best in each other.

What's your real name? I ask.

Umm . . . why?

Are we friends?

Sure, hon. Why?

Then why won't you tell me your name?

I wait for a minute, but she's not even typing.

I'm sixteen, I say.

Nothing. But then she sends a bunch of messages all at once.

You said you were eighteen.

You shouldn't be here.

These are people's real lives you're fucking with here.

I can't talk to you anymore. You're a child.

Everyone keeps telling me I'm a kid. But I don't feel like a kid. And then she's offline.

I thought I could make it work, bring the people from online into my real life, but I can't. It doesn't matter if I know who I am, if I know the words for what I want—that's pointless if there's nobody to use the words with. Trying to make it real was a mistake.

I'm done, I think.

I know I could probably stay here, wake up in my own bed. Maybe Mom would act like everything is normal, like we never fought. She'd pretend I'm still just a little innocent kid. But I know how Mom will look at me. She won't say anything, but I'll know she knows.

$$\wedge\!\wedge\!\wedge$$

WHEN I GET back to Cassie's, the sun's coming up. Alex is sitting alone on the stoop by the back door. She's still wearing her work clothes. She's holding a bottle of Lucky with her fingertips. She uses the bottom of her shirt to twist off the cap, then throws it at me. She misses by a lot and it lands at the edge of the yard.

"I have to go home before work. Wanna walk me?"

"No. I'm pretty tired," I say.

"Hey, remember when we found those porno mags in the yard and Lillian cried? And then someone kept putting the pages in her desk?"

We found them at recess and Lil wanted to tell a teacher but Alex wouldn't let her. Lillian found some of the ripped-out pages in her desk later. It was obvious Alex put them there, but nobody said anything. Lil was so scared someone would see them that she spent the whole afternoon shredding the pages into tiny pieces in her desk. Then she wrapped them in another piece of paper and threw them out in a dumpster behind the corner store on our walk home. The next day, there were more pages in her desk. Women with their legs spread wide, bending over desks, wearing librarian glasses. She ripped those up, too, until they were just bits of skin-coloured confetti.

Alex always wants to talk about when we were little, before things got weird.

"You know I knew that was you, right? You know I protected you? I protected you all the time. I still do."

She tightens up, just for a second, like when you walk through a cloud of bugs, a swarm, an orgy. She acts like she's brave, but maybe she's just as scared as I am. My heart turns to liquid and travels all the way down my body. I can feel it pounding in my knees.

"So?" she says.

"Do you even like me anymore? Did you ever?"

"Do you still like *me*?"

When I don't say anything, she smiles. "Never mind. Don't answer that," she says.

She finishes the Lucky and puts the bottle beside the step. "You know, sometimes I wish I'd get hit by a car so I didn't have to go to work."

I know it's her way of apologizing. Moving on has always been how she begs forgiveness. That's the difference between us, maybe. She can put things in the past. So when she lights two cigarettes with a match and passes me one, I take it. And I sit with her on the concrete step, our shoulders just touching, neither of us saying anything at all. With each exhale, I tell myself I'm letting go.

ᐳᐳᐳ

THE DRAPES ARE open in Cassie's room, so I tie them closed. She doesn't ask where I've been. I crawl into bed next to her and put my arm over her waist, feel her stomach moving up and down because she's alive.

The skin on the very corner of her lip is cracked. Her cheeks look swollen, the skin tight. She stretches out her arm so I can put my head on it, and I nestle right next to her body. Her armpit hair is short, sharp bristles, a new forest against my cheek. I'll never be closer to her than I am right now. When we talk, the words won't be true enough to fix things.

∧∧∧

I NEVER TELL anyone when I get hurt. It's always so embarrassing. Once I went to one of Lillian's riding lessons and a horse stepped on my foot, and I just limped around for a week until it started feeling better. Another time I put my hand down on a nail that was sticking out of a chair. I don't know why the nail was there. Maybe the chair was broken. I remember the blood, trying to clean it off the chair before anyone noticed, clenching a wad of toilet paper in my fist. I don't remember it hurting until hours later—and by then it was already a secret.

I don't know why it's so embarrassing. Except that whenever I get hurt, it always seems at least a little bit my fault.

∧∧∧

WE GET OUT of bed around two. Cass and I stand on the same side of the kitchen island while we eat Frosted Flakes out of matching yellow bowls. Cassie adds extra sugar to hers, pours a little more in every couple spoonfuls. "I can't believe you have any teeth left," Lucy always tells her. But she's the one who buys the sugar.

After breakfast, we go for a walk because we're not allowed to smoke at Lucy's and she'll be home any minute. We wear leggings with boys' extra-large sweatshirts like dresses. We have to roll up the sleeves to stick our fingers out. It's not enough just to look good; you have to look like you don't know it, like you wouldn't care either way.

We end up at the park on the corner. We sit on the swings and plant our toes in the little pebbles underneath.

"I need a break," Cassie says.

"From what?"

"Everything, you know?"

"Me?" I say it like I'm kidding, but I know she can't handle my clinginess anymore. From now on, I'll pull it back. I won't let her see I need her.

Cassie laughs. "No, loser. Just Lucy, the house. The rules, you know? I can't do it anymore."

"You just don't want to do it."

Cassie rolls her eyes and a ringing starts in my head like a fire alarm. I can't tell if it's because I'm mad or because I'm worried Cass is mad. I don't want her to end up hating me.

"I'll just be at my dad's. And I'll be able to go out more, so we can do whatever."

"You don't even like your dad."

She shrugs. "He's okay."

I didn't think I was hungover, but the smell of the cigarettes is making my head fuzzy. I feel wrong sitting down but I don't think standing up will make it better.

"Or maybe I'll go to my mom's."

"Jesus, Cass, she's a crackhead."

Cassie's head snaps toward me. "Your family's a fucking mess—you don't get to say shit about mine."

I say sorry just because you have to say sorry about stuff like that. Both of us know Cassie's mom is a crackhead.

After a minute, Cass starts pushing stones around with her toes. "Do you ever tell the truth?"

"What?" I try not to sound surprised, but I feel my neck get stiff, like I can't move in a normal way anymore.

"You disappeared, Katie." Her voice is soft, like she's trying to get an animal to come to her. "You never even talk about that guy. Sometimes I don't even know if I know you."

"So ask me something," I say. My brain is pounding behind my eyes.

Cassie chews on a hangnail on her thumb. "When you were a kid, what'd you wanna be when you grew up?"

If she'd asked me something serious, something real, I would have lied. But I can give her this. "A vet. I used to put Band-Aids on my stuffed animals."

"Cute."

"What about you?"

"Ginger Spice."

Before we get back to the house, we spray cotton candy perfume and spin around in the mist to cover the cigarette smell. Sometimes people just need you to pretend you're following their rules.

twenty-two

ᴧᴧ

We're walking all the way to Izzy's; you have to pass the *Welcome To* sign to get there. Her house isn't in any place at all. The floors are rotting, and there's no furniture except for a couple mattresses and some white plastic lawn chairs. People love partying there because they can destroy anything and be as loud as they want. The cops never show up. Cass says eventually someone's going to burn the whole place down—she just hopes she's there when it happens.

"Is Nate coming tonight?" Cassie asks.

"I don't know," I say. I've hardly seen him in weeks. I know him and Dresler have started hanging out with a group of grade-nine girls.

"Are you gonna fuck him if he's there?"

When we were kids, Lillian and I made a love potion in her backyard. We collected water and dirt and plants and mixed it all together in this old tree stump. The stump smelled like my feet. We crushed everything up until it was a muddy paste.

Lillian wrote a spell for us to say while we rubbed the potion all over our arms and our legs. We danced around and laughed but I know we both really believed it was going to work. Being a kid is great because it feels like believing in something is all it takes for it to come true.

Nate liked me and I fucked it up. I gave him up; I chose the doctor. I wish I could put all the pieces back together. If I did, maybe I could even stay at Nate's place for a while. Cassie's moving to her mom's in a couple days and I don't know what I'm going to do. Maybe Nate has always been the answer.

"I might," I say. I take my sparkly pink lipstick out of my purse and put it on, then cover it with Blistex so I look extra shiny, brand-new.

When we get to Izzy's, I go straight to the backyard, but I don't see Nate. Ivan's sitting beside the fire. He's dating Jasmine from school now even though she's way too young for him—two years younger than me. Once her mom took her to the pharmacy to buy her a pregnancy test; the girls working there went to our school and recognized her, so they told everyone. Nobody could understand why she'd tell her mom and not just go buy the test herself. I wonder if she's here somewhere.

Ivan passes me a Carling from the case at his feet and I sit down beside him. "I did something weird," I say.

"What?"

"I fooled around with this older guy. I met him online. He hit me and stuff. But I told him he could."

"That's not that weird." He finishes his bottle and opens another. "You know Eddie Devlin?"

I nod. Eddie's a year older than me. I let him finger me once at a party even though he's blond.

"His little brother's in grade nine. Him and his friends went to the strip club and this stripper went home with them." Ivan laughs. "They paid her to sleep with them and now they all have herpes."

I've already heard that story but I laugh anyway. We sit together for a minute saying nothing. It's almost like we're friends again.

I could ask Ivan to hurt me—I know he would—but there'd be something missing. It wouldn't work like it did with the doctor, like I hope it works with Nate. "I miss you," I say. And then Jasmine is on Ivan's lap and kissing him like I'm not even there. He puts his arms all the way around her waist and clasps his fingers together like a basket weaving itself around something important.

〰

NATE FINALLY SHOWS up. I see him sitting on the porch swing. He's smoking a cigarette and laughing. He only smokes at parties. His laugh sounds like a cough. I go and stand just close enough that I know he'll see me, but with my back to him. I push out my hip and tilt my head and type a message on my phone that I'll never send. I feel his breath on my ear a minute later and flip my phone closed. Being sexy is better than sex.

He pulls me to the driveway at the front of the house. Between two cars. He kisses me and it's like everything is back to normal. I kiss him back and he pushes me against a car hood until I'm sitting up on it. His body's between my legs, his bare hands around my thighs. I rub myself, my cunt, against his belt. I feel like I'm too high up and might fall.

There's a car honking. I can feel it all through my body like I'm a musical instrument. I wonder if it travels up through my lips into Nate's, if the vibrations are making his heart beat a little bit faster. He takes my whole chin in his hand and kisses me hard so my lips disappear. He's never kissed me in front of anyone before. And then the car starts to move backward and I almost fall but I find my own feet flat on the ground. Nate and I go back to the party. There's country music playing loud from somebody's truck. There's always country music playing at these parties. Nate shows me his secret hiding spot for beer behind a bush next to the house. He tells me I can have as many as I want. Soon he'll know I want everything.

∿

I GET REALLY DRUNK. Drunker than I've ever been. I take sips from everyone's bottles. I sit in a puddle of beer someone spilled, so my shorts are soaking wet. It seems like that always happens to me at parties. Dresler follows me to the front porch and gives me shots of Crown Royal. He's so high I don't think he even knows who I am. Everyone knows Dresler smokes Oxys. There are some drugs you're only supposed to do in secret.

When I go back inside, I see Nate and Cassie with their heads bent toward each other and wonder if they're talking about me. I go to the bathroom to dry my shorts off. I get period blood on the floor and clean it up with toilet paper. Some drips onto my left shoe. I just bought them yesterday and they were white and new and clean. The drip is dark—someone might think it was coffee or mud. It's not a big deal. I like my shoes even better now because they have a secret.

One of the corners of the mirror is broken and I doubt anyone will ever fix it. This place is shit. My eyeliner is smudged just enough that it looks smoky and on purpose. My summer freckles stand out in a way that makes me look older, my skin is smooth, and my eyelashes are curling. My eyes are dark like two holes someone could fall right into. I feel a buzzing under my skin and I want to let it out.

My ring box is in my purse. I take my sweater off so I'm just wearing a bra. There are cuts up and down my arms, along the sides of my breasts, over top of my ribs. Sometimes I think about what it'd be like to tell someone, maybe someone like Lucy or Miss Ness, but it feels so hard, like I'm carrying a suit of armour.

When I cut, there's a second before the blood starts. In that second, I always wonder if maybe I'm not real. But soon it comes, just like always. I expect to feel better, to feel empty, but this time the buzzing gets worse. So I keep going. I cut until there are lines over lines over lines, but the screaming doesn't stop.

The door opens and pushes me sideways and I drop the razor into the sink. It's Nate. I hold on to the wall because I'm dizzy and I think I might fall over. I need something to hold on to.

"What the fuck?" he says. "Are you okay?"

He's seen my scars before—I've felt the pause while he's running his fingertips over my skin—but he looks afraid. For a second, looking at him, I get that feeling where my stomach drops out, where my heart melts down into my toes. My fingertips tingle.

I look at the blood on the floor, in the sink, the blood all over me, and start to laugh. There are marks everywhere, marks I made on purpose. I want to reach into myself and pull out fingers that are bright and wet.

Nate's looking at me like I'm crazy. He sees it all. He turns around and reaches for the door handle. He's going to leave me.

"No. Please, Nate. Please. I want you."

I push into him, grab his face and kiss him, but when I put my arms around his neck he ducks away. He has my blood on him now, too—smears on his neck, a single fingerprint on his cheek.

If he leaves now, if the door opens, it's over. I know he wants something he's scared of. I've known it since he kissed me with puke all over his mouth, his tongue sour like old beer. Nobody's normal, but most people won't admit how weird they are in real life. He does it all the time—not with words, but with actions—the way he spit in my mouth, licked my armpit, sucked his own come off my face like he was possessed.

I hold his head between my hands and put my tongue right in his mouth. He kisses me back and I can hardly breathe. When we separate, it's like Velcro, and he nuzzles his face into me.

"It's okay," I say. "I know you."

His nose pushes, flattening into my neck like he's trying to smell what's under my skin.

"Hit me," I whisper.

He's quiet. He doesn't understand.

"It's okay. I want you to hit me. I want you to." I need this to be the last time I have to say it, because I don't know if I'll ever be able to say it again. All my biggest regrets are things I said out loud.

"What's wrong with you?"

The question sharpens my breath and the shame hits me in the back of the throat.

He reaches back and locks the door behind him, then turns me around to face the sink, his hands rough on my waist. He doesn't even undo my shorts before pulling them down hard over my hips. I step on them to try to free my ankles, but I slip a little on the tile floor. And then he's holding me from behind. His palm is flat on my stomach and he's kissing my back, right where the bones stick out. Cass loves those bones, her wings. I haven't seen her in hours, it feels like.

He pushes down against the top of my back, so I have to bend over, and he sticks his fingers inside me; it hurts like the throb, the ache, after a cut. I look at our reflection; we look good together. We look like two people who could be in any bathroom anywhere. I lean back into him, put my head on his shoulder. It feels so good to let go, to let my body rest on his.

"You're so fucking wet," he says. "You like this, don't you?"

He's right, but he's wrong, too. There are rumours about guys who fuck girls while they're on their period, but it's always a joke.

He pulls his hand away from me. I see his face in the mirror, his expression when he sees the blood on his hand. "Fuck," he says. "You're so fucked up." He wipes it off on my arm, brown streaks.

Nate pushes up against me from behind. He squeezes the flesh on my sides in his fists like he's angry. And then something hurts and I yell out until he puts his hand over my mouth. It hurts like a burn, like something is scraping my skin raw. It's not a good hurt; it's a warning.

He spits on his own hand more than once—I hear him bringing it up his throat, collecting it in his mouth—and then wipes it on him and on me. And then his dick is inside me; my shit is cleaner than my blood. My chest hurts when I breathe too deep. I can't remember anymore what I wanted.

I imagine I'm a doll. I don't feel anything because my skin is made of cloth and my hair is made of string and my eyes are tiny buttons. *Or maybe I'm another kind of doll*, I think. My mouth is a tight tight O, and I'm full of someone else's breath. *I'm okay*, I think. *I was made for this*. I'm not a person. I'm a collection of orifices. I'm made of holes.

He finally stops. I can see him in the mirror. He picks my shorts up and wipes strings of semen off on the butt, then drops them back on the floor behind me. Someone is knocking. There are bright red handprints on my thighs.

"I'm not gonna be your boyfriend," he says.

∧∧∧

I LOOK FOR Cassie but I can't find her anywhere. Izzy's sitting on the front porch and I ask her where Cass is. She looks at my sweater covered in blood, but she doesn't ask if I'm okay. It's like she's seen it all before. She says Cassie left with some guy to smoke meth, but I know Cass wouldn't do meth because she doesn't want to be anything like her mom. I don't say bye to anyone. I start walking and the sweat on my body dries fast, feels like needles in the cold wind. I feel like I'm never going to get anywhere, but I do.

I get home just as it's starting to get light outside. I know this street so well that I don't even have to pay attention to where I'm going. I've walked down this driveway, put myself to bed in the same room thousands of times. I wonder how many days I've been alive, if I've spent more minutes here than anywhere else.

There's blood in my underwear but I don't know which hole it's from. I wash my shorts and underpants and sweater in the bathroom sink and hang them on my closet door to dry.

It's hot in the house, but I pull a blanket over myself anyway. I let myself sweat, feel all kinds of things leaving my body.

twenty-three

∧∧

When I wake up in the morning, it's like I've been dipped in concrete. There's a rock where my brain used to be, and I think maybe I should stay in bed forever. My skin feels tight, dry like the middle of winter. I have a shower and then lie back down in bed in my towel, all the little knots in my back releasing, winding down and fizzing out like sparklers on a birthday cake. It hurts so much. It feels good.

People will know what happened. They will. Nate will tell someone and that person will tell someone and that person will tell someone else. And then they'll all find out about what I do with boys, with men, that I'm a slut. I'll be the weird girl.

In the kitchen, the fridge is humming. I look around, peek into every room, but Mom's not here. There are dishes in the sink, so I wash them and dry them and put them away. It's almost all mugs and plastic pastel-coloured cups, no plates. It feels strange to be here, like what it must be like visiting parents after moving away.

I leave Mom a Post-it that says I was here and I'll be back soon, and then go for a walk so I can smoke. When I get home she's standing in my bedroom doorway. The house smells like Febreze. "How would you feel about painting in here?" she asks.

The last time we painted the walls was when I was little. Purple stripes. Dad put tape up so the lines would be straight. One of them got messed up—a splotch of purple made it under the tape somehow—and I cried for hours, but I guess I eventually got used to it.

"Are you gonna paint it?" I ask.

She shrugs with just her right shoulder. "Someone will."

"Okay."

"All you need to do is pick a colour," she says. "That's the only thing you need to worry about."

For today, for the next few hours, I let her be right.

〰

ON MONDAY MORNING, I take all my clothes out of my drawers and throw them on the floor, even ones I know I won't wear. I like starting with everything so I can put lots in the *no* pile. It makes me feel like I'm making decisions.

I wasn't sure until I woke up this morning if I'd get up for school or not. But if I don't go, people will still talk. And they'll call me a pussy, a coward. It's harder for people to talk shit when you're standing right in front of them.

I try on six different things before I choose a pair of jeans and a thin, tight, long-sleeved black shirt. It'll hide everything I want to hide, show everything I want to show. It's like something they'd wear on *America's Next Top Model* and it makes me feel skinny, tiny, like someone people might want to take care of.

∿

AT FIRST IT seems like the hallways at school are quieter than usual. Everyone must be whispering about me. But whenever I catch bits of people's conversations, it's always about something else. A few people say hi to me when I walk past. Maybe nobody knows.

When I sit down across from Lillian in second period, she looks at me twice, like she wanted to ignore me but couldn't. "Are you crying?" she whispers.

I reach up to touch the skin under my eye and my fingers come away wet.

"No. Just, my eyes are watering, I guess."

"You have a cold or something?"

"Yeah, maybe." I shrug and put my head down, but my nose is running now, too. I act like I'm resting my head in my hand so I can wipe at it with my sleeve without being obvious.

I can feel it all through class—a slow steady leak from everywhere. I try to keep my head down so nobody sees, but I catch Lillian looking at me a few times. I figure eventually it'll have to stop; there won't be anything left.

My grade-four teacher told our class never to keep secrets because they rot you from the inside out. I pictured blood oozing from my eyeballs, my organs coming out my mouth, my hands getting purple and swollen, my whole body turning completely inside out because it couldn't hold everything inside anymore. I wonder if I'm rotting.

⌃⌃⌃

IN ALGEBRA, we have to switch up our seating plan once a month. Mrs. Walsh, the math teacher, is young—it's only her first year of teaching. She believes we should try things out before making choices. We might think we're a back-of-the-room kind of student when really we'd love it up front. Most people just move over or back one when we have to switch. A sheet with the seating layout gets passed around the room so we can each label our chosen spot. Today, I write my full name in sparkly purple gel pen and pass it on.

When it gets back to the front, Mrs. Walsh looks over the sheet and then tilts her head. She walks toward my back corner. "What is this?" she says, holding the sheet out so I can see it. My name is crossed out; there's a new name in my spot now.

"Vampira? What does that mean?" She looks at me like she wants an answer. Some people laugh, but most just look confused. Everyone's staring at me now. My nose is still kind of runny, but at least my eyes aren't watering anymore.

"I don't know," I say.

She makes me cross out *Vampira* and write my name in again. I feel like I'm falling down flights and flights and flights of stairs.

I sit through the whole class without hearing anything. When the bell rings, I head for the front doors. I can't go out the back in case I run into someone I know. I see Dresler and hope he doesn't notice me. As I pass him, he laughs and tries to look right in my eyes. He pushes his shoulder into mine, whispers, "Here comes the slut." Sticks and stones.

⌃⌃⌃

YESTERDAY, MOM TOOK my clothes off the closet door and washed them. She didn't say anything about it.

Right after the thing with Nate happened, I wanted her so badly that it felt like my body was curling into itself like a wood bug. I wanted her to wrap me up until I was all the way back inside her body, with her muscle and fat to protect mine. Now I never want her to touch me again because she'll feel it through my skin like a memory. It'll ruin her.

She folded my clothes and put them on my bed, clean. The underwear still had some light brown streaks but they just smelled like laundry, like our house. I wrapped them up in a plastic bag and threw them in the garbage.

⋀⋀⋀

BY THE TIME I get home from school, I can feel the sweat collecting, dripping down my cheeks, off my chin. I go down to the computer and sign on to the site; I don't think about it like it's mine anymore. It might not even be a secret now. There's a pop-up asking why I haven't been posting lately. There are a few women advertising Veterans Day specials—panties and socks for only five dollars.

I look at the unopened message from the doctor for a full minute, lining my cursor up with each edge of the window before I finally click on it. But there's nothing there. It's blank. I wonder if it was a mistake, or if maybe he sent it so I'd send him something back. But I try to click on his account and I can't. And he's not on my contact list anymore. He disappeared.

MilkBeaut is online. She must hate me now, but I say hi anyway. I just want to talk to someone.

Hey, she says. *You didn't answer my messages. I was worried.*

That's all it takes, just a little bit of care, of love, for everything to spill out of me. About the doctor and Mom and Cassie and Nate and all the things I thought I wanted, all the things I want. I wish there were so many more words. If I had the right words, if I could just explain everything the way it was, maybe someone would know exactly how it felt. I have to keep pressing Enter because I'm typing so fast and the amount of space allowed in the chat window keeps filling up.

Something is wrong with me. I want to be raped . . . I have dreams about it . . . I want someone to hurt me, I say.

The little bar below the chat says she's typing. And then she's not anymore and I feel so stupid. I want to take everything back, swallow it inside me, taste it all forever to remind me never to tell anyone my secrets.

But she's typing again.

Honey, it's okay to have fantasies. They just mean you're alive, your heart is beating, your blood is warm. It doesn't mean anything except that. Sometimes things just are.

OK, I write, but I don't believe her.

I'll tell you something. I used to have orgasms sometimes when I was breastfeeding my daughter. I was scared to tell anyone because it felt really bad, like I was a bad mother, you know? A bad person.

I spent a lot of nights awake because I couldn't stop thinking I was going crazy. I thought I was some kind of pedophile. I started bottle-feeding her instead. I was scared to even touch her because I thought maybe I was so bad I couldn't even control it. I went to the doctor and told them she was on bottles only and they asked why I switched, and I was so tired that I finally told the truth.

I have that feeling in my stomach, like a snail going back in its shell.

My doctor told me it's hormonal, totally normal. Most things are never as weird as you think they are.

And the last time we talked, I shouldn't have said what I said. I reacted without thinking. I wasn't thinking about you. It's 100% not your fault. I'm sorry for making it seem like it was. People your age are scared. If they feel like they don't belong, they just want to pretend they do. Fuck, most people my age are scared of what they want. You're actually lucky. You already know something about yourself.

She keeps typing, so I just wait.

But you need to talk to somebody. You need to talk about everything. When it's real, it's different. And you can't be drunk or high for this shit. You have to be able to decide what you really want. You can't choose something without a clear head.

It's the first time MilkBeaut has ever really told me not to do something. I don't know what to say.

What's your name? I ask.

There's no answer for a bit. I fucked up. *Never mind. That's stupid to ask,* I write.

No hon. It's not stupid. I'm Angela.

I'm Katelin. Katie.

Okay. I hope I don't see you here for a while Katie, but let me know when you're back. She gives me her email address, says I can always check in.

I think about deleting my account, but I don't. I can decide later. *It's just a break,* I think. Maybe I'll come back when I can love it again. It'll be waiting for me like an answer.

twenty-four

ᴧᴧ

The hour between four and five in the morning always lasts forever. When you're a kid and you're at a sleepover, that's always the hour when people get so tired that it isn't fun anymore—everyone's too sleepy to talk or so hyper they stop making sense. If you can push past it, you're fine, but most people can't. In high school, it's the hour when you run out of coke, when people stop answering the phone, when all you want to do is sleep but you've been high for what feels like days. Your mouth just won't slow down. And then the sun comes out, and you can eat pancakes and go home and watch cartoons on the couch, or brush your teeth and shower off the smell of sweat and smoke. But until it happens, it feels like the sun won't ever come out.

It just hit four o'clock. I know it without even checking the time on my phone. I can't slow my brain down, but I can't stay in my body, either. I get lost in want so strong it's need. That pull where my heart grows too big for my chest, where my nipples tighten until they ache, where my belly button feels like it's connected to my cunt by a phone cord. But I don't know what the need is for. I keep half dreaming that I'm bleeding or pissing or shitting myself and it snaps me awake, but when I reach into my underwear, I'm dry.

The chorus *I let him I let him I let him* runs through me, humming in my veins.

I trace the lines on my hip, smoother every day. The star is fading, disappearing, blending into the rest of my skin like it's never been touched. I thought maybe if I cut it enough times, the same lines over and over, it would stay the way I wanted it, but that's not how things work.

I stop waiting for the sun to come up, and get out of bed. The glass on my window is cloudy, fogged up like someone's been breathing on it with a huge mouth.

∧∧∧

NATE'S BEDROOM HAS its own entrance. He answers the door wearing boxers and a white T-shirt with the sleeves rolled up around his shoulders. I've never seen him wear boxers before, and I wonder if all his underwear are like that now. If he threw out all his briefs and turned into a different person.

It's not even light out yet, but he doesn't look surprised to see me. I wonder if he's been awake all night. I realize I have no idea if he usually stays up late, if he has trouble sleeping, if he likes to get up early in the morning. I don't know what he does when he's not with his friends or having sex. He asks if I want a beer, and I do. He takes two bottles from the little fridge in the corner of his room.

He sits on the floor with his back against the wall, stretches his legs and crosses them at the ankles. I sit down against the opposite wall, with my heels pulled up against my butt. We're close enough that our toes almost touch. He's finally looking right at me. He finally knows who I am. I want to ask him if that's why he did it, but he'll pretend he doesn't know what I'm talking about.

He reaches over and pulls my bare foot into his lap. I let him do it—I don't know why. It's so quiet. He keeps his eyes right on my face. I look at his lap and see his dick rising under the material. He pulls the waist elastic down, and it springs out. There's a drip on the end of it that looks like laundry detergent, shiny like a pearl. He moves my foot against it, more than a hint. The drip smears across his skin and disappears. I know he wants me to rub my body against his, but instead I look toward the window, toward his empty backyard. I pull my foot back.

"Cunt." It takes me a second to realize what he said, maybe because I don't think anyone has ever called me that before. *That's my word*, I think.

I remember the taste of new blood running down the sides of my tongue, clean bright lines on my thighs, the star on my hip, my body a mess of open wounds. But I put them there. *I* did.

He gets up off the floor, his dick hanging over the top of his boxers. I think about what it would be like if I killed him. How I'd do it—with a knife, maybe. With my bare hands. I'd like to see his blood, I think, but not mixed with my own.

I tried to show Nate something—I told him the truth and he didn't listen. He used it to get something else. He never really wanted to know me. My head is quiet. Things are finally empty and clean.

I stand up and kiss Nate and he puts his hands on my waist. His tongue is an arrow stabbing my cheek. I bite down and he yells into my mouth. I can feel his scream travelling down my throat and vibrating and growing, a tunnel for sound, until I'm filled right up with it. He spits blood onto the carpet. I swallow.

∧∧∧

I GO HOME and have a hot shower. I don't scrub my skin or wash my face. The heat just feels right. My cunt is swollen—it hurts to touch. I try pinching it hard with my fingernails, and every time I let go it feels like something is leaving me. When I get out of the shower, I feel like I might pass out, so I sit on the shock-cold floor tiles with my back against the tub. I'm bright red and goose-bumped, like I have a million pimples I couldn't keep my hands away from.

∧∧∧

MY HAIR'S STILL wet when I go down to the basement. A couple minutes later I hear footsteps on the stairs—when the door creaks open, Lillian's standing there.

"Hey," she says.

"Hi."

One of her pant legs is rolled up at the bottom, so she must've ridden her bike here. She sits down on the couch and pulls her legs up under her body.

"What are you doing here?" I ask.

She shrugs. "I was worried about you."

"Why?"

Lillian tilts her head like I'm crazy. "Honestly? We have class together. You haven't been all week."

I didn't think anyone would notice. Mom called in sick for me. It felt like old times, like we were close again. I brought my cardboard box full of DVDs up from the basement and we watched movies on the couch. Last night I sat cross-legged on the floor, between her knees, and she brushed my hair until my scalp felt like mush.

"Why do you care now? Like, all of a sudden?" I ask.

"What do you mean?"

"Why didn't you tell me you had sex?" The words are out before I can stop them.

"When would I have told you that?"

"You could have called me. We could have hung out."

"When? You stopped answering my calls. And when you finally asked me to hang out, Ivan was there. You invited fucking *Ivan*. I didn't want to say anything in front of him, but I would never have come if you told me he'd be there. He's the literal worst. I figured you wanted me to stop trying."

"At least Ivan likes me."

Her face softens. "What?"

"Never mind."

"No. Katie. You think I don't like you?"

"You chose everything over me. Ivan wanted me around."

She pulls on her ear like it's itchy. "I didn't mean to. Honestly? I thought you were tired of me. Like, when I got really busy? It seemed like you got bored whenever I talked about work or the play or Steve. So I stopped telling you, but I didn't know what else to talk about. I felt boring."

I think about Lil feeling bad, and I have to wiggle my nose to stop the sharp burn in my sinuses. "Are you still seeing Steve?" I ask.

"You really want to know? You're not gonna, like, kick me out of your house for talking about him?"

"I actually want to know."

"We're together. He comes home every couple weekends. I visited him at school last week."

"So no more drama closet sex, then?"

She rolls her eyes so far up in her head her pupils basically disappear. I was always jealous that she could do that; whenever I try to copy it I give myself a headache. "We never did that," she says. "We never had sex anywhere at our school."

"Not at *our* school? But his school?"

"I mean, he lives there, so yeah. Except he has a roommate whose bed is literally a couple feet away from his."

"You're such a perv."

"Thank you. I do my best."

Once I start laughing, it comes out in gasps. I'm anxious and relieved all at the same time.

She smiles with teeth, a real one, not her stranger smile. "I'm glad you didn't get too cool for your donkey laugh," she says.

Once Lillian made me laugh so hard that I shit my pants, just a little bit. Lillian made herself shit a little bit, too, because we thought it was hilarious. We told my mom and we couldn't stop laughing. She told us it wasn't funny. She gave us a look like she was reaching right into our brains. So we laughed behind our hands, loving the fact that we had something together we'd never tell anybody else.

Sometimes the world drops something right in your lap. I take a breath. "Can I tell you something?"

〰

SHAWSHANK REDEMPTION IS on Superstation. They'll play it like ten times in one week and then it won't be on for six months. I own it on VHS, but for some reason, it's always better when you find one of your favourites on TV, even with all the commercials. I use the arm of the couch as a pillow. I'm the kind of sleepy where my eyelids feel heavy.

I wake up at four thirty. My phone is vibrating under my body with a text from Cass. *hey! I miss u like a mother bear misses her cubs after they turn into teenagers ... like a year old for bears ... and move to the city and sleep in alleys and spend every night FUCKED on heroin and they forget about her but she still loves them ... thats how much i miss u.*

I'm too tired to text her back. Maybe later. The TV is still on but it's muted. I go to my own bed and dream that Nate starts a fire in my bedroom. Mom is there but when I yell at her to get water, she hardly does anything. She puts her fingers under the tap and flicks water at the flames. So I take the whole fire into my arms and drop it in the sink and we can all breathe again.

Mom likes to say the best things happen when you have your eyes closed. She used to tell me how Dad proposed to her in a hot-air balloon. She told me she didn't even want to go, that she was terrified of heights, but he surprised her and he'd already paid for it so she had to go up. She kept her eyes closed the whole time and she felt him slide the ring on her finger before he whispered the question into her ear. She knew her face was red from the heat floating above her and her hair was sticking to her neck and she was wearing jeans with a hole in the crotch, but she was so light-headed that all of those things disappeared and she was just her, not her body. When they landed, she crouched down as low as she could and my dad rounded his body over hers and the rush in her ears was like a ball flying just past her face. She only opened her eyes when my dad laughed, pulled her up, told her it was safe. They were in a field full of mosquitoes and straw and the sky was grey.

But I don't want to keep my eyes closed. I want my body to exist; I want it to make things. For years, I've thought about my own hip bones and the soft skin right behind my earlobes, the way my hair falls out of a bun onto my shoulders, the sharp arch of my feet and my small toes. But now it also feels good to think about the oil on my nose, the smell of my armpits in the middle of summer, my tangled pubic hair. At some point, the stretch marks on my thighs turned into lightning.

I thought I wanted to know someone else, but maybe I just need to know me.

⋀⋀

I TRIED TO tell Lillian everything, but I know I left stuff out. It's impossible not to. She told me she was worried that I think being happy, being nice, is boring. I told her those are two different things.

When I talked about the doctor, about the men online, she said, "But don't you want someone to be nice to you?" I said it depends, that nice is subjective, that mostly I want someone to listen to me. I told her that rewards are power just like punishment is.

"Do you need to do it?" she asked.

I wanted to really think about it for Lillian, because I felt like she deserved that. With anyone else, I'd just tell them what I thought they wanted to hear.

"I think so," I said.

"Now, though? Does it have to be right now?"

I told her I didn't know. It felt like the most honest thing I could say.

"Do you think I'm crazy?" I asked her.

"No. But I don't think you're taking care of yourself, either. Maybe you need to do something new."

"I don't know what to do."

"That's okay, though. I think most people are just trying their hardest."

I know Lil really believes that's true. It makes me feel like maybe I'm not so bad. People only know parts of each other, but it's impossible to be just one thing, and some of the things are contradictions and don't make sense. And maybe it's okay to feel everything all at the same time.

"I didn't know things were so shit with your mom." Lillian looked really sad about that, more sad than about anything else, and I wondered if I shouldn't have told her, if I'd done something wrong bringing up Mom's business—I told Lil things I don't think Mom even knows about herself.

"Can we tell my mom, though?" Lillian asked. I must have looked confused or terrified, because she said, "I just think she'll know what you should do next. I swear she won't freak out."

"Maybe," I said, but I could feel how hard it was all going to be. How much harder it was to tell the truth. But I also felt emptier than I had an hour earlier, and too exhausted to fight anymore—in a good way, like an untied balloon, like I could sleep wherever I ended up.

Lillian reached over and put one finger on my knee. Her nails were bright pink. "It'll be okay," she said. "Just maybe not right away."

∧∧∧

THE FIRST SNOW of the year is a big one. Buses are cancelled. Lil and I don't go back to bed, though—it's our snow day tradition. Sometimes we hang out with our friends, or with Steve when he comes home on the weekends, but today it's just us. It's not like it was before, but it's not like starting over, either.

I'm supposed to see Mom tonight. I never go to the house; we meet at Boston Pizza or the Chinese food place. She missed the first meeting and I thought I might never see her again. I skipped school the next day and did coke with Cass. It was fun for a few hours until we ran out of coke and it got dark and I realized I might have fucked it all up and maybe I had nowhere to go again. But Lil called me, and I answered, and her mom just said I have to keep going to school. Then she told me to come home. And Mom called me a couple days later to apologize— she's come to every meeting since. Her and Lillian's mom talk almost every day now.

Lillian and I walk to Tim Hortons in the snowstorm. I slip on the ice in my Converse, but Lil falls right on her ass and she's wearing winter boots. We take our hats off and our hair sticks to our foreheads with sweat and static. We order chicken noodle soup and blow on every spoonful. We get hot chocolate to go and then we steal trays and walk to the park. The hill was a lot bigger when we were kids, but even now it's an okay size.

When Lil sleds straight into a tree, I panic. The tray flies off to the right and she goes left. I can tell she hit hard by how far away she landed. I wonder if there's blood, if she hit her head, if she broke something. But when I'm halfway there she starts laughing, just laughing. By the time I'm sitting in the snow beside her, I'm laughing, too, and to anyone watching, we must look like we're nothing but happy.

acknowledgements

ᨆ

ALL MY LOVE and gratitude to:

Stephanie Sinclair, my agent, and Melanie Tutino, my editor. Thank you for believing in this book and trusting where I wanted to go with it. You gave me so much confidence in this story.

Those who read early (and not-so-early) drafts—Jasmyn Galley, Sarah Matheson, Gen Mummery, jesslyn delia smith, Jane Van Nes, Denise Bukowski, Maureen Medved, and Tamara Faith Berger. Thank you for your time and your honesty. I owe you favours for the rest of our lives.

In/Words, UBC Creative Writing, Word and Colour—for the writer's circles, the workshops, the quiet writing time, the drinks, the friendship.

CBC Books and the Writers' Trust of Canada. This story wouldn't exist without the support and recognition your prizes give to emerging writers.

Dick, max, Lexi, and Gwen at *Off the Cuffs*, Erin Pim at *The Bed Post Podcast*, and Dalma Rosa at *The Panty Selling Podcast*.

Doing research for this book was a true pleasure—you made my world brighter.

Sarah, Leanne, Heather, and Helen, for being better friends than any I could dream up. Seeing you every day was the best part of high school.

Mom and Dad, for everything; I promise the next book will be an easier read. Lucas and Coba, for sticking with me. We might be far apart, but I feel like we're closer than ever. Katelin, thanks a million for letting me borrow your name—I hope I made good use of it. I love you all so much.

Leon and Lou, for keeping me warm while I write, for getting me up in the morning. And Ajay, for being the most willing first and second and third reader. And for everything else. I love being your family.

ABOUT THE AUTHOR

LEAH MOL is a writer and editor who graduated from the Creative Writing Program at UBC. Her fiction won the 2018 CBC Short Story Prize and the 2020 Bronwen Wallace Award. She lives in Toronto. *Sharp Edges* is her debut novel.